THE ULTIMATE ACT OF FORGERY!

Shaw sat down and listened, wide-eyed as a child, as Trauber recounted an amazing story. Shaw heard how, under the personal direction of SS Reichfuhrer Himmler a team of top SS officers, including Reinhard Heydrich, Head of the Security Police, and Ernst Kaltenbrunner, had been given the task of perpetrating a plan, approved by Hitler, to organise what was to be the biggest counterfeiting operation of all time. The main objective of the scheme was to flood neutral countries with tens of millions of pounds' worth of forged British currency, thus totally undermining the value of British sterling and causing economic havoc on the money markets of the free world. Shaw listened enthralled as Trauber casually stated that that meant manufacturing one million British banknotes a month in £5 to £50 denominations.

'Five million quid,' Shaw repeated the amount slowly. 'Listen, what's stopping us raiding it and nicking all that money?' . . .

D0767089

The Allies

MAURICE SELLAR

SPHERE BOOKS LIMITED
30-32 Gray's Inn Road, London WC1X 8JL

First published in Great Britain by
Cassell Ltd 1979
Copyright © Maurice Sellar 1979
Published by Sphere Books Ltd 1981

TRADE
MARK

Printed in Canada

To Lorna
who sustained me with her
blood, sweat, tears and tea

ACKNOWLEDGEMENTS

This novel is from the original story *The Allies* by Roy Tuvey and Maurice Sellar.

Maurice Sellar gratefully acknowledges G.I.S. and E.S.; Joe Lyndhurst, Curator Warnham War Museum; Mike Dale, Royal Military Police Museum; Brigadier J.M. (Mad Mike) Calvert; Captain Ivor Roberts, 3rd Parachute Regiment; The Bank of England; H.M. Treasury Department; Imperial War Museum; and Doris Bartlett.

In particular, the author would like to place on record his appreciation of the assistance given to him in the writing of this book by Lou Jones, whose patience, skill and encouragement helped him to 'keep right on to the end of the road'.

Prologue

The provost-marshal tweaked his greying waxed moustache between the thumb and forefinger of his chubby hand, pushed a trayful of papers on the desk away from him in disgust, and glared up at the sergeant-major who stood, ramrod stiff, at attention.

'Makes us look a right pack of twots,' the provost-marshal bristled and his pale blue eyes almost vanished into slits. 'I'm damned annoyed — damned annoyed!'

'Sah!' the sergeant-major bellowed, looking straight at the wall ahead of him.

The provost-marshal quickened the movements on his moustache nervously. 'At ease, sarn't-major!'

The sergeant-major thudded his left boot away from his right and pulled his hands so tightly together behind him that his chest swelled the battledress blouse like a hot air balloon.

The provost-marshal frowned. He was in no mood for parade ground formality.

'Easy! Easy!' the provost-marshal growled irritably. The sergeant-major slackened his muscles but even so, he still gave the appearance of being filled with horsehair stuffing.

The provost-marshal stood up, the ruddy glow on his cheeks dissolving into a pinky whiteness as the fury welled up inside him. He grabbed a brown leather-bound swagger stick from the wire-mesh out-tray and strode briskly across the austerely furnished office to a large map covering half the wall which was clearly labelled in thick black lettering 'Liège Arrondissement'. The provost-marshal stared piercingly at the big man

1

standing erect as a Roman pillar in the centre of the room.

'Know how long I've been in the Army, sarn't-major?'

'No, sah!' The sergeant-major lied. He knew the history of his CO well, but had learnt that it was unwise to admit it. The provost-marshal had to be allowed the indulgence of summarising his military career. It was a necessary prelude to a savage symphony yet to be conducted.

'Served under Kitchener as a boy soldier in 1915. Fusiliers in '28, King's Own in '35!' The provost-marshal smacked the stick into his palm emphasising every statement. 'Transferred to CMPs in '38 — wore the square out at Gibraltar Barracks, Aldershot, through the ranks like yourself, sarn't-major. Commissioned in '41. In '43 I was promoted to a lieutenant-colonel, CO of the CMPs of this entire division!' The provost-marshal circled the map with the stick. The sergeant-major nodded as though he were hearing it all for the first time.

'Not bad for a nipper who came from a family of ten living in a slum in New Cross, eh?'

'No, sah!'

'You don't get made a colonel sitting on your arse — right, sarn't-major?'

'No, sah! You don't, sah! the sergeant-major barked woodenly.

The provost-marshal slammed his stick against the map and it quivered under the impact.

'My manor, sarn't-major, twenty-two thousand, one hundred and three British deserters.' The provost-marshal paused dramatically to let the figures sink in. 'Twenty-two thousand, one hundred and three. If we could catch the buggers we could line every street in Liège with them, and still have enough left over to troop the bloody colour!'

The sergeant-major blinked as the provost-marshal swept past him like a gale-force wind and slumped heavily behind his desk again. He picked up a batch of papers from the overflowing in-tray and selected the top sheet.

'The Yanks are giving us every co-operation, and lately they've been picking up their own scum like potting grouse out of season. Can't let them Doughboys get the better of us, eh?' The sergeant-major made no reply — he knew it was not required.

'Know how they do it?' The provost-marshal tossed his stick

into the out-tray and stood up, clutching the piece of paper. 'They catch the bloody ring leaders — that's how they do it!' He waved the paper in front of the sergeant-major. 'Turn over every bar, every whorehouse in the sector. Find this man Shaw!' He handed the sheet to the sergeant-major who raised an arm mechanically and took it. 'Read his record, study it well. He makes Jesse James seem like Christopher Robin. Pull in anybody who might know where he is. We want him badly, understand, sarn't-major? That's all! Dismiss!'

'Sah!' The sergeant-major smashed himself in the right eye with the back of his hand, leapt to attention, pivoted like a crane and clumped across the wooden floorboards to the door.

'Bloody idiots — they're all bloody idiots,' the provost-marshal muttered under his breath as the sergeant-major left. With a heavy sigh, he started to pore over the mountain of paperwork piled up before him.

1

The stench of stale urine in the concrete pill-box was almost
overpowering. An odorous reminder that previous occupants
had also been incarcerated in the cold stone-like tomb. There
were, too, other more visible signs of their recent residency.
Scattered around the muddy floor were crumpled chocolate-
bar wrappers, rusting empty meat-cans, and cartridge cases
everywhere. On the walls, carved with care by the sharp points
of bayonets, the names of loved ones, messages, bawdy
barrack-room slogans. Under a well-drawn figure of a nude
girl with her legs spread open provocatively was the phrase:
'*Mädchen mach die Beine breit, der Führer bralicht Soldaten*'.
Shaw assumed it was the German equivalent of 'Kilroy was
here'. Not that he cared much what it meant. He was cold,
thirsty, hungry and, God, so tired! He stroked his unshaven
face with earth-blackened fingers, ran his tongue over the
coated teeth that had not been brushed for days. His hatless
head was streaked with mud and small fragments of foliage
that remained entwined in the matted blond hair after his
painfully scrambling, on hands and knees, through fields of
spiky hedgerow. The British uniform he wore was torn and
mud-spattered. The sergeant's stripes, with the winged
Pegasus above, almost obliterated by the caked hard earth.

Sergeant Walter Shaw, of the 1st Battalion Parachute Regiment, pressed his weary head against the pillbox slit and
peered out. The wind, whistling through the narrow opening,
tore at him, his dark indigo-blue eyes, red-rimmed from days

without sleep, began to water. He blinked to clear them. In the thin fading sunlight that lingered almost lovingly over the rain-sodden fields outside, his attention fixed on a small clump of natural hedgerow about three hundred yards from his position on the top of the hill rise. He could sense they were there, and as if to confirm his thoughts, a startled brown bird soared out of the bushes and flew up the side of the hill, almost brushing the tips of the surrounding grass in its frantic flight.

On this wet October afternoon in 1944, in the war-ravaged countryside of Belgium, the solitary figure of Shaw paced up and down in the abandoned pillbox, a man desperately trying to stay awake, anxiously glancing out of his concrete sanctuary to the fields below. The open wild land that spread out beneath him like a patchwork quilt of marshy green and brown plains, formed the outskirts of the small but important Flemish town of Liège, the town that, until a few days ago had been his home, a home he might never see again. He was almost delirious with fatigue and hunger. 'Christ!' he said aloud, 'I could kip for a year.' Yet he knew he must not sleep. He knew they were out there, waiting for him. He was beginning to acquire the instinct of a hunted animal that warns when a predator is near. Yes, they were there all right! Like a bloody fool he'd signalled his position by firing at them as he retreated up the hill. Now they were patiently waiting, biding their time, knowing it would soon be impossible for him to fight off that inevitable state of unconsciousness.

'Concentrate, concentrate!' he breathed between clenched teeth. He forced himself to read aloud the German writing on the walls. It struck him as odd that all enclosed men behave in a similar fashion. They find an irresistible urge to make an indelible mark, to communicate. He decided it would be another method of fighting sleep if he, too, were to add his name to those of his prolific unknown adversaries. He took a sharp knife from the webbing belt that also supported a service revolver strapped firmly in a webbing holster. He crudely cut into the rough grey wall, inscribing the first stroke of the letter 'W' just under a girl's name, 'Hannah', when something, perhaps just the faintest sound, made him swing to the pillbox slit again. Yet it would have been impossible for him to have heard anything, as the nearest point of cover was so far away that any slight noise would have been inaudible to the human ear. It had to be that strange sense that civilisation has made

6

dormant — dormant, that is, until fear awakens it.

Shaw narrowed his eyes to sharpen his view. His gaze focused on one of the larger bushes that made up that rugged, yet strangely well-ordered natural hedgerow. There was a movement almost imperceptible in the long grass just in front of the bushes, but it was enough for Shaw to tighten his grip on the stock of his Bren gun. Then he saw him. Out of the shadow of the patchy green undergrowth, weaving a path on elbows and belly, hoisting a Sten gun aloft, face down, nose almost ploughing the moist soil, his khaki uniform blending so subtly into the rough autumnal landscape, he was barely visible in the half light of the early evening. Shaw could now pick out others. Like mobile mounds of cinnamon earth, silent and snakelike, the soldiers squirmed up the hill. 'The bastards,' Shaw growled, glancing at an expensive gold wristwatch. 'In another hour it'll be so dark they wouldn't be able to find their cock if they were holding it!'

Shaw could now clearly define the leader of the approaching men — a corporal, not much more than a youth. A bright ginger border of hair surrounding his red beret like an oval frame, the two colours contrasted so vividly it was almost physically jarring. The white shoulder and belt webbing of the British Military Police flashed like beacons against the dull tones of the shadowy field — luminous chalk stripes in a strangely twisted pattern winding upwards towards him.

Shaw turned his head momentarily in the direction of the pillbox entrance. There, lying untidily where he had dropped them, were the two camouflage-green smoke canisters. The presence of the metal cylinders gave him a slightly comforting feeling. They were part of his constant personal armoury, along with his razor-edged commando knife, his Smith and Wesson special service revolver, two hand grenades which swung from belt loops at his side, and his Mark 4 .303 Bren gun. His pocket bulged with spare magazines, and, clipped around his belt, were several rounds of .38 calibre shells for reloading the cumbersome revolver. The burden of the extra weight of these weapons — the Bren alone was nearly twenty pounds — was easily compensated by the confidence they gave him. They were more important to this battle-hardened warrior than food or water. In his hands they were worth a platoon of men.

He quickly considered the situation. It was no use waiting

7

for the cover of darkness now. The ginger bastard and his mob had made their move. The redcaps were determined to get him this time. They were not going to let him slip away in the rapidly failing light. The hounds had sniffed the scent and were nosing in, eager for the kill. It was a scent, Shaw dryly observed, of a cornered fox shitting himself.

Shaw gently raised his Bren gun and silently let the tip of the barrel rest on the pillbox shelf. His unshaven cheek flattened hard against its bulky stock, his finger tightened slowly on the trigger and, suddenly, he was squeezing it and all hell broke loose! He smoothly swung the blazing gun through a ninety-degree arc and back again. He was not aiming at any particular target, just spraying the entire area below with the fiery silvery messengers of destruction. The noise inside the pillbox was ear-shattering as the sound of the discharging bullets reverberated round the stone-grey concrete walls.

Outside, in the field, the corporal was shouting at the top of his voice, his pale blue eyes bulging like a toad's, as he bellowed, 'Cover, take cover!' The small unit was almost ahead of their leader's command as they hurled themselves down the hill again, rushing for the protection of the nearest earthy mound or clump of bushes — anywhere out of the line of fire Two of the men did not join the hasty retreat of their companions. One lay completely still, a huddled heap devoid of any movement. The other, a dark, curly-headed youngster with full lips and protruding ears, was sitting in a grotesquely bent position, his ghostly face twisted with pain, groaning intermittently between sobs that his leg was shattered. A sudden feeling of remorse swept over Shaw. The agonised young voice, the same tortured cries, the same sound of helplessness, the sick fear in the weakening shouts. It was all gruesomely familiar, like some devilish gramophone record where the needle had stuck in a scratched groove, and the same nauseating phrase kept clicking back monotonously, over and over again . . .

*

'Sarge, sarge, me belly's all bleeding — oh, God, Sarge.' He could still hear the boy's anguished call. He'd heard it above the deafening bangs of shells exploding, the crackle of buildings that blazed all around them, the crunching and squealing of the tank tracks, the rattle of the light machine guns, the whip-lash snap of small-arms fire, the burst of mortar bombs, the whistling of bazooka rockets — the shrill utterance of distress seemed to penetrate the whole cacophony.

Nicholls was only nineteen when he had joined Shaw's platoon a few weeks earlier. A shy lad with a broad Bolton accent. Shaw remembered winking at him as he gave him a friendly push on the shoulder at the jump-off from the plane, and the toothy grin he received in return as he leapt into the cold morning air. Now, here he was, two days later, lying only eighty yards from that accursed Arnhem Bridge, totally immobile and bawling like a child.

Shaw swung round to Spud and Connolly, who were loading a hand-held mortar with the two-inch calibre missiles. 'Give me cover over there,' he shouted to the pair at the top of his voice. 'I'm going to get him.'

'Don't be a berk, sarge,' Connolly yelled back at their leader in ringing Scouse tones, 'you'll get your fucking head . . .'

Shaw didn't hear the rest of the sentence, it was never finished. A tank shell screeched above and crashed just behind him. The blast hurled him forward, and where Spud and Connolly had been, there was now only a large smouldering black cavity. Lumps of earth fell from the sky, bounced on his back and knocked his helmet sideways, but apart from a thunderous noise that seemed to rock the brains inside his head, he realised he was all in one piece.

Pushing his helmet tightly on again, bent almost double, he dashed across the devastated strip. He leapt over crumbling piles of rubble where the dust still hung in the heat-filled air, circled sprawled-out blood-stained relics of humanity that stank like an open sewer, dodged past burning trucks where the flames licked like tongues of Hell, as they reached out for him, and finally skidded to the young paratrooper's side. Nicholls was gazing up at the thick multi-coloured fumes in the sky, singing, seemingly unaware of all the chaos around him,

> You must remember this,
> A kiss is just a kiss.

'Hold it, lad,' Shaw said gently, lifting the babyish face and supporting the back of his head in the crook of his arm. 'Save it for the Hippodrome.'

9

He looked down at the ashen cheeks with the bright red trickles coming from the corners of the mouth and thought bitterly how appropriate his last remark had been, for the face staring up at the heavens no longer seemed human, but strangely resembled a horrific ventriloquist's doll, the mouth opening and shutting woodenly, as he continued, in a tuneless voice '. . . apply . . . as time goes by.'

Shaw let Nicholls' head fall back against his chest and placing his hands firmly under his elbows, slowly started to drag him backwards. He had gone only a few inches when the wounded man let out a chilling piercing shriek. Shaw stopped immediately and came to his side. The blood-drenched combat jacket had pulled away to reveal his stomach. Shaw visibly winced as he saw that it had been split open like the skin of an over-ripe tomato, glittering fragments of metal were embedded in the tubes of his exposed intestines, and blood was oozing from the gaping chasm, forming a crimson pool in the dusty earth beneath him.

Nicholls stopped screaming and turned to look at Shaw. A flicker of recognition flashed across his face as he peered briefly up at the rock-like features now full of compassion leaning over him. He opened his mouth to speak, but no word came out. Then Shaw watched the light go from behind his eyes, and a blind lifeless stare take its place. There was a gurgling gasp, a faint sound of breath being expelled, and a final jerk as the body slumped into a crumpled, useless heap . . .

*

A dull metallic ring brought his thoughts back to the present grim reality. God knows how long it was since the magazine shed its last bullet; his finger had gone white pulling the trigger of an empty gun.

He quickly surveyed the scene about him. The MPs were scampering down the hill in complete disarray, diving behind a gnarled tree here, a smattering of hedgerow there. He had to make the break now. He pulled back the slide of the Bren to release the burning-hot spent container, snatched a fresh magazine from the battledress map pocket, slotted it into place over the barrel, and slammed it forcibly home with the palm of his hand. He ducked low and sprinted to the entrance of his temporary hiding place. He laid the loaded Bren on the cratered floor, picked up the smoke canisters and ripped the activating tabs from both of them. Then with all the strength he could gather, he flung them from the doorway, one to the right and one to the left. In a second, smoke was gushing from the open tops of the dark green cylinders, like the massive cloud that surrounds a pantomime djinn as it begins to materialise, billowing all around the top of the hill, engulfing the pillbox in a swirling denseness. Shaw grabbed the Bren, threw his arms across his face, and rushed blindly through the protective haze. In a few seconds he was only yards from where the soldiers had taken cover. The red-haired NCO was spluttering out commands to his confused, coughing bunch of men.

Shaw heard the MPs clearly as he sped past their position, but he knew that in the fog still pouring from the canisters he would be totally invisible to them. He stumbled and zigzagged as he almost tumbled down the hill, maintaining a precarious balance until he reached the flat soggy meadow below. As he raced across its morass-like surface, the soft gluey earth clung to his boots and pulled at his legs like a giant magnet. He willed his aching limbs to take him on faster, but his muscles were stiff and unresponsive, and it required all his strength to sustain him. Everything ached. He could swear there was not a part of him that had not been bruised, scratched or cut. It was as though he had been swept in on a surging tide and battered viciously against sharp, jagged rocks.

'Faster, you bastard, faster,' he grunted under his breath, as he drove himself on . . .

*

. . . 'Good old Wally!' There was Pongo, and Streaky, and Woofer, the three closest members of his gang, cheering him, urging him onwards as he thundered round the track. Faster and faster, past this chap in a blue vest, those two in white and green stripes, only the tall youth with fair floppy hair and long spindly legs with that number '3' flapping irritatingly on the red vest continued to show him his skinny bum and grubby white running soles.

'Wally, get him! Wally, get him!' The chant started by Pongo spread to others from his school. Mr Melluish, the

History and Games master was there, right on the rails. Gone was his normally cool, sardonic manner. In its place, an excited, gesticulating silver-haired figure with gold-wired spectacles and a bulbous pitted nose. Looking surprisingly agile, he almost physically tried to sweep the young Shaw round the arena waving a tweedy arm in a scything motion, his crinkly fingers looking like the white-gloved hand of a French *gendarme* on traffic duty. The tall flaxen-haired boy in front started to wobble, his running shoes didn't lift so high, the rhythm in the legs was uneven. Young Shaw knew he had him. So did the crowd from his school, wildly howling his name. They were all for him now, now he was tearing his guts out. Despite his youth, he had become something of a cynic. Ever since he could remember, life had been a battle ground where he had to prove constantly that he was tougher, stronger, and more courageous than any of his pals. No one, it seemed, would just like him for his own sake.

He recalled the time when, as a shy boy, he first arrived at the grammar school, a scholarship entrant from a poor home, mixing with youngsters who were better dressed, spoke 'posh', had plenty of pocket money and who regarded him as something of an oddity. He had had very little contact with these well-off middle-class kids, and he felt ill at ease in their presence. There were no lines of communication. To young Shaw, it seemed that they had everything and he had nothing.

So he became a loner, and preferred it that way. He spoke only when he had to, as the boys would often mock his cockney accent. Some of the teachers could be cutting too, and seemed to resent him as an unwelcome guest in their cosy little establishment. They would delight in correcting his pronunciation whenever he gave an answer to a question.

'Crom*well*, Shaw, not Crom*will*', or 'Enlighten us, will you, Shaw; let us see why the authorities, in their wisdom, have deemed it fitting that you should have joined us.' And there was the time at a term-ending when they were discussing the new books required after the holidays; 'You've a books allowance, haven't you, Shaw?' and then a long pause while the master waited for his 'Yes, sir', then a half-heard mutter, 'Mm, pity the grant doesn't extend to your clothes', and laughter from the class as they picked up the remark.

He was only too aware that his clothes were getting threadbare, that his flannels were shiny and his blazer, which started off two sizes too big, was now a couple of sizes too small. But Mum had said he'd have to make it last until the end of this term at least, and there was not a damn thing he could do about it. He hated the lot of them, but, paradoxically, he wanted them to like him. He had to prove himself once and for all, otherwise he'd be treated just like the other minorities' groups at the school: the fat boys, the swots, the boys who shied away from sport.

He had learned from the tough kids in the Hackney streets where he lived that if you wanted to gain a reputation and respect, pick on the biggest bloke around and beat him up. If the method worked in the alleyways of East London, he reasoned, there was more than a chance it would succeed at this sissy school. He selected Davis, a beefy youth who, having prematurely acquired a downy black moustache, looked years older than he was. The rest of the class kept well away from Davis as he would take great delight in trying to pull the ears off any unfortunate boy whom he considered to be 'tiresome'. He had a laugh to match his size, and it was always heard above the rest when a master made a particularly vitriolic remark. He had irritated Shaw for some time now, and he felt it would be a popular move to give him a good thumping. At first Davis was reluctant to soil his hands on this cheeky upstart whom he regarded as infinitely his inferior, but egged on by the other boys, he agreed to teach the common little sod a lesson. They arranged to meet at the end of the day behind the cycle sheds, and the word had gone around like wildfire that there was to be a fight that evening. A good many of his class came along and formed a human ring circling the two adversaries as they faced each other. Davis was no easy opponent — for one thing he could box, and Shaw only had the ability of a street fighter: head butting, kicking, and wrestling were his special skills. But he attacked with a terrifying ferocity. He became a crazed animal, and it was not long before he had hammered Davis into blubbering submission. It was a revelation to the well-brought-up young onlookers. They had never before witnessed such aggression. He had more fights after that, bigger boys from other forms, anyone who doubted that he could lick 'em! He beat them all, and won a grudging admiration from the other boys. He would never be accepted socially, of course, or be invited to their homes. He was a bit too common for that, but he was a good bloke to be seen around with at school.

He earned a reputation as a rough diamond, some even called him a lout and a bully, but one or two of the more astute masters noticed he had begun to acquire a following that bordered on hero worship, and wisely stopped using him as a target for jokes. They encouraged him, instead, to channel his physical energies into organised sport. Mr Melluish felt he would make a good miler, and set about the task of training him. The hunch paid off. It was not long before young Shaw won the school title in near record time and had entered for the event in the inter-school games. He took the honour very seriously and straight after lessons he would run lap after lap of the playing field's perimeter. Even that number who still disliked him watched him pound the grass and conceded he had guts. After his gruelling day's grind at school, he would return home, rush through prep, and then don his father's heavy leather-studded boots over several pairs of socks and go clattering round the echoing side streets until late into the evening. When he arrived at the stadium he was staggered to find that virtually the whole school was there to support him. He won his heats by a good margin and, apart from a bellyful of butterflies, was feeling supremely confident when he lined up for the start of the final.

Now the only barrier between him and victory was this gangly youth who was visibly crumbling in front of him. He had to pass him. All his struggles at school to maintain that thin veneer of popularity would have been in vain should he fail. He gritted his teeth and reached inside his very soul for a spark of remaining energy. It came from somewhere, and a feeling of power surged through his young body again. Strength flooded back into those heavy feet, the bloody taste in his mouth was not so noticeable now. With a mighty effort he accelerated. In seconds he was shoulder to shoulder with his one remaining obstacle. The fair head turned to look down at this impudent intruder, and a flash of despair showed on the face. A moment later it was all over as young Shaw streaked past and threw his barrel chest at the tape.

Pongo was hugging Woofer and leaping in the air. Mr Melluish was an ear-to-ear grin. The Hackney Stadium was a great roar as the East London schoolboy, one-mile champion, trotted into a quiet corner and heaved his lungs up . . .

He had driven himself to the limit then, and that same sick feeling was with him again. The hammering chest, the jelly legs, the thick dry taste in the mouth, the eyeballs that nearly fell from their sockets, but this time there were no cheers. No pats on the back, no 'Well done, Shaw!' — nothing now but run or you're dead, or if you're lucky, the glasshouse for evermore where you're kicked around from arsehole to breakfast time by a bunch of moronic sadists.

He stopped running and stood still, panting like a greyhound. His eyes were still stinging from the smoke, and streaming tears blurred his vision. He lifted a grubby khaki sleeve to his face and wiped away the sticky fluid on the rough surface of the cotton stripes. He glanced around quickly at his new position. Just below him was a small ditch — an oasis with withered golden leaves bobbing and rippling on the black surface. Shaw fell to his knees almost like a man in prayer and rolled clumsily into it. There was a muffled splash and his pain-racked frame made contact with the cold water that covered the bottom of the muddy trough, its icy coolness soaking through the sweat-stained uniform, surrounding, soothing and caressing his fatigued body. He lay quite still on his back and allowed himself the luxury of not moving for a long time. Then he cupped his hand and splashed his stubbled face with the brown water. He opened his mouth and tasted its gritty sweetness. Sitting up now, legs astride, he slowly began to collect his scattered thoughts as feeling returned to his numb body. He cursed himself aloud for getting caught like a nun with her knickers down. They must have had a tip-off, that was the only possible explanation. They were waiting for him. Who knew he was going to do that NAAFI again? He'd only raided it four nights earlier, and Shaw had never returned to the same place. He should have realised himself that it was a trap when he first discovered how easy it was to spring the lock of the stockroom door. But a sleepless night with Evelyn and a few cognacs on an empty belly had put an end to any logical thought. Christ! He'd told Evelyn! It suddenly dawned on him. She'd asked him to get her some soap and stockings, and he'd promised he would. Of course, it had to be her — she'd ratted on him. I'll kill the cow, so help me! I'll strangle her! Shaw raised himself on one elbow angrily. He was one of the most wanted deserters in the British Army — that was fairly common knowledge in most of the bars and whorehouses of Liège — but surely they hadn't resorted to offering a reward for him, or had they? It wouldn't take much to get her to talk. She'd sell her baby for a bar of chocolate. Well, he'd sort that *poule* out when he got back. It would give him a goal to aim for. He'd enjoy seeing the surprise on her face when he confronted her. Yes, he'd get a kick out of watching her squirm in her hot camiknickers, the dirty little bitch! If she had shot her mouth off, he'd shut it for a long time to come.

Shaw lifted his head wearily and peered up at the hill. His eyes were still stinging and the skin on his face felt as taut as a drumhead where the tears had made bright ruts through the film of dirt and dust. His face now had a strange resemblance to an African dancer wearing a terrifying mask, the haunted blue eyes darting from side to side behind it, watching hawk-like the activity now taking place above him.

The smoke around the area had almost cleared and the soldiers had re-formed and were again advancing up the hill. The corporal and three of his men, armed with Stens, had raced several yards ahead of the others and were moving steadily in towards the pillbox, dodging from cover to cover, firing in short, sharp bursts as they did so. The bullets from their chattering guns were thudding into the walls of the concrete blockhouse and kicking up the surrounding black mud, splattering it in all directions as they cautiously neared their target. Protected by this front-line attack, the remainder of the platoon had quickly gone to the aid of their injured number. A couple of them were gently lifting the man with the wounded leg down the sloping bank as he twisted and grimaced in pain, while two others had slid to the side of the slumped lifeless form. They turned him over and almost jumped back as the man suddenly sat bolt upright, shook his head, and looked all around him with a dazed expression, seemingly unhurt, just stunned by a chance bullet grazing his temple. Under the advancing cover his comrades gladly helped him as he clambered unsteadily to his feet.

As Shaw viewed the scene, a faint smile came over his grimy features. At least he'd not done for 'em, he thought.

2

The corporal arrived first at the pillbox. The white smoke had
hung more heavily here. Angrily he fired three bursts from his
Sten into the dying vapour, knowing full well it was a useless
action, and that his quarry had fled. He entered the empty
blockhouse, gun at the ready, two other MPs behind him. The
corporal scratched the back of his carrot-coloured neck. His
face was white with rage, and the freckles on it stood out like
splashes of dirty engine oil. He kicked viciously at the scattered Bren cartridges on the earth floor as though that could
nullify the anger within him.

'The bastard,' the corporal spat.

'I heard he was at Arnhem, corp,' the younger of the two
MPs proffered, hoping this comment in some way would
pacify the seething NCO.

'Lots of blokes was at Arnhem,' the corporal snapped back.
'A lot of 'em still there! There'll be daffodils as big as sodding
sunflowers at Arnhem next year.'

He squinted through the pillbox slit. In the distance he
could see a puff of smoke on the horizon, accompanied by the
muffled sounds of heavy gunfire.

'Fucking marvellous, ain't it! Our lads are out there fighting
Jerry, and we're up here, chasing a lousy deserter!' Then,
bracing his shoulders back, he bawled: 'All right, at the
double!' The dejected bunch trotted in step down the hill to
join the others.

Shaw watched them as they faded into the distance and

disappeared; then cautiously he clambered out of the ditch and stood shakily on its lower bank. From his new position he could just make out, in the descending twilight, what was once a farm track. It had been a long time since it had been used for the purpose of husbandry, and indentations showed that heavy tanks had recently churned their way across the yellowish clay strip. As he plodded towards it, an overwhelming tiredness suddenly seemed to weigh him down. He was, for the time being anyway, out of danger, and he yearned for sleep. As he marched wearily on, he spotted the shadowy shape of an army truck which loomed up in the distance. It was tilted precariously on one side and had obviously been hit by a powerful missile as it was badly charred, and most of the rubber tyres had been burnt away. What he could see of the blistered markings showed it had been an American troop transport vehicle. He climbed exhaustedly into the rear and braced himself for an expected shift in its position, but it had ploughed well into the mud which acted as a sort of pillar, and the angled truck remained firmly in place. He stretched himself out on one of the hard bench seats where only the blackened metal framework remained after the fire had finished all it could devour, curled his legs up under him, shivered violently and fell into a restless sleep.

❋

. . . He flicked open the catch of the little wooden gate at the side of the house, turned briefly to Pongo and Streaky, who were moving on, and shouted, 'See you about six.' The two retreating friends waved back their acknowledgement. Almost before he started to walk the path that led to the back door, he was yelling at the top of his voice: 'I won, Mum!' He pushed the peeling red door open, lifting the silver cup above his head like a victorious Roman emperor waving a regal banner. It was much more than a sporting trophy, it was a symbol of achievement far greater than this. It represented the fulfilment of a struggle over what, to one of his tender years, were major obstacles. The threadbare clothing, the lack of money, the fact that his father drove a removal van and was not a solicitor or worked in a bank. These all counted for very little now. His new-found popularity would wipe them all out like a duster on a blackboard. He had won through. He saw

18

the admiration in their eyes. He had been accepted— he could relax, work hard for his matriculation certificate, and get a good job. Use his brains, not his hands, like his Dad had always said. He'd make his parents really proud of him. He acted modestly as his pals recalled every moment of the race again for his benefit, almost as though he'd never been there.

The kitchen was strangely disordered. The table had not been laid for supper, and when he looked around the small room he noticed that dishes from breakfast still stood, unwashed, on the wooden draining-board. He knew at once that something was wrong.

'Mum, Mum!' he shouted as he bounded up the stairs of the tiny terraced house. He poked his head into both of the bedrooms and saw the unmade beds. He bolted down the stairs and just avoided colliding with Mrs Stokes from next door, who was standing there.

'I thought I 'eard you, Wally,' the stout woman with the kindly face said. 'It's yer Dad. He's 'ad a serious accident. Yer Mum's wiv 'im at the 'ospital. She left . . .'

'Where? What hospital?' the boy interrupted, dry with fear.

''Ackney General — Accident Ward. She said you was to . . .' but the boy had gone, still clutching the cup. He ran through the crowded streets, bumping into irritated workers returning home. 'God, don't let it be bad. Please, God, don't let nothing happen to him.'

His mother sat alone on a long wooden bench outside the ward. He would never forget the way she looked that day. Whenever he was to smell that pungent hospital antiseptic again, his mind would flick the memory back to him. She was wearing a sun-faded old camel overcoat, and although it was buttoned, he could see, in the gaps, the bright floral colours of her apron underneath, which, in her her haste to leave, she had forgotten to remove. A brown beret covered most of her greying hair and emphasised a face that had once been pretty but had been remoulded by the pattern of a life spent in constant worry. The deep lines in her forehead, the tired eyes, and the once soft and sensual mouth that was now tight and colourless. As he stood in front of her, panting for breath, she looked up at him, saying nothing. Then suddenly she grasped both his hands and almost squeezed the blood from them, clutching on as though, in her despair, she had found a soul-saving raft.

"Wh— what happened, Mum? I mean . . .' the boy blurted, and really did not want to hear the answer.

'Please, God, I'll pray all the time if you don't let him die.' What if he did, though? Wally was an only child His parents had almost given up trying to have kids, 'but one day you came along' his mother used to say in one of those rare happier moments, and proudly plant a kiss on his cheek. When he had got his scholarship, she had looked like a young girl again, and had promised to save from her housekeeping to buy him a bicycle. Dad was cock-a-hoop too. Took the day off work and spent all the money he had on him at the school outfitters. Dad never spoke a lot, but the big man expressed all his inner joy when he said to the shopkeeper, 'No, I want the best satchel you have. It's not every day your youngster passes for the Grammar, is it?' His Dad had wanted him to better himself. 'You don't find educated men in those dole queues,' he used to say.

'He was changing a wheel on the lorry— he'd got it propped up on a hill with a brick or something. He was underneath when it rolled over him. Oh, Wally!' The woman sobbed quietly into her handkerchief.

They sat there in silence and his heart leapt everytime a footstep sounded near them.

After an age, it seemed, the grim-faced doctor came through the doors. 'I'm sorry, Mrs Shaw, we did everything we could.'

The young nurse put an arm round his mother and the doctor looked at the boy, and at the cup, and said nothing, but his eyes revealed how useless he felt.

'Oh, Wally, what are we going to do?' His mother broke down in a flood of tears.

It was the summer of 1932, and he had just turned fourteen. He held on to the frail woman, and knew that his school days were finished. His victory over adversity epitomised in the silver award that stood shining on the bench beside him was all without meaning now. He picked it up. 'Don't worry, Mum,' he said quietly, 'I'll look after us.' He stared at his reflection in the gleaming cup, breathed on its mirrored surface and watched the distorted image of his face vanish— along with his youth.

●

... Shaw awoke with a jolt. A rusting metal screw from the hard seat was digging into his back, and the steady rain was dripping on to his face as it ran down the twisted metal supports that had once held the burnt-away canvas top. He sat up, shaking with cold. His bones cracked like dry twigs as he swung his legs over the bench to let his squelching boots down on to the floor of the lorry. Picking up the Bren gun that lay at his side, he moved to the rear and jumped to the soft ground below. The night air was cold and cutting, with just the hint of a breeze gently moving the foliage above him. The blackness was interrupted here and there by the light of a distant star, allowing just enough visibility to observe the path of a farm track ahead. He pulled back his sleeve and glanced at his watch. It was twenty-two hundred hours. He frowned, then listened to it. He'd forgotten to wind the bloody thing up! He started walking carefully, feeling slightly more refreshed but now very hungry. He looked for places on the track where the land was a little firmer, but now and again his wet boots wouldn't quite find their mark, and he would slide into the icy mud up to his ankles. After a while, he even stopped cursing when it happened.

Occasionally, without warning, he would be plunged into almost impenetrable darkness as thick overhanging branches would blot out the faint source of light. When this happened, he would stop, put his hand out in front of him and feel ahead like a blind man, then walk on again with short careful steps, until a few seconds later his route would once again be illuminated by a faraway constellation. He must have progressed for more than a mile like this, with the stillness of the night being disturbed only by the sound of his sludgy tread and laboured breathing, when suddenly the silence was pierced by the solitary trill of a bird. He froze for a second, realised what it was, then continued walking. It was joined by an answering call, and another, and soon all around him was an incessant babble of chirping song.

'Happy little buggers,' he muttered through panting breath, and he realised he was smiling. He had escaped. He was weak with hunger, he ached all over, and his skin was crawling with lice, but he was still free, and— Christ only knew why— he felt good.

As if to share his new found spirit, God produced His most awesome miracle, slowing dissolving the inky blackness into the grey of a new dawn. The birth of a new day would always fill him with wonder. Perhaps this would be a day when he might not have to run, when he could find food and temporary shelter. This thought gave him fresh vitality, and he marched along with renewed energy, softly whistling a tune, the title of which he had forgotten.

About twenty yards ahead of him, the track along which he had been steadily plodding widened and veered off sharply to the left. The tank and the tyre marks continued along it for as far as his eye could see, and it confirmed his feeling that this improvised road had, in the not too distant past, been the scene of some amoured vehicle activity. He surmised that a main highway lay ahead where the track undulated and vanished over a hill rise about two kilometres from his position. What he could not be certain of was whether it had been German or Allied transport that had taken this route. He knew that there had been some fierce resistance from German tank units in the area, and that they had stubbornly refused to be pushed back. He had been told that large Panzer divisions had been deployed to defensive positions on the other side of the River Meuse, and towns like Aix-La-Chapelle and Bastogne, not too far away, were under constant bombardment. It was vaguely possible, he reflected, that he might be in enemy-occupied territory. Of ths two evils that confronted him, this would certainly be the worse. For the past few months the Germans had not been taking prisoners, and any Allied servicemen unlucky enough to fall into their hands, would be tortured for information and then shot. At least if he were captured by American or British Military Police he would not be executed. He had not deserted in the face of the enemy, merely taken off from a military hospital on a permanent spell of AWOL. Yes — he would be allowed to live — if he could call having the shit kicked out of you daily living. Either way it was not an enviable position.

The morning light had spread to an even flood and the birdsong reached an orchestral crescendo as he approached the broad section of farm track. He observed that immediately to his right, almost hidden by a tall poplar tree, a narrow path turned off and stopped abruptly in front of a broken, but incongruously closed, five-bar gate. Looking cautiously all about him, he placed his Bren against the post, swung his leaden legs over it and landed with a wet plop in the waterlogged field on the other side. Just where the ground dipped, he could see the dilapidated outbuildings of the farmhouse. He splashed his way towards them, his Bren poised for instant use. As he got closer, he could get a clear view of the farmhouse itself. Like its surrounding barns and stabling blocks, it was many years old, ravaged by time as well as by the war which had passed that way. Red slates from the broken roof lay splintered all around on the cobbles of the yard. The windows were glassless, the frames hanging loosely askew from their twisted hinges. The front door had been nailed in with criss-cross pieces of wood, banning entry. An air of desolation hung over the whole place. Even the chit-chat of the birds was strangely absent here. It was eerily silent. Treading very carefully and constantly watchful, he walked into the yard. All at once he stopped dead in his tracks. It was just a half-heard sound. He swung round full-circle to face it, aiming the Bren in its direction. He saw him at once — a man in a farm worker's clothes, dashing from the door of a crumbling barn towards the farmhouse, like a frightened cat in the night.

Shaw raised his gun to fire, and shouted, 'Halt! *Arrête*!' The man stopped immediately, and thrust his hands in the air in a gesture of surrender facing the farmhouse. Shaw held his position, and called to the man again. 'Come here,' he commanded. The man stood still, rigid as a statue.

'Er . . .,' Shaw paused, '*Avance ici . . . toute suite*!'

The man turned round, arms stretched straight up to the clouds, and nervously walked towards Shaw.

'Belgique, Belgique,' he said in a quavering voice. Shaw shot an edgy glance around the yard. He listened attentively but heard nothing. The frightened man, shaking visibly in front of him, appeared to be alone. Shaw allowed his Bren to drop slightly from its menacing position as he studied him. He was aged about forty, short but stocky, with big shoulders and a chest that had responded well to clear country air. His thinning brown hair lay wispily uncombed and strands hung over a furrowed forehead. His sad brown eyes were deep set above the cheekbones, and the cheeks themselves, although now pinched white with fear, still managed to display the ruddy bloom that comes from a life spent in the open, daily battling against whatever weather Nature, in all her fickle moods, decided to throw at him. The years of ploughing, reaping and gathering were all there, chiselled into the square rustic face, and sculptured on to those calloused hands with the cracked skin and broken fingernails. Shaw had many questions to ask him. What was this labourer doing on this abandoned farm? Where exactly was this place? Who was in the area — British, German, or American soldiers?

'*Parlez-vous anglais*?' he said firmly, but in a more friendly tone. The Belgian shook his head and broke into a broad grin, exhibiting a row of uneven yellow teeth. A foul smell of bad breath and garlic wafted under Shaw's nostrils. It was so powerful it almost made him retch. Shaw stepped back a foot and was about to speak again when he heard a distant whine of a truck in low gear. He signalled to the man for absolute stillness, and listened attentively, head cocked like a spaniel. The sound was coming closer. He pushed the Belgian forward and prodded him in the back with the barrel of his gun to the shelter of the farmhouse wall. He looked around hurriedly to find a hiding place. The outbuildings, he felt, were too exposed to give safe cover, and even though he could gain access to the main building by climbing through one of the broken windows, he was certain that that would be the first place a patrol would search. Then he noticed that just in front of the farmhouse was a heavy oak trapdoor which had been let into the earth. It was the entrance to an underground storm cellar. He motioned urgently with his Bren to the Belgian to help him, and together they grabbed at the huge rusty iron lifting ring and pulled it with a mighty tug. The trapdoor refused to budge. Shaw took a deep breath and they both heaved again. It gave a little. He leaned right back with the heels of his boots dug firmly into the ground, beckoning the farm worker to do the same, and, with a massive jerk, they wrenched the ring upwards. This time, with a creaking moan of protest, the door slowly opened. Shaw peered into the gloomy hole. The daylight penetrated just enough for him to see the uneven grey stone steps that led down to the floor of the cellar. He placed a forefinger against his lips, indicating silence to the Belgian, spun him round and prodded him in the back with the tip of the gun. The Belgian cautiously descended into the musty basement, Shaw following a pace or so behind. When his head was just below the surface of the ground, Shaw reached up and lowered the heavy door over them. Taking the strain of the weight on his shoulder, he kept it an inch or so ajar, his ear pressed against the narrow opening. He heard the sound of the vehicle crunching over the rutted track as it came closer. At its loudest point it screeched to a halt. He listened, hardly daring to breathe lest he miss the faint snatches of conversation barely audible above the noise of the running engine.

'Sure thing,' he heard one man say, then some laughter, followed by indistinct chatter. Heavy footsteps started to come nearer, but stopped suddenly, then dialogue at much closer range.

'Ain't going to find no lousy AWOLs here. It's a goddam morgue.'

'Well, maybe we should just take a look around.'

'You take a look around — I ain't going to get shitted up in all that mud. Took me half the night to whiten these sonofabitch gaiters!'

'Well, just as long as we're here, let me say "goodbye" to a bladderful of Shlitz!' The man chuckled and almost simultaneously Shaw heard the stream of water splashing against the earth. 'Wonder why you shudder when you piss?' the man continued. 'Know what some wise guy wrote over the NCO Club latrines?'

'What?'

'You don't buy the beer round here — you rent it!'

'Ain't that the truth. OK, guys, let's go.'

Shaw listened as hasty footsteps were followed by the roar of an engine being revved up. He raised the door an inch or so more and just caught sight of the rear of the small canvas-topped Army truck with the large white painted star, and the 'Caution, no signals' sign boldly underneath it. He breathed a deep sigh as he watched it rock from side to side and disappear. He smiled to himself, and released the grip he had on the Belgian's arm. They were snowballs on the prowl for deserters, but their presence confirmed that he was in an American zone. He nudged the Belgian to help him lift the door again, and they began to raise it above their heads.

'*Hände hoche*!' The voice cut sharply through the darkness below him, and Shaw's stomach plummeted to his boots as he went cold all over.

'Shit!' was all he could manage to say, as he let the door crash back again. After all his recent ordeal, to fall into German hands at this time was just about the worst piece of stinking luck he could imagine.

'Place your gun on the step behind you, and come down here,' the voice continued in almost perfect English. 'I advise you, do nothing foolish, we have more than one gun aimed at you.'

Shaw reluctantly complied, and pushed the terrified Belgian ahead of him, using him as a shield as they moved slowly into the black void.

A beam from a torch flashed from somewhere onto the two intruders, making them blink in its blinding light. From another part of the cellar Shaw heard the scrape of a match and the smell of an oil lamp being ignited. Soon its glow had brightened to illuminate the whole area. A tall man standing at his side clutching a Luger was dressed in a badly creased olive-green uniform of a Wehrmacht Oberleutnant. Another man, a good bit younger but similarly dressed, was leaning back in a chair training a light machine gun right at Shaw's heart. A rotund figure of a German private was holding an oil lamp at chest level. It was a large cellar, and had a lived-in look about it. Shaw observed the variety of its contents. There were oddments of furniture, blankets, boxes of ammunition. A brace of game birds hung from the ceiling, casting their shadow over an incongruous ancient wind-up gramophone with half the protruding horn missing. On one side was a neat pile of well-worn gramophone records, on the other side an almost floor-to-ceiling stack of large round cheeses which leaned precariously against an even taller column of wooden crates that contained fruit or vegetables, and had '*Ferme Bromberger*' stamped indelibly on the splintering frames. Approximately in the centre of the room was a crude table made of up-ended packing cases which bore the remains of a disturbed meal. Shaw looked hungrily at the food on display— two long dark loaves of bread, a big hunk of cheese with some unpeeled onions, two opened bottles of wine and a half-consumed fowl. His mouth watered at the sight of it.

'Walk forward slowly, hands very high,' the officer commanded, jabbing the tip of the Luger into Shaw's ribs for emphasis. Shaw grimly obeyed and the Belgian shuffled nervously at his side. The young German aiming the machine gun at them got up casually from his chair, handed the weapon to the private and strolled arrogantly over to Shaw. He prodded him forcibly in his stomach and indicated that the belt had to be removed. Shaw unclasped the brass buckle and it clattered to the stone floor, taking the grenades, revolver, knife and ammunition with it. The officer smirked silently at him as he kicked the belt to one side. He then patted Shaw's battledress tunic, searched his pockets, and relieved him of three spare Bren gun magazines and a dog-eared letter. Shaw moved forward to retrieve it, but halted as the Luger dug deeper into his side.

Satisfied that there was no further threat from the British sergeant, the officer started to search the Belgian. He found a clasp knife in his pocket and tossed it into a corner. He then walked back to his chair and snapped his fingers. The plump German soldier came waddling back and handed over the weapon. The young officer took the gun and once again directed it at Shaw. This ritual completed, the tall man motioned with his Luger to the Belgian to stay where he was, and turned to Shaw. He pointed to a wooden box which served as a seat at the improvised table and said pleasantly, 'Sit down.'

Shaw, with hands still raised, did as he was told.

'We heard a truck,' the officer went on, 'they were Americans, yes?'

'That's right,' Shaw replied flatly, and studied his interrogator thoroughly for the first time. He was more than six foot tall, with dark, well-oiled hair that was neatly parted in the middle. He had large greyish eyes that revealed a mature intelligence and strangely contrasted with the rest of his face which was dominated by a well-flattened pugilistic nose. Shaw put the man's age at about thirty-five.

'You were running from Americans?' he said, lifting his eyebrows in surprise.

'Yes,' Shaw replied coolly, but inside he was cursing himself for getting captured.

'Why would you wish to hide from Americans?' his inquisitor probed, and leaned in closer to Shaw, intrigued now by what he might learn.

'I'm on the scamper,' Shaw replied, matter of factly. The officer frowned, not understanding the term.

'I've resigned from the army,' Shaw went on. He could see that the tall German looked puzzled. 'They think I should have waited till the war was over.'

'I see. But a sergeant of the Airborne a deserter? I find that hard to believe.' The officer responded with the glimmer of a smile, and scratched the bridge of his nose, as though this signalled his doubt.

'Then don't believe it,' Shaw said defiantly. He didn't at this moment give a monkey's arsehole what this Kraut believed. A swift flash of annoyance came over his questioner's face. 'Why did you desert?' he snapped irritably.

'Why did I desert?' Shaw looked up at the German and stared right into his grey eyes. What a question! Did he want his life story in a few minutes? In any case he had no simple answer. Nothing he could rattle off pat. A bloody long list of good reasons, yes— but no real answer. He thought it odd that if he had ever been captured by the MPs and the inevitable court martial had followed, he would have had a pretty poor defence. Hundreds of blokes had had their families wiped out in air raids back home — that was no excuse. Thousands of blokes got wounded and saw death at its most inglorious. Those were no excuses either. There was just one day when he'd had enough— that was all. And as for trying to explain that to a bunch of Krauts — well! One of his few remaining convictions was that the entire German race should be wiped out, and he firmly believed that the world be a better place if that happened.

'You've got a couple of days to spare?' Shaw answered eventually. 'If you have, I might be able to tell you why I buggered off!' He paused for a moment. 'I was at Dunkirk . . . Italy . . . I was dropped at Arnhem. . .' He slowly bent down to raise his right trouser leg, and exposed an ugly twisted line of scarred flesh. 'That's where I copped this little beauty, *Flammenwerfer*, I think you call 'em. Let's just say I've had a gutful,' he concluded bitterly. He shook his leg and let the rough khaki fall back to cover the wound. He raised his hands once more, examined the faces of his captors and tried to assess by their expressions what effect his words had had on them. He needed to play for a little time, just enough to get the right opportunity to blow these Krauts back to Hell.

Shaw felt that the older of the two officers seemed to believe him, but the younger man looked totally indifferent. Shaw could now see that his rank was the equivalent of a British major. He was probably no more than twenty-four, of slight build with carefully clipped white-blond hair. His light blue eyes were small and piercing, and his skin was pale and soft, like a woman's. Shaw felt that there was something about this

28

man that was decidedly dangerous. An ever-present nervousness showed in all his movements, and he looked as though he could erupt into uncontrolled fury without a moment's warning. Shaw thought he would watch this one very carefully.

Almost as though he were trying to distract his attention away from the younger man, the tall German, who had been observing Shaw closely, took two long strides to the side of the Belgian. 'What about him?' he said, looking over in Shaw's direction, but nodding at the farm worker who was licking his dry lips.

'I just found him in the yard,' Shaw replied, with a candour that had no hint of deception.

'Uh huh!' the officer murmured, and ran a hand absent-mindedly over his shining hair. He then pivoted on one heel, turned, studied his captive briefly again, then walked over to his two comrades.

'*Was meinst Du dazu*?' he whispered to the young blond officer who raised his machine gun even more pointedly at Shaw, as he scrutinised him with those cold penetrating eyes.

'*Ich weiss nicht. Vielleicht können wir etwas erfahren.*'

'*Ja, eventuell —,*' the tall man scratched his broken nose again. '*Aber was machen wir mit dem Belgier?*'

'*Erschiess ihn,*' came the unemotional reply.

Shaw had suspected from the time that he could first see around the cellar that these men were no ordinary German soldiers. A further look at the contents of the underground store had confirmed his feelings. Whilst they were engaged in the brief conversation, he had carefully lowered his raised hands to behind his neck. As he heard the sound of the German officer working the slide of the Luger, his right hand flashed with the speed of a snake's tongue, and dipped inside the back of his battledress tunic. In an instant he had snatched out a grenade that was clipped behind his collar, whipped out the pin, clutched the lever tight against its bevelled casing, and held the armed explosive aloft.

'As you were!' he barked at the surprised group who, for a brief moment, had temporarily lapsed their guard on him. The tall officer was caught in the middle of turning round with the primed Luger and the other officer's attention was focused, for a split second, on his commander's action. Shaw made certain that they could all see the grenade by waving it slowly in front of their astonished faces. This old trick that he'd learnt from an American Army pal had got him out of other tight situations, but, he reflected, it had never been more effective than now. He dangled the grenade pin in front of their eyes, riveting their attention, hypnotising them with the small metal ring. He paused for several seconds, then tossed the pin casually among the loaves of bread on the table.

The cellar at once became still, silent, cryptlike. No one in the room knowing what to do next. The lofty officer made the first move; he slowly sat down, keeping his Luger aimed at Shaw.

'What do you call this?' he said quietly, as though not daring to break the deathly hush. 'Stalemate?'

Shaw leaned forward, rested his right hand on his knee and held the grenade out in front of him, permitting the Germans a closer view of the small iron sphere that could destroy them all.

'I call this grasping each other firmly by the short and curlies, mate,' he said with just a touch of cockiness.

The Belgian, who still stood exactly where he had been ordered, began visibly to relax at this sudden turn of events, and flicked some stray hairs away from his eyes with a large flat hand. The tubby private anxiously looked over at his two officers, a little bewildered by the way the initiative had suddenly switched to this scruffy English paratrooper. There was no doubt that Shaw had taken control, and he knew it.

'Now, I've got a couple of questions. What are you doing in charge of a cellar? And how come you, Oberleutnant, are senior to the major over there?' He nodded over towards the younger man, who was tapping his slender fingers nervously on the butt of the light machine gun.

'Not so,' the German replied quickly, waving his Luger to make his point. 'My English is better than his, that is all.'

'Bollocks,' Shaw spat out contemptuously. 'I'll tell you what you are, shall I? You're all on the bloody run like me — I can see it in your faces. I can see what you've been thieving.' Shaw cast his eyes at the mountain of dairy produce.

The tall officer pinched the end of his squashed nose and stared at Shaw, stony-faced, giving no indication of an answer. His comrade bent his cropped head over his gun, dropped his eyes shamefacedly, and continued to fidget with the barrel. The private glanced at his superiors, looking for a sign, trying to fathom out what on earth was taking place.

'What are you?' Shaw continued, 'Oberleutnant or a private?'

The tall man shrugged his shoulders. 'Oberscharführer, SS. A sergeant,' he answered, and as an afterthought, 'a sergeant like yourself.'

Shaw thought it ironic that he should be wearing his correct uniform and rank. In the past few months he'd had more outfits, stripes, pips and flashes than hot dinners. Oh, Christ! He mustn't think of food.

Shaw glared at the blond German. 'I don't blame you for ditching your SS uniforms around here. All SS, were you?'

The Oberscharführer weighed his reply carefully before he spoke.

'Leder was,' he said, cocking his head slightly in the direction of his younger comrade, 'and I, too, as I told you. But Winkel over there, our well-fed fellow, he was Wehrmacht.' The plump private nearly clicked his heels at the sound of his name. 'I am Trauber, Horst Trauber,' he concluded with a flashing smile.

Shaw nodded a brief acknowledgement. 'Wally Shaw, First Airborne, retired!' he responded without so much as a glimmer.

Carefully keeping the Luger aimed at Shaw, Trauber half turned towards the table, and with his left hand picked up one of the wine bottles. It shook a little as he splashed some wine into a mug. He then replaced the bottle on the table and turned to face Shaw again.

'The British and Americans now control this area?' Trauber said, more as a statement than a question.

'I reckon so,' Shaw responded and looked in the direction of Leder, who now seemed to be taking a renewed interest in the conversation. He leaned forwards slightly, hunched over the stock of his machine gun, and stroked it lovingly. Trigger-happy bastard, Shaw thought as he observed the action. Yes, he would definitely have to watch this one.

Trauber shifted his seat towards Shaw, a positive gesture of friendship implied in the movement.

'You know this area?' he said, fixing him steadily.

'Well, where the hell are we?' Shaw asked.

'We are situated about four kilometres east from the town of Malmédy.'

Shaw straightened a little. Had he run that far in three days?

31

His leg had stood up well, considering, he thought. 'We're what? Twenty, twenty-five kilometres from Liège?' he said, brightening.

'Correct.'

'The town of Liège I know like the back of my hand,' Shaw said with a touch of pride.

'Good, good, I guessed as much. You see, the way things are at the moment, it is not so easy for us to get around here now,' Trauber said with a sigh.

'That's your hard luck,' Shaw muttered irritably.

His hand was going white from clutching the safety lever of the grenade, his arm ached from holding the explosive above his head, and that bloody food on the table was driving him potty.

'You live by stealing, like we do?' Trauber went on in a confidential manner.

'Yes,' Shaw replied sharply.

'Here we have shelter, guns, ammunition,' Trauber enthused with the air of a man sharing a great secret, and paused slightly, knowing his next words would perhaps have the most impact on the famished-looking deserter, 'and food — plenty of food — we live well.'

Shaw shot another glance at the feast on the table, and remembered that he had eaten nothing for three days.

'All right, what's the point you're trying to make?' Shaw said, trying to take his mind off his stomach.

'With our strength of numbers and specialised knowledge, your ability to move about, your contacts and our contacts, we should be able to see the war out here in comparative safety.' Trauber was bringing Shaw into his scheme with all the measured cunning of a fisherman with a prize salmon on his line. 'Together we would make a formidable team.'

Shaw searched the faces of the 'formidable team'. Trauber appeared to be in earnest. Winkel seemed harmless enough. Leder was listening intently, but his expression indicated nothing. The more Shaw looked at him, the more he was puzzled why such a textbook Nazi type should have gone over the wall.

'And the war is over as quickly as that?' Shaw directed his remark at Trauber, and knew that the tone of his voice contained a ring of disbelief.

'For us the war is already over,' Trauber replied philosophically. Then warming to his subject he continued with enthusiasm. 'Look — it may at first seem preposterous, but you will find we have a lot in common. We are all disillusioned men. Our Führer has brought our country to its knees, and your leaders get fat at the expense of your dead. Whatever motive you have for desertion — and I assure you that that is your own business — you will find, I suspect, that it is not so vastly different from ours.'

'Keep talking,' Shaw said with more interest. Despite his first violent reaction, he felt he was in no position to rule out even the most ludicrous propositions. It seemed they weren't bluffing. He could see how he could be useful to them; the question was could they be of any use to him?

Trauber reached over behind where he sat and grabbed the mug of wine from the table, holding it in his hand as he spoke.

'We have done pretty well until the situation became almost impossible. You see we have a good stock,' Trauber indicated the booty by the wall, 'but we are worried that a lot of it may perish. We find we are virtually trapped here, thanks to over-zealous military police.'

Shaw nodded — he could well believe that. The MPs, American, British and Canadian, had really cast their nets wide in the last few weeks. He could count himself very lucky that he had just managed to slip through. Trauber offered the mug to Shaw who reached out a muddy hand to grasp it. He sat silently looking down into the ruby liquid. He knew that a lot of Krauts had gone on the run in Paris, he had heard there were a few in Brussels, but he was surprised to find them around this area. Like the thousands of GI AWOLS or Tommies on the run, the German deserters lived in the twilight world of the *marché noir*. Stealing in the main military supplies and selling them to the local gang bosses who supplied the restaurants, whorehouses and bars with booze and fags, or food shops with a variety of fare from caviare robbed from officers' clubs to spam swiped from the NAAFI. . .

Shaw spoke slowly and deliberately. 'If — and I say *if* — I decide to give you the benefit of my knowledge, what can you do for me? Whom do you deal with, for instance?'

'Well, we work with Caminade. He takes everything he can get from us. We mainly cover the farms — meat, bacon, cheese, butter. We grab it en route to the city, but occasionally we tackle an army supply truck. That's where we get most of our ammunition,' Trauber replied, animatedly waving his free arm in the air.

'Why are you dressed in those uniforms, then?' Shaw heard the fatigue in his own voice.

'If we get captured, we're merely POWs. If we're found to be black marketeers and ex-SS at that— ping!' Trauber raised two fingers to his head in a gun imitation.

Shaw nodded. He knew that any SS flotsam was strung up without hesitation. His mind was a jumble of contradictions. All his instincts seemed to be saying 'Play for time and get out' — yet, somehow this ridiculous scheme might work. It was going to be hotter than a barrel of mustard in Liège for a while, but he had to survive and that was his only hunting ground. Working with these men could prove an advantage, even just on a temporary basis. Trauber could see Shaw was deep in thought again.

'With all due modesty, we are pretty dependable. Leder is a marksman, first class, Winkel is an extremely able driver and mechanic, and I myself know a trick or two about explosives.'

'Caminade, you say?' Shaw said eventually. Trauber nodded. Shaw had heard of Claude Caminade. He was one of the big shots, a Belgian 'Capone' who controlled most of the bars and whorehouses from Blankenberghe right through to Brussels.

'You deal with him directly?' Shaw said in surprise.

'No. We have met him on a few occasions, but mostly we do our business indirectly, with one of his cronies. Well, what do you think?' Trauber eyed Shaw anxiously.

Shaw made no immediate response, but ran his eyes around the cellar and fixed them finally on Leder who was still fidgeting with the machine gun.

'Your friend playing with his Schmeisser doesn't look too happy about the idea.'

Leder rested the gun on his knee and stared firmly back at the British sergeant.

'I am not,' he replied in good English.

Shaw lifted his eyebrows, surprised to hear the man speak in the language. Leder reached over by the loaves of bread and picked up the grenade pin. He stood up, allowing it to dangle at his side, and marched more than walked, to where Shaw sat.

'But,' Leder paused for a moment, 'I can understand why it should be so. I think you will need this,' he said holding the pin in front of him.

Shaw held up his free hand. 'I'll have the letter back first,' he replied determinedly, 'then the pin.' Leder took the letter from his dark green tunic pocket, glanced at the torn envelope quickly, and handed it to Shaw.

'The letter — it is important to you, eh?' Leder said, with a slight glint in his small blue eyes as he let the grenade pin fall on to Shaw's lap.

'Yeah,' Shaw said, placing the letter in the top pocket of his battledress.

Trauber looked interested. 'From your girl friend?'

'Wife,' Shaw answered softly, and an image of her laughing face flashed through his mind.

'Letter from your wife,' Trauber chuckled, 'Why is that so important?'

'There won't be another one, that's why,' Shaw replied almost inaudibly. He looked up at Trauber and stared pointedly at the Luger. Trauber smiled and slipped the safety catch on, rammed the gun firmly back in its holster and snapped the black leather flap over it. He then picked up his mug and started to drink.

'I'll be a lot happier when that Schmeisser's out of the way,' Shaw said irritably, nodding towards the machine gun Leder still held. Leder lifted his eyebrows for a moment, then placed the gun on the table, but Shaw noticed his fingertips still rested on the stock, and he moved them gently up and down it, as though he were fondling a kitten.

'I think I should inform you about this gun,' Leder said, addressing Shaw with an air of knowledge. Shaw frowned, wondering what was coming.

'You called it a Schmeisser — it is a mistake even some of our own people make,' Leder paused dramatically before continuing, 'this is an Erma — the lightest machine gun in the world.'

Shaw caught Trauber's eyes which, for a brief moment displayed amusement at the way Leder was warming to his subject.

'No wood is used at all, instead a new substance invented by us called "plastics". Hence this weapon weighs a mere nine and a half pounds.'

Heil bleeding Hitler, Shaw thought, but knew his first assessment of this man was correct. The fanatical way he spoke revealed that he was close to being unbalanced.

'You British and Americans have nothing to compare with it,' Leder concluded. He turned from the weapon and puffed out his chest proudly. Shaw wanted to ask 'So how come you're doing so badly?' — but felt, under the circumstances, that it would have been unwise.

Instead, he picked up the grenade pin and eased it slowly back through the two small holes. He then reached to the back of his neck and hooked it once more beneath his collar. The grenade had served its purpose, but in any case he was now convinced that he was much more useful to these men alive. The Belgian dropped his hands to his side and relief visibly spread across his weatherworn face. He felt secure in the presence of this tough British soldier. He was greatly impressed by the way he had got these German dogs firmly under control.

Winkel, feeling the tension in the cellar unwind, ambled over to the table. He slipped a bayonet from a sheath in his belt and hacked off a good-sized slice of cheese. Shaw watched him with interest as he replaced the bayonet, took one of the brown loaves between his large dimpled hands and tore it in half. He turned to face Shaw, handed him the food, nodded courteously, stood back and grinned.

Shaw flashed a smile in return as he grabbed at the offering. The rounded Winkel looked anything but a soldier. He was well into his forties, and was one of that band of late conscripts who knew less about the tide of events and twists and turns of warfare than the majority of the civilian population who were made aware of it through personal suffering every hour of the day.

'*Sprechen* English?' Shaw aimed his question at Winkel, who stood with arms folded in front of him.

'*Nein,*' came the reply, accompanied by a heavy shrug and a broad grin.

Shaw ripped off a great portion of bread, thrust it into his mouth and chewed it, slowly savouring its taste. He ate with relish, delighting in the contrasting flavour of the rye bread and the strong cheese that bit into the tip of his raw tongue. As Shaw wolfed the meal, Leder rose from his sprawled position in the chair and strolled towards the Belgian. He looked him up and down, examining the man from head to toe. The Belgian grinned nervously into his face. Leder pulled his head back sharply and turned the corners of his well-shaped nose up in disgust.

'*Der Mensch stinkt wie eine Sau*,' he spluttered at Trauber.

'Yes,' Trauber replied thoughtfully, addressing Shaw, and indicating the Belgian. 'What about him?' Shaw could not answer for a moment, his mouth was full of food. He munched on it as he pondered the question.

'It's your cellar, mate,' he replied finally, and swallowed hard, 'but he seems harmless enough to me. I think he should go.'

'That is stupid,' Leder blazed, 'if he is allowed to go free, in no time at all he would reveal our position here.'

Shaw considered this, and knew that Leder spoke good sense. 'Perhaps we could use him.'

'How?' Trauber asked, believing Shaw might have a sound idea.

'I dunno — running errands, keeping watch. He speaks the local lingo, he could be handy,' Shaw replied, not very persuasively. 'I reckon we should think about it.'

'*Überlasse das mir*,' Leder said quietly to Trauber, plainly ignoring Shaw.

'Now, hold on a minute,' Shaw retaliated angrily. 'I don't know what you said, but I don't like the sound of it. And another thing — cut out all this speaking in German. If we're going to work together, you talk English — OK?' Shaw could feel his blood rising.

'I agree,' Trauber said pleasantly, 'Martin, from now on we speak only English among ourselves, unless of course we are addressing Winkel — all right?' Leder nodded a sulky affirmative.

Trauber took Shaw's mug and filled it to the top with wine, emptying the entire contents of one of the bottles. He lifted the other bottle and repeated the process with his own mug. He raised it amiably, 'Bung-ho,' and creased his face in a smile. Shaw clicked his mug against Trauber's — '*Prosit*!'

The two men eyed each other over the chipped rims and drank deeply. Suddenly Trauber set his mug firmly on the floor with a force that almost split it in two, got up, swallowed audibly, motioned to Shaw to stay where he was, and strode briskly towards the gramophone. Shaw sipped the wine and looked on, puzzled. Trauber searched impatiently through the stock of dusty gramophone records. A wide grin appeared as he found the one he was looking for. He placed the record on the turntable and rapidly cranked the ancient mechanism. He looked at Shaw and his eyes twinkled with anticipated pleasure. He coaxed the steel-pin pick-up point onto the start of the record. The machine wobbled violently as a tinny sound came crackling through the broken horn:

> I've got sixpence,
> Jolly, jolly sixpence,
> I've got sixpence
> To last me all my life.
> I've got tuppence to lend,
> And tuppence to spend,
> And tuppence to take home to my wife.

Shaw paused, the mug at his lips, and he took another drink as he listened. He smiled, the smile grew broader, as he drank it became a laugh as he half choked on the wine, and a bigger laugh. Trauber laughed out loud, a great roaring bellow. Leder giggled selfconsciously as the scratchy song continued. Winkel shook his great girth up and down like a buoy on a rough sea, threw back his head and shrieked. The Belgian, caught up in the hysteria, joined in.

Shaw rocked backwards and forwards, helpless with laughter, eyes closed, stupidly overcome with weariness and relief at the uncoiling of tension. It all flooded out as the wine dribbled from his lips and traced a red path down the stubble of his chin.

The machine gun's rapid hammering made Shaw jump quickly to his feet. He spun round and saw Leder standing over the Belgian as he fell, clawing the air inches above the black leather boots of his killer. Leder's eyes were murderous as he lowered the smoking Erma and watched his victim twitch uncontrollably, then move no more.

'You lousy bastard!' Shaw yelled as he lunged forward to Leder. Leder calmly raised the gun again, and Shaw stopped still in his tracks.

'Are you to be next?' Leder said menacingly. 'This man was a great danger to us. These farm labourers haunt the farms where they used to work. They are acting as caretakers. Do you honestly believe we could have trusted him to leave and not report our position here?'

Shaw stood his ground, seething.

'He's right,' Trauber said softly as he lifted the arm of the gramophone from the swishing record. 'We would never be safe if we let him go.' Trauber poured some more wine and drained the bottle into Shaw's mug. Shaw took it and shook his head slowly, a silent expression of sadness at the inevitable flitted across his features. Shaw knew the poor bastard farm worker would have been a great risk had they released him. To himself, perhaps, even more than to the Germans, who would merely be regarded as POWs. It was the cold-blooded way in which it was carried out that upset him.

'I've got to get out of this clobber,' he said, choosing not to refer to what had taken place. 'I need a bloody good scrub down, shave, fresh clothes.'

'Good, good, we will boil up a couple of buckets of water right away,' said Trauber helpfully. 'I will go to the well.' He clambered up the wooden steps and pushed the cellar door open.

'Wait a minute, I'll go with you,' Leder shouted after him, 'but we need some help first.' He turned to Winkel and continued in German, 'Winkel, *hole die Schaufel und ich will die Leiche tragen.*'

'*Ja, ich werde das sofort tun,*' Winkel almost came to attention at the command, then crunched across the stone floor and noisily rummaged through a collection of paraphernalia, eventually selecting a rusting spade. He moved to the body of the Belgian, lifted it under the armpits and dragged it along to the base of the stairs. Puffing and grunting with the effort, Trauber and Leder lifted the legs and all three struggled awkwardly as they hauled it up the stairs, one at a time, until they had gone through the cellar opening and out of sight.

Shaw hardly moved a muscle as he watched them leave, and when the cellar door slammed down the only sound he could hear was his own stomach loudly grumbling at the intake of food, lately unused to the process of digesting it. 'I've been in some oddball situations,' Shaw thought, 'but the idea of going into partnership with these Krauts really takes the biscuit!' It was a dangerous existence at the best of times, but he had always just managed to stay one jump ahead of the MPs. Until three days ago, that was, when he heard that several cases of best Scotch whisky was due in at the NAAFI. It was only a short while before that he had pulled a job there with the aid of two pals and got away with a half-gross of fags, several cater-

39

ing sizes of ham and a load of powdered eggs. All good saleable stuff. Shaw ruefully recalled that it was 'Two-Way Wilson', a black GI, AWOL, who had given him the wink on the whisky consignment, and had agreed to go on the job with him. After discussing how they would raid the place, Shaw had gone to 'Antoinette's' for a skinful, and to wait till the NAAFI was closed. There was a fairly good selection of tarts at Antoinette's and Evelyn was the first to make 'Come wiz me, Wally' noises. At 2 a.m., pissed as a fart, he had decided that he'd rolled in the sheets long enough with the hungry redhead. He had dressed in his uniform, and staggered down the stairs of the noisy bar to meet a fuming 'Two-Way'.

'Shit, man, where you been?' the big Negro said, hopping mad.

'Fighting a war on the Red front,' Shaw replied with a silly grin, and rubbed the sore fingernail tracks in his back, 'and I think I lost!'

'We're going to be too late, Limey,' the Negro complained.

'Listen, it was only a couple of days ago Harris, Ginger and me did it. They'll never expect lightning in the same place twice. Golden rule— you don't go back. Right? No one would do that NAAFI for a while. Everyone knew we pulled a big one there. It'll be a piece of cake. Calm down,' Shaw rambled disjointedly, as the room swum with a sea of smoke and smeared faces.

'I'll remember those lines, soldier boy, when they're kicking my ass around the stockade,' Two-Way said glumly.

Two-Way swung the van to the entrance. The NAAFI building was still and silent, the ghosts of choruses of 'We'll Meet Again' and 'Roll out the Barrel' had long returned to rest in the out-of-tune piano. The NAAFI was situated about a mile from the nearest Army Post, which was occupied almost exclusively by members of His Majesty's Royal Engineers, and the two boys selected that night for picket duty were sound asleep at the doorway.

Shaw nudged the Negro. 'See,' he whispered, 'we don't even have to sing them a lullaby.'

Two-Way beamed a wide white smile.

'It's a straight-forward nick. Keep 'em covered and I'll slip round the back.'

Two-Way pulled an automatic from his pocket and just watched the snoring soldiers while Shaw, soft-footed as a cat,

40

went to the rear of the building. There was no light here at all, and he flicked his Tommy-lighter to find the small window that led to the latrines. The idiots had left it slightly open, just as before. 'They deserve to be done,' Shaw smiled to himself. He lifted the window silently and dropped in, just touching the porcelain rim with his boots. He crept through the main hall avoiding tables and chairs with the aid of the flickering lighter, and made his way to the storeroom. He tried the handles, placed a long piece of stiff wire in the lock, forced it inward and the door clicked open. 'God, they must have had a hell of a piss-up tonight,' he thought, 'they've even forgotten to throw the second lock.'

The light filled the room, like a sudden bursting of the sun through a black cloud.

'Hold it, soldier!' the redcap shouted, 'there's no way out.'

The grinning faces of the MPs holding their Stens on him made his heart crash through the floor. They'd been waiting! The whole thing stank! He'd been set up. He should have got it in his fuddled brain that it was too bleedin' easy. Since when had he ever broken into a place like walking through the front door of a Lyon's teashop?

The MPs grabbed him by his arm roughly.

'Well, well, it is Mr Shaw, I believe,' said a six-foot-two bull-headed sergeant. 'You will notice I address you in the civilian vernacular.' He poked his bamboo stick straight into Shaw's ribcage, winding him with the force. Another MP grabbed him by the shoulders and kneed him straight in the balls. Shaw doubled over in agony.

'You will notice I address you in the army knackers,' the redcap said with a Scottish accent, and chuckled at his own wit.

'Don't damage him, gentlemen,' said the sergeant, 'we've got a lot to talk about — haven't we, Mr Shaw? Let's get him on the wagon.'

They dragged him on his bootcaps across the floor out into the cold night. The shots rang around his ears as Two-Way emptied the automatic at the redcaps. There was a clumsy confusion as his escorts ran for cover. Shaw realised for a split second that he was free, and painfully hobbled into the covering blackness, running blindly away from the store . . .

. . . And he had hardly stopped running since, as patrol after patrol pursued him from one haunt to another until they eventually chased him into open country and up to the pillbox

41

from where he had made a last desperate escape.

Was that only three days ago? God, it seemed like three lifetimes. Now, here he was, face to face with these Germans, and they wanted to do a deal with him. What an absurd situation! Nevertheless, Trauber had spoken a lot of sense. They could survive and let the war bypass them as a team. They were obviously fairly efficient. Caminade, who was just a name to him, would have no truck with them if they weren't, and after all, if this man, a one-time resistance leader and on the Gestapo wanted list, was doing business with them, why not him? Any alliance he might form would be purely on a temporary basis anyway, and right now without assistance and with the MPs hot on his arse, there wasn't a great deal of choice.

There were a few advantages he could see that had not already been outlined by Trauber. The redcaps and snowballs had been co-operating a lot lately, and had mounted an intensive campaign on GIs and Tommies who had gone over the hump. It had, of late, proved unnervingly successful because they only had to catch one unlucky bastard and kick his balls in before he couldn't stop blabbering about his pals, the gangs they worked with, names, addresses, the lot! At least these German deserters would not be known to the Military Police Special Investigation Bureau, or the local Belgian Gendarmerie. They had a contact with Claude Caminade, which he didn't, and judging by their larder they seemed to live pretty well. What he must do now, even at this stage, was to establish himself as the boss! He'd have no problems in that respect from Winkel and Trauber, but Leder might not leap at the idea. From the heels of his jackboots to the top of his Kraut head, he was a Nazi. But the type weren't just confined to the German Army, he reflected. Every battalion had its share of men like that, and there was a heavy concentration of them in the Military Police. However, he felt he could handle him. He'd make the bugger jump! If he were true to pattern, he'd respond well to precise, loud orders. Anyway, Shaw mused, what the hell had he to lose. He would get a good scrub down, wash his filty clothes, and have a good night's sleep. Then he would get them all enthusiastically involved with a plan for a fairly simple raid. Perhaps a parachute job would act as a good introduction. It would give him a chance to take command and see how they got along together.

3

The jeep bumped along the cratered road, and all around them as they travelled were the monuments of war. The burnt-out tanks of the Panzer Corps, the blown-up American armoured cars, the bent and broken British self-propelled guns; dotted among the giant hulks were a collection of smaller smashed-up transporters used for troops and supplies, the crippled echelon lorries, the charred coaxial machine guns, the shattered recovery vehicles, an endless variation in international weaponry, all designed for the sole purpose of destroying all that God had created and man had built. And the evidence of how successfully this havoc had been wrought was everywhere. The lifeless scorched trees and shrubs, the piles and piles of rubble, the mountains of bricks and splintered slates with an occasional ripped-open mattress, crushed wheelless pram or cindered armchair jutting out through the pyramids, like so many pitiful signposts stating that people had once lived in these streets, when the bricks lay tightly together and the bright red tiles sat proudly on top of the little houses, surrounding the sounds of families, laughing, weeping, loving.

Shaw moved restlessly on the wooden seat as the jeep twisted and jolted. Now and again a military vehicle travelling in the opposite direction would flash its light in a friendly acknowledgement. At first Winkel ignored these sporadic greetings but as his confidence mounted, he began to return the signals. Shaw glanced at the three men as they bounced up and down in the jeep. It was now five days since he had first

43

encountered them in the abandoned farmhouse cellar. In that time he had learnt very little about his new allies. Trauber seemed open enough, but was not to be entirely trusted. Leder was still aloof and at times plainly hostile, and there wasn't a lot to be said about Winkel, except that he now knew he was a reckless driver and appeared just as absurd in the uniform of an American GI as he did when he was wearing the Wehrmacht equivalent.

Trauber, leaning back casually, chewing gum vigorously, looked absolutely the part of a dog-faced veteran of Uncle Sam's army, and oddly enough, so did Leder. With his crew-cut hair, skinny frame and fair complexion, he seemed every inch the all-American college boy. Shaw felt comfortable in the uniform of a top sergeant. The jacket was a little tight under the arms but otherwise it was a perfect fit. The acquisition of the jeep and uniforms had been relatively simple. The former occupiers were drunk as skunks anyway when they staggered from the truck to remove the big slab of masonry blocking their path. It was an easy matter then to overpower the Americans, strip them of their clothes, tie them up and dump them unconscious in a field about eight miles from the village of Beaufays. Shaw felt certain that they would still be sleeping off the effects of the booze and gun butts on their heads— he smiled at a mental picture of the men waking up in their underwear in a mound of cowshit.

Obtaining the passes they required to gain entry to the base had been a more complicated affair. Shaw dared not risk a visit to Liège for the time being, even though getting the necessary faked papers would have presented little problem there. Instead they had travelled at dead of night to the village of Faimes and to the tiny thatched cottage home of an elderly crippled artist known simply as 'Mafi'. Occasionally the painter would supplement his meagre earnings from the sale of his works by a little surreptitious forgery. Shaw had met the man once before and knew he could be a temperamental old cuss and would only tackle the painstaking task of counterfeiting if he felt in the mood. Armed with a couple of bottles of good wine, two large cheeses and a box of vegetables, Shaw managed to persuade Mafi to work through the night until he eventually produced an authentic-looking permit which would have withstood even the closest of scrutiny. For a few francs extra, Shaw also got the artist to juggle about with the

ID cards they had stolen with the uniforms, and with a little clever touching up here and there, he had transformed the photographs into passable likenesses of the four men.

'OK, slow down,' Shaw ordered suddenly. Winkel drove on relentlessly, not understanding the command. Christ, he'd forgotten he couldn't speak a bloody word of English. 'Tell him to slow down,' he snapped impatiently at Trauber.

'*Fahren Sie langsam*' Trauber responded and leaned forward and waited to make further translations as Winkel lifted his foot from the accelerator and reduced speed.

'Turn left up that hill,' Shaw continued, making sure his instructions were clear and precise.

'*Links abbiegen und dann den Berg rauf,*' Trauber echoed in German. Winkel obeyed at once and juddered up the steep incline.

'Right, stop and switch off,' Shaw said after they had proceeded about two hundred yards.

'*Hier anhalten. Drehen Sie den Motor aus.*' Winkel slammed his foot down, wrenched back the handbrake and cut the engine. He relaxed, reached into his top pocket and pulled out a packet of 'Luckies', grinning broadly as he offered them around. He was more delighted with this find than he was with the scrip dollars, chewing gum and Hershey bar that were also in the jacket pockets. Shaw and Trauber took the cigarettes and lit up, Leder raised a hand and shook his head.

'Now then,' Shaw said, after a long draw, 'just over that hill you'll see the airstrip.' Trauber nodded slowly, Leder listened and unclipped the flap of the revolver holster.

'You won't need that yet,' Shaw said sharply, observing the action. 'And when you show it you don't use it, right? Keep it just as we planned.' Leder made no reply. Shaw swung round to Trauber hotly. 'Look, you tell this gun-crazy friend of yours there's to be no shooting. I've done dozens of places like this and never had to resort to any killing. Just use the guns to threaten with, that's all. They'll be no bother. It's not their personal stuff we're nicking.'

Shaw pulled himself together. He couldn't afford to let them see his calmness slipping. He must learn to ignore this Leder 'needling' him.

Trauber turned to Leder and started to speak, but was interrupted almost before he had opened his mouth.

'All right, you're not talking to Winkel now,' Leder said

irritably, 'I heard what he said.'

'Good,' Shaw said, fixing Leder with a determined glint, 'then do it!'

'I still think we should have waited till dark,' Leder said sulkily. Shaw did not reply, instead he gave him a look of sheer contempt. He'd spent a long time, too bloody long, explaining why their first raid together should take place in daylight. He'd told them it was as black as a nigger's armpit on the airstrip at night, that no one present, apart from himself, knew the layout and that, odd as it may seem, they were much more security-conscious at the air force base after sunset than they were during the day. It was then that a twitchy picket was liable to blow the head off anything that moved. There had been too many nocturnal robberies over recent months from various military headquarters, and they had tightened up the watch on all roads. Dressed as GIs and with good forged papers, they would be able to gain access and mingle with the air force personnel without arousing a lot of suspicion. He thought this had been fully understood when they planned the exercise. Now here they were, about to raid the place and Leder was still arguing the toss. If he raised any more stupid objections, as he had done the previous night, he'd call the whole damn thing off!

Trauber read Shaw's thoughts almost uncannily. 'Martin — he has told us why. Let us not have any last minute doubts now.' Leder permitted himself a slight smile and nodded slowly to Shaw.

'OK,' said Shaw, taking this gesture as a final acceptance of his orders. 'Let's go.'

Trauber leaned over to Winkel, arched like a bridge, and spoke to him in German. Winkel switched on and after a couple of grinding attempts to get into gear, the jeep lurched up to the top of the hill. It seemed to pause at the summit for a fraction of a second as though it were a gull hovering in flight. Then suddenly it plunged crazily down the incline, over a white painted sign in the road that read 'Positively no unauthorised admittance', and levelled out as it sped towards the airfield entrance.

The big guard in the sky-blue greatcoat and white helmet left his box at the side of the horizontal single-barred gate and strolled over to the jeep as it screeched to a halt with its engine still shuddering noisily on. He leaned over the driver's door, rested his cane on the bonnet and addressed Winkel in a deep southern drawl.

'Where yo'all heading'?

'Motor pool, Mac,' Shaw responded brightly and waved the forged permit at the guard who took it in a mittened hand. Shaw threw a sideways glance at Winkel and noticed that little beads of sweat had started to appear above the full lips as he stared blankly in front of him, tightly gripping the wheel. The guard cast a cursory look at Leder and Trauber who sat in the back trying to appear nonchalant, ran his eyes quickly over the document and handed it back to Shaw.

'Uh huh,' You make a right by the third, no fourth, hangar. Motor pool lies back a-there.' The guard pointed out the direction with his stick. Shaw nodded, the guard span on his heel, returned to his box and wound the gate up. Winkel made no attempt to drive on. Shaw nudged him heftily in the ribs with his elbow. Winkel released the handbrake and slowly moved forward. Once the other side of the gate, he started to turn left, but Shaw reached over, hastily grabbed the wheel and swung it to the right. Winkel acknowledged the assistance with a nervous grin.

There was a lot of activity at the air base that day. Huge petrol bowsers trundled across the field towards the Flying Fortresses lined up on the tarmac like a group of sombre roosting eagles. Two bomb-loader trucks laden with 500-pounders criss-crossed a path and just missed each other as the airman sitting astride the triangle of missiles laughed and shouted obscenities. Admin. staff ran from one hut to another carrying sheaves of paper with orders in duplicate and triplicate, mechanics with black-smudged faces bent their backs in contorted positions as they tapped and tested the rivets and lovingly injected their charges with oil from huge grease guns. The aerodrome buzzed with anticipation. Shaw was pleased with himself. His timing had been perfect. They had arrived right in the middle of preparations for a heavy air raid. Little wonder, he thought, that they hardly got a raised eyebrow from the duty guard when he said they were for Motor pool. It was even possible that extra mechanics had been requested from another base.

He was about to explain their good luck when he caught sight of the Germans' faces. They wore a thoroughly dejected look and he knew what they were thinking. They had realised that the destination of the deadly cargo was their beloved Fatherland. Shaw could not help feeling a certain satisfaction as he gazed at their crestfallen expressions, but he decided not to add to their misery and said nothing.

Suddenly he felt there was something familiar about the place. He shook Winkel's knee. The German's cheeks wobbled as he turned to Shaw to await the instruction. Shaw waved his hand in a slow-down motion and Winkel duly obeyed. They continued to crawl along the clean grey road when Shaw became certain they were where he wanted to be. He had been straining to read the markings on the row of huts they were passing, when he saw it. It was a good bit larger than the surrounding huts and the words 'Equipment Stores' were clearly picked out in yellow on the dark green door. He grabbed Winkel's arm and pointed to the building. Winkel slammed his foot on the brake and they stopped just a few feet beyond.

'All right, Horst, and. . .' Shaw hissed and then broke off as a Negro airman came out of the stores, closed the door behind him, selected a key from a jangling bunch on a metal ring, turned it in the lock, tested the handle, and, satisfied it was secure, walked jauntily off, whistling and swinging a mess tray in time to the tune.

'Fuck it, that's all we need,' Shaw cursed in exasperation. Then he saw that heading in the same direction as the Negro was a steady flow of personnel. They all carried mess trays and chatted animatedly as they ambled along in groups of twos and threes. Trauber glanced at the black-dialled chronometer on his wrist. 'Lunch, eh?' he murmured pensively and squeezed his flattened nose.

'Yeah,' Shaw growled, and his mind raced on to his next move.

'Do we have to wait till he returns?' Trauber queried anxiously, his grey eyes narrowing.

'Not bleeding likely,' Shaw retorted, 'this could work out better for us. It won't be a straight pick-up job like we planned — but we could have a clear field. When these buggers go for grub, they all go.'

'All armies are the same,' Trauber said, with a glimmer of a smile.

'I wonder if we would have this trouble at night?' Leder uttered smugly, and adjusted his forage cap on his blond hair, although it was already perfectly in place.

'No, we wouldn't have,' Shaw glared at him, 'they'd have shot us.'

Leder's face dropped. A few airmen strolled by their jeep, and one of them threw a puzzled glance in their direction.

Shaw observed this and turned to the Germans. 'We're going to attract a lot of attention if we don't make ourselves a bit busy.'

'Doing what?' Trauber grumbled and his frame seemed to stoop like a giraffe looking over a fence.

'You'll find a tool bag under that panel,' Shaw turned and addressed Leder, 'Get some spanners out, screwdrivers, anything.' Leder lifted the corrugated metal plate just behind the rear seat and pulled up a canvas tool case.

'Good,' Shaw said when he saw it, 'OK, lift the bonnet — make out like we're fiddling with the engine — we shouldn't get any interruptions — no one's going to miss their dinner to help us.' Trauber chuckled. In a few seconds all four men appeared to be engrossed in their work.

Shaw looked round. Apart from some late drifters who were heading for the mess in a different direction and by-passing the stores, the airfield which, only a few minutes earlier had been a buzzing hive of movement, now seemed almost deserted. Shaw appeared satisfied that he could tackle the store without too much disturbance.

'All right — me and Horst will go in,' he turned to Leder, 'get Winkel to rev up the engine just before I blast the lock.'

In two strides Shaw was at the door of the stores. He tried the handle and scrutinised the lock. 'Piece of cake,' Shaw grunted at Trauber who had joined him. Shaw took the revolver that was attached to a green lanyard from his holster, examined the full chamber, aimed the gun closely at the lock, was about to nod to Winkel to crash his foot on the accelerator, when he heard the heavy crunching of boots on a gravel path at the side of the hut. He quickly hid the revolver behind his back, and turned to Trauber with a fixed grin as though sharing a joke. He felt the drops of sweat fall from his armpits and run down his sides. A puffing airman in fatigue denims, carrying a full pack on his back stood breathlessly in front of him. He looked no more than eighteen. His face was scarlet from exertion and he was scared stiff.

'Sarge,' the young airman panted as he addressed Shaw,

'I've done ten circuits of the field and I'm kinda lost.'

'Where do you have to be?' snapped Shaw. He felt sorry for the kid, but was so keyed up himself, the agitation showed in his voice.

'I gotta report back to the Provost Hut,' the airman blurted out.

'Well, goddam it! Does this look like the Provost Hut?' Shaw barked, pointing at the Equipment Stores sign.

'N — n —no, sar — sarge . . .'

'I dunno why they gave you detail, boy, but I bet you sure as hell deserved it.'

'Yes, sir, er, sarge.'

'Do another two circuits — run this time, keep your eyes open — don't let me see you back here — understand?' Shaw bawled. 'What are you waiting for?'

'Er . . . nothin', sarge,' The airman crunched over the gravel and into the field.

'Phew!' Shaw looked at Trauber who said nothing, but his eyes showed admiration at the way Shaw had dealt with the situation.

Shaw once more aimed the revolver at the lock and nodded to Winkel who, with Leder, had witnessed the incident, wondering what the outcome would be. He pressed his foot firmly on the accelerator and the ensuing roar made it sound as though six more jeeps had joined them. Shaw blasted two shots straight under the handle and, close as he was, could barely hear them above the noise Winkel had created. As the smoke rapidly cleared, Shaw pushed the door. It swung open easily. He beckoned with a tilt of his head for Trauber to follow him in.

The interior of the stores was in complete darkness. The one window at the end of the hut was blocked in by what seemed a huge obstruction. Shaw felt for the light switch and found it almost at once. He looked round the room and saw that piled up against the window was a column of bedding, blankets, bolsters, pillows, sheets. His eyes roamed across the variety of equipment that lay on the slatted metal shelves which were attached to a wall behind a long wooden counter. Canvas packs, webbing-rope, mess trays, cutlery, neatly sectioned and labelled. Above, an assortment of clothing, fatigue denims, webbing belts, fur-lined jackets, boots and gloves. On the floor stood tins of paint, oil and disinfectant. Buffers, mops, brooms and dusters lay nearby. It had that distinctive smell of all QM stores, an odd mixture of dust, polish and new clothing. Near the bedding were three rows of parachutes stacked so high they nearly reached the roof. Shaw walked straight over to them and picked up an armful. He rushed out and threw them into the back of the jeep. Trauber followed close behind him with a similar load. Leder got the parachutes in some kind of order while Winkel, from behind the wheel, kept a nervy watch. The process continued until they had removed all the parachutes which Leder calculated to be about fifty.

Shaw was pleased with the quantity of the haul, but saw at once that there was now no room for anyone to sit in the rear of the vehicle.

'Look, we're never going to get out with this load. Let's find the Motor pool and nick something larger,' Shaw said a little breathlessly. Somehow the four men squeezed up into the front. Winkel was about to drive off when Shaw stopped him. 'Hold on a minute.' Shaw eased himself out of the crush, jumped to the ground and raced back into the stores. He appeared seconds later carrying a bundle of blue denim overalls. 'Get these on,' he said, as he threw one to each man and struggled into the one he retained. 'We're going to look like we're a fatigue party,' he said, addressing the Germans who quickly followed his example. He noted that all the overalls, including his own, were voluminously too large. They were bloody well-fed, these Yanks, he thought. 'Let's get over to the pool.' He leapt in beside Trauber. 'It's behind the fourth hangar as we came in — that's what he said, didn't he?'

Trauber spoke in German to Winkel and they sped in the direction Shaw had indicated, passing the great gloomy open hangars that echoed with the noise of their engine as they went by. Winkel was the first to spot the group of vehicles that made up the pool; he pointed to it excitedly. He swung the wheel hard into the bay where a selection of vehicles stood in various stages of being dismantled. Some of the lorries and bikes were in so many pieces, Shaw realised, that it would be hours, even days, before most of them could be reassembled. The only possibility of anything that looked faintly mobile was a US Army Air Force ambulance that was still resting on a pneumatic jack with the wheels from the front axle lying on the ground.

'Can Winkel fix that pronto?' Shaw asked hastily. Trauber

posed the question to Winkel, adding an even greater sense of urgency. It was answered with an enthusiastic nodding.

'Right — let's get these 'chutes in the back while he starts work,' Shaw ordered and flung the rear doors of the ambulance open. He poked his head quickly around the inside and saw that it had been stripped bare of all medical equipment. There only remained two long wooden bunks. He heaved a huge bundle of parachutes in the back, Leder and Trauber followed with the lot they were carrying, and started to stack them neatly against the walls of the ambulance. Shaw returned to the jeep, picked up another load — and went cold inside as he saw them.

The two air force snowballs were standing on the corner talking to one another. One of them turned his head and stared over at the activity by the ambulance, creased his forehead in a scowl and started to walk towards them. His companion fell in at his side. There was no time for Shaw to alert the others who were too occupied with the business in hand to notice the MPs approaching. The snowballs were both as tall and broad as trees, and although Shaw was only half an inch short of six foot, they towered above him. The one who seemed the most interested in what was going on pushed his steel-framed service spectacles back above the bridge of his nose.

'Where you guys takin' them 'chutes?' he said in a voice that contained as much curiosity as his face displayed. The three Germans froze like figures in a waxworks.

'These have been tested and rejected,' Shaw replied as calmly as he could, but he was not too happy about his American accent.

'That's not what the man asked; he said, "Where you taking them," buddy.' Shaw looked up at the MP who had just spoken. If anything, he was even bigger than his sidekick, and he noticed, as he leaned in towards him, that his blotchy white skin was full of holes and weeping red pimples.

'I got the transit order somewhere,' Shaw said, fumbling inside his denims till he found the flap of the holster and got a grip on the revolver. But with his other hand he made a lot of patting movements to the top pockets to distract the MPs' attention.

'How come you're using this ambulance?' the MP with the specs asked the grimy Winkel, walking over to him.

52

'That was our orders,' Shaw jumped in quickly. Winkel stood up from the wheel. He had got it on the axle but had not tightened the nuts.

'I'm still waiting to see 'em,' the MP said dryly.

'Ah, here they are,' Shaw mumbled as he pulled the revolver from under his denims and stuck it hard into the ribs of the pock-marked snowball who stood at his side.

'Hell, he's got a piece on me, Del,' the surprised MP exclaimed feebly, addressing his spectacled partner, who made a quick move towards his gun.

'You do and he gets it,' Shaw said tersely. 'Get those guns off them and bung them in the back.' Leder and Trauber sprang to the command and pushed the MPs into the rear of the ambulance. Leder, grinning unpleasantly, held his revolver on them while Trauber tied their hands behind their backs with the gleaming white lanyards he had ripped off their battledress blouses.

'They'll throw away the key of the stockade, boys!' The spectacled MP grimaced as the cord cut into his wrists.

'Say listen, don't be goddamned idiots — you go easy on us and we'll tell the Provost Office it was just a bit of horseplay, OK?' The pockmarked MP lied badly.

'Shut up or I'll put knots in your head,' Shaw snarled and threatened with the butt of his gun. He turned to Trauber and Leder. 'OK, chuck these bums right up the front end and build the 'chutes into a wall round them so they can't be seen from the arse end.' The Germans grasped the parachutes and carried out Shaw's orders. Shaw moved round the ambulance and came to Winkel's side. 'It's good?' he said, pointing to the tyre. Winkel stood up holding the spanner, wiped his blackened hands on the denims and nodded, 'Ja, Ja, it's good.'

Trauber and Leder now joined Winkel and Shaw.

'They should be all right,' Trauber addressed Shaw, 'We have secured them safely.'

'Right, ditch these fatigues,' Shaw ordered and started taking his off. The Germans followed his example and wriggled out of the overalls.

'Now we're going to take it nice and easy — no panic — smoothly, understand?' The men nodded. 'Horst, Martin, in the back – and watch those snowballs, they're cunning bastards. OK, let's scram.'

Trauber and Leder raced to the back of the ambulance,

climbed in and slammed the doors behind them. Winkel, surprisingly agile for his size, jumped in behind the steering wheel. Shaw lifted the bonnet, found the two wires leading to the battery and sparked off the ignition. Winkel pumped the accelerator. In a few seconds the rotor turned over as the engine sprang to life. Shaw grinned at Winkel, slammed down the bonnet and jumped in beside him. Winkel spun the wheel round and the ambulance rocked its way along the flat terrain of the airfield perimeter towards the gate. The guard they had met on their entry gave them a strange look.

'Say, weren't you guys for Motor pool?' he said in a deep lazy voice.

'Sure, but this ambulance is needed in a hurry. We've got to get to a field hospital right away,' Shaw replied, chewing non-existent gum.

'Hey, I didn't know the 10th got posted up these parts,' the guard said, staring at Shaw's armoured corps flash with the tiger's head prominently above. 'I got a brother serving in Tiger's in Bastogne.'

'Great little outfit,' Shaw said pleasantly, and thought all he needed was to engage in small talk with this Texan idiot. He glanced edgily at Winkel and noticed that little droplets of sweat were forming in the creases of his bulging neck.

For a brief moment Shaw breathed a sigh of relief as the guard seemed about to step back to allow the vehicle through, when all at once from inside the ambulance there was the noise of boots being kicked against the thin metal structure, followed by muffled shouts and the sound of a struggle.

'Go!' Shaw yelled at Winkel, '*Schnell!*' He did not have to be asked twice. The ambulance jerked forward past the startled guard, who just managed to jump aside. Shaw heard the blast of his whistle and saw in the mirror that he had run to the guard-box telephone. His only thought now was how fast the crate could go, but his doubts were soon dispelled as he was tossed back and forth, desperately clutching on to the seat, whilst the ambulance screeched around corners and careered hazardously along. Trauber had not exaggerated — Winkel was no amateur when it came to driving. At times there were barely two wheels touching the ground. The commotion in the back of the ambulance had now ceased, and Shaw turned his head awkwardly and held on grimly to the door for support as he tried to look through the small glass communicating panel.

He had half turned when he heard two dull thuds that appeared to come from behind following each other in rapid succession. He glanced in the driver's wing mirror and saw what looked like a pair of sky-blue coloured sacks in the road, getting smaller by the second, as they raced on. One of them got groggily to his feet and Shaw spotted the white gaiters of the Military Police.

'What the hell was going on?' Shaw shouted, just managing to turn in the cabin again. Trauber's voice from the back could just be heard above the roar of the engine. 'You were right, Wally— they were poor travelling companions— we decided to drop them off!'

Shaw smiled resignedly — served 'em bloody right! He despised all MPs. As Winkel spun the vehicle round and negotiated a sharp bend, Shaw could see the road behind them. Apart from a horse and cart and a few farm workers on bicycles it was quite clear. If they were being followed there was no sign of their pursuers. Shaw reasoned that Winkel had opened up such a gap that by the time the air force MPs had rounded up enough of a party to give chase, they would not know what direction to take. He felt it more likely that patrol waggons would be alerted to keep a sharp look out for the stolen ambulance, but this would not be so easy, since large convoys of vehicles, including many ambulances, were constantly to be seen traversing the highways. To stop every one would be a difficult, not to say an impossible, task. Nevertheless, there was no room for complacency, and every so often he would dart a quick look into the mirror.

Winkel still maintained the same breakneck speed but as the surface was flatter the ambulance was holding the road more evenly. Shaw thought his view in the mirror was limited, and he slid the window aside and gingerly poked his head out to look down the road as it snaked out behind them. The wind howled and struck him in the face, numbing his cheeks with its icy breath. He desperately held on to his forage cap while he strained, with half-closed eyes, but he saw nothing to alarm him. He resumed his position in the cabin and signalled to Winkel to drive a little slower. Winkel eased his foot off the pedal and the ambulance moved at a steadier pace. Shaw was now concerned with getting back to the farm as soon as possible and offloading the parachutes at the first opportunity. But at the moment he had no idea of their position. In their hasty get-away he had not noted the road Winkel had taken. Then, by sheer luck, as he glanced through his window he noticed a small stone road sign stuck at an odd angle in a grassy verge. Its weather-worn letters read 'Durbuy 5 kilometres'. They were less than twenty kilometres from their base, and heading in the right direction. He breathed deeply, sat back, stretching his legs, reached into his blouse pocket and fished out a crumpled packet of Camels. He handed one to Winkel, thumbed his tommy-lighter, held it shakily under Winkel's cigarette, and then lit his own. The job had not gone as he had planned, but his new 'allies' had proved themselves efficient and professional. There had been no panic when things started to go wrong. They had improvised well and never questioned his orders. If he could learn to live with an ever-present feeling of guilt, this strange teaming up might just work. He puffed a long thin trail of smoke through the open window and watched the trees go swishing by. Saw two pretty girls with brightly coloured headscarves smile and wave at them from their bicycles, and decided that things could be a darn sight worse!

4

The tailor's shop off the rue Dartois was quite deserted when Shaw and Trauber, still dressed as American soldiers, strolled casually through the brown wooden door. The little bell above jangled tunefully as it announced their presence. Shaw swung a bulky duffle bag on to a small dusty glass counter and looked around. A few rolls of indifferent-coloured cloth rested against a fading yellow painted wall, pinned to which were several curling pages cut from magazines displaying photographs of mannequins parading in sleek pre-war styles. By the counter stood a headless tailor's dummy on a metal stand. A sleeveless 'Prince of Wales' check jacket was draped over it, and Shaw could see white cotton tacking and heavy lines made with marking chalk on the unfinished lapels. He felt the garment and nodded approvingly. Only a rich black marketeer could afford a handmade suit in stuff like this, he thought, a little enviously. Trauber watched him with amused interest.

'Beautiful, eh?' said the stooped, wrinkled old man coming through an outer door. 'I'm making it for a two-star general. It's going to set him back a few francs, I can tell you. Still, you Americans can afford it.' The tailor shuffled over to the dummy and admired his handiwork. 'Well, messieurs, what can I do for you?'

'Don't you recognise me, Max?' Shaw said, taking off his hat and coming closer to the old man. The tailor squinted into Shaw's face through his thick-lensed tortoiseshell-framed glasses and slowly broke into a broad smile.

'Wally, Wally!' he said happily, and threw his arms round

Shaw's waist. Shaw was moved — the old man seemed over-joyed to see him. 'But they said you were dead!' And his face became a frown as he turned back to the door through which he had come, opened it and shouted in an emotional voice, 'Henriette! *Kom hier, wy hebben een onverwachte bezoeker.*'

The tailor then moved to the shop door, pulled a canvas shutter down, threw the lock and shouted again, louder this time, 'Henriette, *waar zyt gy? Laat ons niet zolang wachten, mens!*'

'*Ja, ja, Il ben er al!*' a woman's voice replied impatiently as she appeared wiping her wet hands on a vividly coloured apron. Shaw gazed at her for a moment. She had not had time to put her false teeth in, and her screwed-up sallow features resembled a football with the air let out. He smiled at her warmly and she knew him at one. 'Wally,' she cried and rushed across to plant a wet kiss on his mouth. Shaw hugged the small round woman and remembered that he had first met these kind people whilst hanging on to the neck of the bony little American, Les Harris, who had hammered at the door and dragged Henriette out of bed at some godforsaken hour of the morning. 'This is my buddy, Wally,' he had said, peeling some notes off a bundle and handing them to her, 'he's got a rotting leg and needs looking after.' He turned to Shaw with a broad wink and said, 'You'll be OK here, Limey. They're great folk.' He kissed Henriette and vanished into the dark.

In the following weeks Shaw had grown very fond of the old couple and had learned that before the war Max Cordier was a master tailor with a top clientele, while his wife, Henriette, was in the haute couture class as a dressmaker. When Belgium had capitulated he had subsequently been reduced to becoming an alterations and repair hand for German officers, while Henriette had to confine her talents to creating gaudy gowns for their girl friends and bar-room tarts, who were the only females who could afford such luxuries. Their son, Georges, a soldier, had been killed in the first German onslaught in the May of 1940, and the heartbroken couple promptly offered their services to the Belgian FFI. Max, as befitted his profession, had a good line of chat and would prise from what seemed harmless conversation with some of the more talkative officers little snippets of news which he would duly note. Henriette, not surprisingly, found the hens clucked even more than the cocks. A demand for a dress uniform to be altered to allow for its owner's expanded waistline would be enough of an incentive for Max to go into verbal action. With a series of seemingly innocent questions he could often establish both the time and the venue of the forthcoming occasion. If he learnt it was to be a top brass affair he would contact the 'underground' at once. Thus many a merrymaking gathering came to an abrupt end as its participants were blasted in pieces through the windows of a finely gilded room, after opening that 'special' bottle of vintage champagne. Or an urgent request to make a lady's expensive travelling outfit by a 'stuck-up' high-class tart would indicate that 'Mon General' was requiring extra comforts in a private compartment of a train bound for a vital battle zone. Armed with this kind of advance knowledge, the Résistance could ensure that the train would never reach its destination. The method Max used to convey the information was ingeniously simple. His contact was a clerk in a small wholesalers in Brussels who supplied him with thread, yarn and sundry tailoring materials. Max would fill out the firm's standard order form for supplies he genuinely needed, but in addition he would sometimes request a dozen reels of black cotton. This would mean that a high-ranking SS Official was to attend the party for which he was preparing a uniform. Or in the case of the general on the train, this message was transmitted by a return-of-post order for six bobbins of red machine threads and a new tape measure. Max was also able to disclose the departure time of the train by converting the hour numbers to francs and adding them to a cheque in payment of an invoice.

Never once were these leaks even remotely connected with the little tailor's shop off the rue Dartois. In fact the only time old Max ever had a visit from the Gestapo was when a suspicious and ambitious officer asked him questions about a superior who, it seemed, had a different suit for every hour of the day and who used to come to the shop to get them hand-sponged and pressed.

In the last six months or so, when the German armies were pushed back over their own borders, there had been no call on the Cordiers from the Résistance, and, like most of their fellow countrymen, they turned their attention to the thriving *marché noir*. Although, strictly speaking, black market dealings were illegal, an official 'blind eye' was cast on virtually the entire operation. It would have been impossible to do otherwise as everyone from the Préfecture de Police down to the lowliest customer looking for an ounce of real 'coffee' was, in some way, involved in its activities.

At the time Shaw was first introduced and made welcome in the Cordiers' home, they were running a successful fencing operation for the *marché noir* in Liège. Max was a tough negotiator and would haggle just as vehemently over the price of a single tin of powdered eggs as he would over a whole truckload of cigarettes. But although he drove a hard bargain, once a deal had been struck, it was always cash on the nail.

During the time that Shaw stayed with the Cordiers, they arranged for a doctor 'who could be trusted' to treat his leg and change the dressings regularly, while they themselves attended to his every need. Henriette cooked him nourishing meals made from good meat, vegetables and fruit, all of which were in very short supply, and they would both take it in turns to keep him company at his bedside. At first Shaw assumed they were just exceptional people who cared for all of Harris's deserter friends in the same way, but then he began to feel that their concern for his welfare seemed to be far deeper rooted than merely making sure that he regained his health. One evening, while he was enjoying a particularly delicious dinner, he told Henriette that he was frankly puzzled by their boundless generosity. Without a word, Henriette left the room and returned a moment later with a photograph of a young man wearing the uniform of a Belgian soldier. Their dead son, Georges, bore a vague likeness to himself, especially the way he smiled. The woman looked at the photograph with misty eyes, and Shaw said nothing, but he now understood why . . .

When he could walk properly again, Max introduced him to a strange new world of commerce and Shaw received an education on what was saleable and what was not. Parachutes were, as Max would say, always *'très, très'*. What he learned later was that selling almost anything was fairly simple, getting it quite a different matter.

✻

Shaw noticed that Max was staring pointedly at Trauber who shifted about uneasily, and had taken off his cap to smooth his already glass-like hair.

'You don't know him, Max,' Shaw said, then quickly, 'he's

newly over the wall . . . er . . . Harry—from Poland.' Trauber nodded courteously with a smile, and old Max beamed.

'Listen, what's this "they told you I was dead" stuff?' Shaw looked quizzically at Henriette.

'Yes, yes. Some of the girls from Claudine's", I think—maybe it was "Antoinette's"—I don't know—anyway they said the MPs had shot you.' Henriette laughed piercingly, 'So you must be a ghost, yes!'

'Wasn't a little redhead among them, was there?' Shaw asked and felt his blood rise.

'Do you know, *chéri*, I cannot remember,' Henriette replied, with no hint of evasion in her voice. 'There were three or four girls, all jabbering away—you know what girls are.'

'Yeah,' Shaw replied slowly, 'one in particular, anyway.' Trauber had moved further down the room as he felt the conversation did not concern him, and he busied himself by idly looking through an obsolete pattern book that hung from a hook at the end of the counter.

'Your friend, Leslie, came in pretty wobbly. He was very very sad when he heard you were *mort*.' Max laughed, as he continued, 'I can't wait to see his face when I tell him you are very much alive!'

'Listen, I want you to do me a favour,' Shaw said conspiratorially, 'don't tell a soul you've seen me. If Les calls in, OK, you can mention it to him, but explain he's not to breathe a word to anyone.'

'We shall be like *des huitres*,' Henriette giggled.

'You will have a drink?' Max asked, a smile still on his face.

'No, not now, Max, thanks,' Shaw said hurriedly. 'Got a bit of business—*beaucoup de parachutes*.' Shaw loosened the cord of the duffle bag and tugged at the parachute packings. As he did so he glanced at Max, who was looking anything but enthusiastic.

'Parachutes, I said, Max,' Shaw repeated with a tinge of surprise.

'Yes, I heard you. You know, Wally, the market isn't so good for 'chutes these days,' Max said with a shrug.

Shaw frowned and Trauber looked at him a shade bewildered.

'You see, we're getting some good cloth in from Paris now for those who can afford it, and what with the handling and the dyeing of these—well, it's hardly worth it now,' Max offered in explanation.

'Max, you told me parachutes would always sell.' Much as Shaw liked the man, he couldn't keep the annoyance from his voice, remembering that the parachutes had not been an easy snatch.

'That was true, my friend— a few months ago — but, well, things change all the time — now, tobacco, soap, choc——'

'Hold on,' Shaw interrupted impatiently, 'I know about that, but I've . . . we've got fifty bloody 'chutes in best silk! Are you telling me they're worthless?'

Max sighed. 'No, I did not say that — I said only that they were a lot of trouble now.' Henriette had taken the flap from the parachute pack, pulled some of the silk from the case, draped it over her shoulder and looked into an upright mirror. She turned and postured, and stroked the material lovingly.

'Max, we should have them,' Henriette smiled and winked at Shaw.

'Well,' Max was dithering.

'Please,' Henriette pouted persuasively.

Shaw saw Max take a deep breath, then he looked at him through those frosty lenses that made his eyes look twice their size, and spoke in a businesslike voice.

'How many you got?'

'About fifty,' Shaw replied and saw that Trauber was a shade more relieved.

'Mmm — four thousand francs a piece,' Max said eventually. Shaw bristled— he knew they were worth more than that. Friendship or not, he wasn't going to let Max put one over him, and he certainly wasn't going to show Trauber that he was easy meat.

'Don't force me to be rude, Max — I've got too much respect for your wife,' Shaw said gruffly.

'Look, Wally, you see . . .' Max stammered, and Shaw knew the old fox was weakening.

'Five thousand each,' Shaw stated firmly.

'Impossible! What are you trying to do? Put me out of business?'

'Four and a half— I'll bring them tonight,' Shaw said in a no-nonsense voice. He had learned in his dealings with Max the more you argued, the more he enjoyed it, and he was in no mood to play games.

'What time?' Max asked resignedly.

'After dark.'

The business was now concluded, and Shaw noted that Max suddenly seemed tired and beaten. Shaw softened and broke into a wide smile. Max looked at him as a father does a son, and responded with a grin that displayed a few broken nicotine-stained teeth and an expression that silently conveyed the statement 'I have taught you too damn well!'

While Shaw and Max had been discussing the deal, Trauber was quietly charming Henriette with talk of Paris before the war, and she was giggling like a schoolgirl at an anecdote he had recounted. She left Trauber's side and came over to Shaw, still wreathed in smiles. 'You will eat with us tonight— and of course your *ami*?'

Shaw thought, as he watched her acting coyly, if only she knew my '*ami*' was a German, and SS to boot, the meal would have been laced with a large dose of rat poison. Shaw hugged her to him tightly. She had once shown him some photographs of herself when she was young and had a figure like Hedy Lamarr. Now her lovely contours had vanished under a parcel of flesh and it felt as though his arms were surrounding a bulging bale of cotton.

'Nothing I'd like more,' Shaw said and kissed her fondly on her forehead, 'but not tonight. I've got some unfinished business I must deal with.' Henriette's expression hardened. She pouted like a child, but although it was in fun, Shaw knew she was disappointed.

'Another time, eh? Tell you what, Harry,' Shaw addressed Trauber, 'this is some cook, believe me.' Shaw kissed his finger tips and sniffed in ecstasy at an imaginary aroma.

'Oh, get on with you!' Henriette laughed and pushed Shaw's chest good-naturedly.

'He doesn't exaggerate,' Max turned to Trauber, and tapped his rounded belly.

'I hope you will be kind enough to invite me again,' Trauber smiled and bowed like a tree in the wind.

'Oh, by the way, Max,' Shaw broke his hold on Henriette, 'can you get me a uniform for tonight? Something good— I'll settle with you when I bring the 'chutes.'

Max nodded and Shaw shook his hand firmly. He kissed Henriette again, as Max unbolted the door and he and Trauber left with the sound of the bell jingling in their ears.

5

Shaw descended a short flight of stairs and opened a narrow door. The smoke-filled air with its mixture of five-cent cigars, cigarettes and cheap perfume grabbed him at once in its sweaty embrace. A laughing, shouting hubbub bombarded his ears as soldiers of various nationalities tried to make themselves heard, in an assortment of languages, above the noise of clinking glasses and an old radiogram blasting out the Andrews Sisters' frenetic rendering of 'Boogie-Woogie Bugle Boy of Company B'.

Shaw's eyes vainly searched the room for familiar faces and, finding none, he elbowed his way through the jostling throng towards the bar. He met with little resistance as heads turned in his direction, and men moved out of his way, for that night he was dressed in the uniform of a REME captain, and officers were not frequent visitors at 'Antoinette's'. When he got to the counter, Françoise was pouring a beer for a British lance-jack and fighting a losing battle trying to keep her long chestnut hair from falling into her eyes. She swept it aside with her free hand and half turned towards Shaw, sensing a presence staring at her. The full mouth fell and her large blue eyes widened in surprise as she recognised him. Shaw nodded for her to come from behind the bar and her smile said she understood. He watched her with growing excitement as she handed the drink to the soldier, gave him some change, brushed his hand away as he tried to hold on to hers, whispered urgently to another harassed girl who was pouring wine into tall-stemmed glasses, wiped her hands on a towel, straightened her pencil-slim black skirt, swept her hair from her eyes once again, and moved round the bar to where Shaw stood.

'Ello, Volly — I never thought I would see you again,' she flashed an even row of white teeth, and Shaw noticed that some of the crimson lipstick she was wearing had smudged on to them. 'I was told zey had shot you.'

'Yeah, I know. Can you get away?' Shaw almost commanded, but softened a second later with a flicker of a smile.

'*Non, chéri*, impossible — we are two girls sick and we are crowded like fish.' Françoise took Shaw's hands tenderly. 'Wait for me — you know, when we are closed.'

'Yeah, I'll do that,' Shaw shouted above the din that seemed to get even louder. She made him feel as horny as a rattlesnake about to strike, but he remembered that was not why he had come to this place. He spoke as coolly as he could in the surrounding drone of chatter and blaring music.

'Is Evelyn around?'

'*Cochon!*'

'What?' Shaw scowled.

'*Pauvre* Evelyn,' Françoise's doe-like eyes filled with tears.

'What about poor Evelyn?' Shaw grunted and looked steadily into the delicate white face that wore too much rouge.

'She go wiz zis *cochon*,' Françoise went on in a voice trembling with rage, 'then she find out 'e is from SIB. 'Ow was she to know? Ze man, he is dressed in dobies.'

Shaw became more interested. The SIB were the Special Investigation Branch of the Military Police, and often wore civilian clothes or 'dobies', as the Yanks called them. He was keen to learn more.

'Well, go on.'

'He find out she have a baby,' Françoise's face became hot with anger.

A sweating British corporal, egged on by a group of his mates in the artillery, almost fell between Shaw and Françoise.

'Come on, darlin',' the corporal, thick-tongued with booze, 'we're still waiting for them beers.'

Shaw scowled at the corporal, and Françoise waved a hand at him impatiently.

'You won't get nuffink there, corp,' a voice from the group shouted, 'she's officer bait, ain't she?'

There was some raucous laughter mixed with a few jeers

and whistles. Shaw grabbed Françoise roughly by the arm and steered her past the swaying corporal to a small space he had seen in a corner.

'This baby — what about the little bastard?' he said testily.

'Zis man threaten to tell the authorities she keep ze baby here — unless . . .' Françoise bit her lip as she gazed up at Shaw.

'Unless what?' Shaw snapped irritably.

'Unless she tell him all about ze deserters she sleep wiz.'

Shaw frowned — Françoise wasn't making much sense.

'You see, now we have Belgique Government again, Inspector for Health forbid any children to live in a brothel.'

'So?'

'Evelyn work here since she was twelve years old. She knows no other life. Her baby was born here.'

'Well, where is she now?' Shaw was not entirely convinced, but Françoise did not appear to be lying.

'She have to pack up and go fast, anyway,' Françoise replied bitterly, lowering her voice.

'What?' Shaw could not hear her. His ears were getting blocked by the continual sound of the merrymaking. Françoise repeated her answer, almost shouting it.

'Why?'

'Some *amis* of deserters zey catch come looking for her,' Françoise's eyes blazed. 'Zey say zey will cut her tits off.'

'I'm not surprised,' Shaw muttered gruffly. 'Where did she go?'

'I do not know, and if I did I would not tell you,' Françoise stared at Shaw defiantly. 'She's had enough!'

'She's had enough,' Shaw thought. He looked down at Françoise's slender loveliness, and slowly the anger seemed to drain from him. It was a lousy war. A dog-eat-dog existence. Everyone fighting to survive, by tooth and claw if need be. Could he really blame Evelyn for talking if she thought it would save her and the baby? He was at fault for opening his bloody big drunken mouth in the first place. He nodded, smacked Françoise playfully on her firm round bottom and smiled. 'Get me a good beer — I'll be sitting over by the usual place. I may wait for you here if I can stand this racket.' Shaw watched her face light up and felt a bulge in his pants as her eyes promised the delights of her body. He pushed his way past a couple of very drunk Canadians, and heard her voice call after him. 'Volly, your *ami*, he is over there,' Françoise said gaily, and pointed in the direction Shaw was going. He turned to ask her who she meant but she was already swallowed up in the crowded room. Shaw made his way slowly towards his favourite spot, and then he saw him.

He had a permanent bluish stubble on his face that resisted even the sharpest razor blade, and his vigorous dark curls were firmly held in place by an excess of oil that reflected the wall light he sat under like a wavy black mirror. His sad brown eyes, far too big for the round face they were set in, always seemed the same even when he laughed. A smoothly curved nose guarded full lips that resembled a fish leaping for a fly and missing it, and his short neck seemed to have fought its way out of shoulders that sloped like the sides of a pyramid. Leslie Harris was reading *Yank* and chuckling over the strip cartoon 'Sad Sack'. Harris loved the army as much as he hated it. That night the love affair was on again — he was dressed in his correct uniform, that of a PFC in the 2nd Infantry Division, or 'Indian Heads' as they liked to be called. He looked up, still smiling at what he was reading, as Shaw sat opposite him and placed his cap on the table.

'How's your arse?' Harris said with a voice that displayed genuine pleasure at seeing his friend again.

'Beautiful,' Shaw replied dryly.

'I like the suit,' Harris looked at Shaw's uniform admiringly.

'Like it?' Shaw's eyes shone with humour. He had almost forgotten that his original purpose for calling at the bar was to seek a soul-soothing revenge. In the last few days the thought of coming face to face with the little whore had eaten into his guts — now it didn't seem to matter much any more. It was a strange existence all right.

Harris was feeling the lapels of his uniform. 'A nice piece of schmutter,' he nodded approvingly.

'Two bottles of Scotch and a parachute,' Shaw grinned. 'Half a case of Spam on top of that, I could have been a general!'

'What I like about you, Wally, you never was ambitious.'

Shaw looked at the man who had possibly saved his life, and certainly his sanity. Shaw remembered his first encounter with Harris . . .

*

One sleepless night, when his leg was playing him up like hell, Shaw crept to the night sister's small annexe at the end of the long slumbering ward. It was well known among the patients that she was shacking up with an English dental officer, and, as he got to the tiny room the sound of bed springs creaking noisily was competing with her muffled gasps and the dentist's empty 'I love yous'. Shaw silently took the RAMC uniform from the chair in which it had been hurriedly thrown and crept out. He changed in the latrines and left through the main gate, where he was saluted by a sleepy private on picket duty. He'd headed at once to the 'off limits' area of the town, and was happy to find that the dentist had a wallet bulging with Belgian and English notes. After that, events were a bit hazy. For several days he lived in a sweet nightmarish world of women and booze, as he fell from bed to bar in an almost continuous cycle. He was throwing up some bad cognac violently into a gutter on a cold drizzling evening when the American major came up behind him and said politely, but firmly, 'I'd like to see your ident papers, lieutenant.'

Shaw muttered something about not having them with him and vomited again. The major pulled a gun on him and said he had reason to believe he was an AWOL in a 'borrowed' uniform. Shaw told him to mind his own fucking business and aimed a wild punch at his head. It missed by a mile and he remembered no more until he found himself sitting at a table in a quiet bar with the major opposite him, and a head that ached almost as much as his leg.

'Your leg is in a bad way, Limey,' the American major said and his voice showed real concern. Shaw noticed that the man no longer had a gun on him and he got up to leave, but fell back into his chair in agony.

'Don't be an idiot,' the major said, 'You wouldn't get two blocks with that leg.'

The man then introduced himself formally as PFC Leslie Harris and explained that he was a deserter like Shaw, and had been in and out of the stockade almost since the Americans had landed in Europe. He told him that he'd gone to fight for a cause that included wiping out the evil of anti-Semitism, represented in all its horrors by Nazi Germany. But he found that Jew-baiting was not just a German prerogative and he had to take insult after insult from one sadistic NCO after another because of his faith. One day, a loud-mouthed sergeant was spouting off that Hitler had the right idea screwing all the young Jewesses and knocking off the rest of the race. Harris calmly picked up a baseball bat and hammered the man's head in. He'd spent six months in the stockade after they eventually caught him, but had, while over the hump, been introduced into the life of the *marché noir* — which, he'd explained to Shaw, had suited his style down to the ground. Before the war he'd been a reasonably successful forger and con-man, and had learned from his alcoholic father, a vaudeville magician, how to make playing cards 'leap up their arse and back again'. It was after one particularly crooked poker game with a murder-minded bunch of victims hot on his tail that he volunteered to join Uncle Sam, and got out of the USA. He offered to teach Shaw the *marché* business, but told him that 'first you gotta get that leg fixed good', and took him to the Cordiers' little tailor's shop. When Shaw was fit again, Harris was as good as his word and the two men became inseparable.

*

Harris neatly folded his copy of *Yank*, laid it carefully on the table, gripped his tumblerful of Belgian whisky, took a slug, contorted his face in disgust as he gulped it down, and stared steadily at Shaw.

'Heard that some crummy *poule* did more than open her legs regarding your goodself!'

'Very true,' Shaw replied evenly, 'I gather you've seen Max?'

Harris nodded slowly. 'They got Two-Way you know.'

Shaw felt the colour drain from him. He had been so concerned with his own problems that he hadn't given the big Negro a thought. 'I didn't,' he muttered weakly.

'Yeah, when you made off, he gave himself up, but a snowball bastard said "fuck the nigger" so they kicked his ass and used him as target practice.' Harris paused and took another sip from his glass. 'When they fished him out of the river, he had more holes than a clarinet.'

Shaw felt sick. 'How do you know he gave himself up?' he said eventually.

'One of the snowballs told another nigger — a buddy of Two-Way. They was working over in the stockade,' Harris replied. 'They also said they got you.'

69

'Well, if it wasn't true about me,' Shaw said grimly, 'why should it be about Two-Way? You know, I mean about giving himself up. Maybe this loudmouth MP was just sounding off, trying to scare the geezer.'

'Yeah, maybe,' Harris nodded. 'But I don't believe that — do you?'

Shaw shook his head, 'No.'

'So, anyway, listen — what you been up to?' Harris said more brightly.

'Oh, you know — this and that,' Shaw answered evasively, 'bits and pieces.'

'OK, so tell me,' Harris's eyes bored into Shaw with the look that he reserved for a poker opponent when he was calling his bluff.

Shaw considered Harris to be his closest friend. He liked the man immensely and had far too much respect for him to resort to lies. With as much diplomacy as he could muster, he recounted the events of the last few weeks, and of his teaming up with the Germans. Harris reacted as Shaw had feared he might. He was furious, his mouth stretched into a white snarl.

'Are you kidding — Germans?' He slammed his glass down on the table top.

'These blokes are not so bad,' Shaw decided he would not refer to Leder at this stage.

'You're not Jewish! I thought you were my buddy,' Harris seethed, 'and here you are, working with Nazis!'

'Les, they're not all Nazis,' Shaw said evenly, but Harris's attitude jolted his conscience again.

'Balls!' Harris uttered contemptuously.

'Look, Les, these fellows are as pissed off with the war as we are,' Shaw offered by way of explanation. 'They know the game — they've got some pretty good contacts. I've done a caper with them and they're good.'

'Well, bully for you,' Harris blazed.

'I was going to ask if you would join us,' Shaw said, mimicking Groucho Marx and flicking a non-existent cigar in the air.

'That'd better be a joke, Limey.' Harris didn't smile.

Although Shaw had suggested it light-heartedly, he had hoped that Harris might have considered the idea. Shaw sat silently for a while drumming his fingers on the table to the strains of the 'Cow Cow Boogie' that blared from the crackling speaker. He wanted to say something that might break the

70

tension that had suddenly developed between them, but could think of nothing that would not make the situation worse. After what seemed an interminable lull, the American picked up his glass and looked at Shaw steadily.

'Wally, I think you're out of your skull,' Harris had cooled a little, 'but that's your business. If you need ration books, ident. cards, passes, you got 'em. Anything for you I'll make. For them nothing — understand?' Shaw nodded, there was no point in pursuing the issue when Harris was in this mood. Perhaps some other time, if he was still with the Germans, he would be able to talk with more conviction. He remembered, as he had shared out the money with Trauber, Leder and Winkel, how he had said they would tackle a PX next, and Shaw had told them he would get some information on the most suitable one in the next day or so. The three Germans seemed happy with their first pay-out, and had gone back to the farm to await his return.

'I'm thinking of turning over a PX.' Shaw leaned on the table and fiddled with his cap. 'Max said chocolate, gum, hooch, fetch ridiculous prices now.'

'Yeah, true enough. The one at . . . cr . . . oh, Jesus, what's it called, Pepinsten, could be good. It's pretty new, they took over some kids' school and turned it into a military base. Some of the guys from 75th Infantry are holed up there. Far as I know, it's never been hit.' Harris was almost enthusiastic.

Françoise arrived at the table, winked at Harris and placed a large bottle of beer and a glass under Shaw's nose. 'About bloody time,' he growled with a crooked smile, as he pulled a note off a bundle, gave it to her with one hand, slid his other hand up her skirt and gently squeezed her crotch. She giggled, pulled his hand away and fought her way back to the bar.

'That's some chick, eh!' Harris said enviously.

'Yeah. Listen, any idea of the layout of this joint at Pepinsten?' Shaw queried.

'I'll try and find out for you, palsy,' Harris pulled another face as he took a swig from his glass. 'Nazis — Wally, I can't believe it.'

Shaw began to protest when the whiff of strong perfume drifted under his nostrils. He turned and saw two girls smiling down at him. They were a couple of tarts who normally hung out at the Coq d'Or. He had a feeling that he had slept with both of them, but he wasn't too sure. They were somewhat alike, their sameness constructed from the fashions of the day; Alexis-Smith hair, Betty Grable lips, Lana Turner tits. Harris stood up politely, Shaw remained seated.

'You're a bit off your beat, aren't you?' Shaw smiled and aimed his question at the taller of the two girls.

'The *gendarmes* have closed the Coq D'or, *chéri*, didn't you know? the girl replied.

'How come?' Shaw wasn't really interested.

'A zigzag GI knifed the barman, Adolphe — he died. They shut the place up.' Shaw nodded, he still wasn't very interested.

Harris sat down again. Shaw racked his brains to think of their names. 'Meet er . . .'

'Jacqueline and Nikki,' the tall girl said helpfully, and smiled at Harris. 'A couple of goers,' Shaw added.

Nikki moved behind Harris, chewing gum and clicking her fingers in time with the music. Shaw and Harris watched her gyrate.

'This one's still going,' Harris's brown eyes were bulging like two large chestnuts.

'Hi, Joe,' Nikki pouted at Harris, and wriggled in beside him.

'Les,' Harris corrected her. Shaw looked at Harris with a bemused expression.

'I always tell 'em my real name,' Harris replied to the silent question. 'I like to hear it in bed, otherwise it sounds like they're with some other guy, and when I'm paying for it, that makes me real mad!' They all laughed, but Shaw knew the girls did not really understand what Harris meant. Shaw saw Harris hand Nikki a stick of gum, and then offer one to Jacqueline, who had snuggled in at his side. Shaw moved up to make room, but she made sure her thighs were still touching his.

'*Merci,*' both girls said together and giggled as they peeled the wrappers off the gum.

'My pleasure,' Harris acknowledged courteously.

'Nobody ever said a truer word,' Shaw took another gulp of his beer. It tasted foul, and he'd told Françoise to get him a good one. The annoyance showed on his face. Jacqueline saw his expression and came closer to him.

'We go upstairs, *chéri*?' she half whispered in his ear. Shaw looked at his watch. 'Later, maybe. I want a few drinks first.'

He stared over the crowded room and contemplated making his way through it again. He noticed, in the sweltering mass of babbling humanity, a big man in a belted overcoat. It was unbuttoned and he saw him reach into his jacket pocket, take out a lighter and flick it under a cigarette that was dangling from his lips. His eyes quickly searched the room and his gaze momentarily fell on Shaw. He turned away, puffed out a cloud of smoke and gathered his coat around him as he casually left the room. Shaw remembered what Françoise had told him about the SIB, and he started to feel jumpy.

'Listen, Les, silly question, I know,' Shaw said urgently.

'Absolutely definitely no, I will not work with your lousy Krauts,' Harris countered quickly. Shaw ignored the interruption. 'Are you AWOL at the moment?'

'You're right, it is a silly question,' Harris spluttered on his whisky and smiled at Nikki.

'But you're wearing your proper clobber!'

'I know that, Limey. They were taking me to meet the nice provost captain over a little matter of being sixteen days AWOL.'

Harris put down his drink and Shaw saw him slip his hand under the table and watched, amused, as a startled Nikki sat up with jolt. 'Naturally, I had to be attired in my best going-away suit— thing was we had conflicting ideas on which way I should be going. After careful consideration I decided to extend my vacation.'

'How did you pull that?' Shaw asked with a grin.

'I just happened to mention that I thought I got a dose of syph, so this captain says get the dirty little Yid up to the doc, we don't want him poxing up our nice clean cooler.'

Harris rubbed the furrows on his forehead, and Shaw noticed he seemed tired. 'Anyway, this doc was only a kid, a rookie. He hands me this beaker, sends me into a side room and says 'fill it up'. Well, this room had a little window. For all I know the quack is still waiting for me to come out holding it!'

Shaw laughed. 'Well, you mean you've not got yourself some dobies by now?'

'Wally, they've caught me so many times, I'm thinking of hiring myself out as "basket-ball",' Harris wisecracked. 'Naw! You don't catch me in dobies again, nor impersonating an officer. I got too much of a record. Buck private— that's me, baby, so if they grab me all they can hit me with is an AWOL charge. Right?'

Shaw shook his head. This was the man who had taught him nearly all he knew about the art of switching roles and identities in the constant quest to stay free. Harris could be a strange case sometimes. Shaw knew that he desperately wanted to be a good soldier. If only the snowballs and the other vicious sods had left him alone, he would have been.

'I got a feeling we're going to have a visit tonight, that's all,' Shaw said pensively.

'Aw, come on, relax,' Harris slipped his arm around Nikki, who was running her fingers round the rim of his glass. 'This broad gives me a hard just sitting by her. Want to come beddy-byes — Daddy give you lots of —— '

It started with the shrill piercing of whistles which cut through the incessant chatter. It was followed instantly by the door being smashed in and a swarm of MPs, both British and American, poured through the small entrance like a turgid khaki custard. They pushed, they shoved, and used their sticks viciously on anything or anyone. The screams and shouts only seemed to accelerate their frenzy as they grabbed soldier after soldier and pinned them against the wall. The man Shaw had seen in the overcoat was with them and pointed to where he sat. Immediately a group of MPs came in his direction, kicking over tables as they struggled, with hate-filled faces, to get to him. Jacqueline and Nikki screamed as they approached. Harris tried to bolt for it, but a snowball leapt at him and pulled him to the floor. Shaw quickly raised his hand to the wall behind and felt for the fuse box. With a practised move he slammed the switch down. The room was plunged into a sudden darkness, and, for a split second, there was an uncanny silence. Then the screams and shouts commenced again even louder as panic swept through the room and hysterical people tried to fight their way out.

When the lights went on again, Shaw had gone.

A burly American MP was forcing Harris to bend over a table by ramming his arms tightly up behind his back. Harris winced, but made no sound. The snowball snapped a pair of handcuffs on his wrists and grinned spitefully as he did so. Elsewhere in the room the MPs had taken complete control as they hustled girls into a far corner and were roundly cursed for their trouble in choice words of Flemish. Other MPs were dragging bleary-eyed servicemen and tarts in various stages of undress from rooms upstairs and pushing them to the centre of the mêlée. The women were then roughly ushered to the section where the others stood, some sobbing, some adjusting their clothes, some just screaming abuse. Another area of the room near the bar had been cordoned off by a ring of chairs and tables. Inside the circle several soldiers and civilian 'suspects' had their arms raised while redcaps and snowballs systematically searched their pockets and checked identity cards.

The man in the belted raincoat emerged from somewhere in the bustling commotion and came over to Harris who was still being held by the snowball doubled across the table. As the man approached, the MP released his grip on Harris and allowed him to straighten up.

'Where is that . . . officer . . . you were with?' the man asked Harris coldly as he searched his pockets and studied his ID card. Harris made no reply.

The man waited for a moment and repeated the question more forcibly. Harris shrugged non-committally. The man nodded meaningfully to tho MP who acknowledged the silent command by poking Harris heftily in his back with the cane towards a group of men being herded outside to a line of waiting trucks . . .

*

The red bedside lamp swathed their naked bodies in its warm glow. Jacqueline grimaced as the drunken Yank pawed her ineffectually. Saliva hung from his mouth as he lifted his head from her breast and listened to the approaching clamour. The four snowballs burst into the room nearly breaking the door off the already loose hinges with the impact. The Yank looked up at them and burped loudly as his head swayed from side to side like a slowed-down metronome. Quickly the MPs searched the pockets of his uniform which lay strewn across the carpetless floor. Then they poked about with their sticks under the bed and inside and behind the wardrobe. One of the snowballs opened up the dusty windows and stuck his head out, and looked left, right, and up and down.

'Wassamatter?' the Yank hiccuped and felt for the half-bottle of vodka that stood on the bare boards near the bed. A snowball held up a pass that he had fished out from the soldier's clothes whilst his colleagues scrutinised it thoroughly. Satisfied it was in order, the MP handed it to the

Yank who grabbed it with one hand while he lifted the bottle with the other, took a long swig and offered it, with a smile, to the nearest MP. It was greeted with a surly look and the four snowballs stormed out of the room leaving the door wide open. Jacqueline got off the bed at the sound of their boots retreating down the creaking floorboards of the corridor and slammed the door hard.

'*Cochon*!' she spat venomously.

The Yank seemed to sober up considerably as he looked for his clothes and slowly started to dress.

'Ten dollars, OK, Joe?' Jacqueline said in a businesslike manner.

'What — are you stupid?' the Yank replied.

'Ten I was told — ten!' Jacqueline made the point firmly. She flounced to the bed in a temper and began to pull the covers off angrily. 'Goddam you — you all the goddam same!'

The Yank looked sheepish. He walked to the door and locked it. 'OK, ten,' he said finally. Then he watched the girl as she tugged off the sheets and blankets and threw them carelessly on the floor behind her. When the bed was completely stripped, she slipped her long fingers behind a thin groove at the top of a padded board which was inserted in the mattress and lifted it up. Shaw stretched stiffly and blinked as he raised himself from the 6' × 3' × 3' foxhole in the mattress. What air there was in the blackness had been foul, and he took a deep breath as he climbed out.

'How much?' Shaw looked at Jacqueline hazily, his eyes not yet accustomed to the light.

'Ten,' Jacqueline replied.

Shaw felt for the bundle of notes in his back pocket and peeled off two five-dollar bills and handed them to her. Jacqueline turned to the Yank and thrust them into his open palm.

'Thanks, lady,' the Yank slurred, acting drunk again, 'any time!' Shaw watched as he weaved to the door, unlocked it, turned back to Shaw, saluted shakily, winked broadly, and almost fell back out of the room as he hung on to the handle, closing the door as he left. Shaw straightened himself, spread his arms wide, and heard his neck creak with the movement.

'You like me to get dressed again?' Jacqueline purred provocatively. Shaw seemed to notice her nakedness for the first time as she undulated sensuously towards him. The threat now

76

averted, his blood began to race as he gazed at her.

'Hardly seems worth it!' Shaw felt the excitement mounting inside him as his eyes roamed over her creamy skin, over her small but firm breasts with the dark-chocolate nipples that stood out as he gently squeezed them. His eyes fell to the almost perfect triangle of brown silky hair that contrasted so startingly with the whiteness all around it, and offered such flimsy protection for the well of pleasure he was soon to explore. Jacqueline pressed her body tightly against him and slid her hand to his trousers, unbuttoning them, tauntingly taking her time. At last she had loosened them, and Shaw let out a gasp as the cool slender fingers found his rampant swelling.

'I can feel Tommy is coming to attention like a good soldier,' Jacqueline whispered nibbling his ear. I wonder how many hundreds of times she's used that line, Shaw thought, and the idea of it slightly dampened the first strong arousal. But it was only momentarily as Jacqueline's lips fluttered down his face with the softness of a butterfly's wings until they found his. Then opening her lips she searched every part of his mouth with dagger-like thrusts of her tongue. Glued together like this, she steered Shaw back to the unmade bed. Deftly she peeled away the underpants that were the only barrier to the goal of her breathless desire. Her eyes seemed to burn, as, just for a fleeting moment she looked hungrily at him, then with an animal moan she lowered her head and fell over his pulsating hardness. Shaw saw the blonde hair with the dark roots bobbing like a beach ball on a raging sea, and felt the darting moistness of the warm waves that lapped around him, sweeping him in on a quickening tide that could only disperse in a final gratifying explosion.

When he could stand it no longer, he grabbed her head from him and threw her back onto the bed, 'Oh, *oui, oui*!' she uttered with a tortured cry and swept long legs round his back pulling him into her . . .

Shaw noticed the glistening sweat in the valley between her breasts as he rolled to his side panting, and as the heat left his body he shuddered with a clammy coldness. Jacqueline leaned over and kissed him on the mouth and muttered an endearment in French, but he didn't really listen. He was spent, and her touch repulsed him. He stared up at the fine cracks in the plaster ceiling, and in the dimly lit room the spidery lines seemed to form familiar cartoonish shapes: there was Humphrey Bogart complete with bent trilby, a large woman with one enormous tit and one smaller one, and a broken cricket bat leaning against the wing of an aeroplane. He shut his eyes . . .

The shadowy corners of the room merged into one and waved like a black banner across his mind. Tiny threads of red cotton broke the starkness; the threads, now no longer cotton, were rivers of blood flowing from a leg without skin; faceless bodies on cindered grass. A sickly stink of frizzling hair and sweet flesh roasting, smelling like pork. A hissing streak of white flame. A lightning strike of searing pain. Hands coming towards him out of a smoking inferno. Thundering bangs, distant voices yelling, 'Medics, medics!' and another voice, louder than everything screaming straight from Hell, filling all the air. It echoed through an endless tunnel, shrill, incessant, increasing in pitch, beating its way into his consciousness, as yet another voice, soft, warm, feminine, smoothed the agonised cry and surely stifled it.

'*Chéri, chéri,*' Shaw opened his eyes and saw Jacqueline's silhouette in front of the lamp. She was gently shaking him. '*Chéri,* you are having bad dream — you shouting like crazy.'

Shaw sat up and felt the clawing dampness on his back, the salty sweat on his lips and his heart trying to crash through his ribs. He pummelled a pillow to form a back rest and pulled some bedclothes that Jacqueline had retrieved in the night around him. He felt lost and utterly alone. He stretched out an arm to bring Jacqueline to him, but she had turned on her side and in a few seconds Shaw heard her deep breathing broken occasionally by a single snore. He sat there, quite still. There would be no sleep for him that night.

6

An icy morning wind scattered the curling golden leaves around Shaw's ankles. He blew noisily through his cupped hands and felt the warmed air bring tingling life back to his numbed fingers. He leaned against the huge petrol bowser and watched the two RAF men reluctantly remove their uniforms while Leder impatiently tapped his foot and pointed the Erma threateningly at them. Shaw observed that Leder's face had taken on the appearance of a sinister clown's, its whiteness highlighted as it was now by two crimson ears and a red-tipped nose. About twenty yards to the rear of the vehicle Winkel stood in the middle of the lonely road keeping a sharp lookout for anything that might be approaching, and engaging in a series of exercises that included jumping up and down and swinging his arms round his barrel-shaped girth. When the airmen were down to their underwear Shaw walked over to them and offered them a cigarette. He could see they were shaking with cold and goose bumps stood up quite clearly on their chalky flesh. A bony-faced youth with thick black hair cropped atop an almost depilated neck that made him resemble a chimney sweep's brush, stuck out a trembling hand to accept the cigarette. His sturdier companion, whose eyebrows seemed to join together over a beak-like nose pushed the hand away angrily before the youth could take it. 'Stuff 'em,' the man snorted, 'we're having nothing to do with bleedin' deserters. That's what you are, ain't you?' Shaw made no reply. He removed his top sergeant's blouse, dropped it on the ground in front of him, and donned the still body-warm

RAF jacket. This action, coupled with the freezing temperature seemed to enrage the beak-nosed man even more. He leaned forward like a fighting cock about to attack and pointed to a group of hills on the horizon. 'There's our mates over there getting their heads blown off and you bleedin' deserters nicking this juice — what they need. Well, you know what I hope. I hope they bleeding catch you and hope they bleedin' bump you orf!'

'Yeah,' the thin-faced youth jeered, joining in the defiant mood of his comrade. Shaw, now dressed in the RAF uniform tossed the other discarded one to Leder who caught it expertly with one hand, while still training the gun on the men with the other.

'Bleedin' quislings,' the beak-nosed man breathed savagely between chattering teeth as he watched Leder putting on the jacket with the LAC's stripe he had worn so proudly.

The man's remarks stung Shaw. He could feel completely at ease with his conscience when his activities were in direct conflict with the Military Police. But the man who had spoken so scathingly had an accent he could identify with at once and had the kind of cockney courage he knew so well and admired so much. The words got right through to him, and for the first time since he went over the wall, he felt rotten.

Shaw swung the giant steering wheel and guided the heavy bowser around the treacherous corner of the snaking road. Leder, who sat at his side and had been silent for most of the journey, turned towards him as he struggled to steady the vehicle. 'Difficult to handle, eh?'

'You could say that,' Shaw replied flatly, and peered into the driver's mirror to see that Winkel was still following closely behind in the jeep.

'Still you are coping admirably,' Leder said with genuine approval. Shaw did not answer. A picture of the beak-nosed RAF man waving his fist at them and shouting, 'Bleeding quislings,' as he set off with his skinny companion on an hour's jog to the nearest village kept coming into his mind. He sometimes felt a sense of achievement when he pulled off a job. Apart from the resulting proceeds of these commando-type raids there was usually a feeling of satisfaction. On this occasion for some reason there was none. He glanced at his watch. The second hand was sweeping towards the 08.32 mark. If there were no more snags he assumed that Trauber would now be going through his well-practised routine of bargaining over the sale of goods they had stolen from the PX at Pepinsten. An aide of Claude Caminade, one of the very few who knew their hideout, had agreed to meet them at the farm the previous evening and make an offer for the booty which included Bourbon, french letters, chewing gum and chocolate, but had not arrived. Some hours after he was due they were alerted by a loud knocking on the cellar door and a fresh-faced kid of about thirteen shouted down that his papa had to meet Monsieur Caminade on important business in Brussels, but would be along immediately on his return in the morning. Before they could ask him any more questions, the boy had climbed on his bicycle and ridden off into the night. The hijack of the petrol bowser had been arranged some days before. Leder had told Shaw that over a long period of observation of the area he had seen a heavily laden gasoline truck head in the direction of a small RAF station about thirty kilometres from the farm. It always took the same route at the same time, 08.35, and was never escorted, but came regularly once a week. Shaw knew that on the *marché noir* petrol was valued almost as highly as gold, and he decided that the delay in the disposal of the haul from Pepinsten should not interfere with their plans. The vehicle's weekly trip was on the following morning, and he was determined they should be there to greet it. The plan itself was simple enough. They would bring the jeep up to a tree as though it had smashed into it. Winkel would lie in the road with a greatcoat over him and groan in agony. Shaw would frantically wave the driver and his mechanic down and ask them to help him get his injured buddy to a hospital. Leder would then spring from behind the jeep and hold the airmen up with the machine gun. All would have gone smoothly had it not been that Winkel had chosen to have a long piss in the bushes when the vehicle turned the corner ten minutes ahead of schedule. Shaw grabbed Winkel and threw him on his back in the road, where for a second or so he looked like a whale spouting a steaming yellow jet. Even the normally stony-faced Leder broke into a smile, but there was no time to appreciate the absurdity of the situation as the truck, after swerving round the bend, began to gather speed at an alarming rate, and a terrified Winkel just had time to roll out of the way when it was plain it had no intention of slowing down. As it reduced speed momentarily and the driver changed gear to climb a sudden incline, Shaw leapt at the bowser and just managed to get a precarious foothold on the side while he hammered desperately on the glass. The driver who was deeply engrossed in conversation with his mechanic, nearly lost his grip on the wheel as he saw Shaw's face staring at him through the window. When he eventually brought the vehicle to a shuddering stop, Shaw went through a hastily revamped story until a breathless Leder sprinted to the other side and stuck his gun through the window forcing the occupiers to climb out.

At first the RAF men seemed utterly bewildered at being held up by these 'Americans' and then it slowly dawned on the elder of the two that they had been ambushed not by 'Yanks', not even by Jerries, but by 'bleedin' deserters'.

Shaw flattened the pedal against the floor as the monster groaned, hissed and raced on. They had earmarked a clearing in the woods about eight kilometres from their hideaway where they would camouflage the bowser with leaves and foliage until they could arrange for a suitable buyer to take it off their hands. In the meantime they would have a good supply of petrol for the jeep and for that reason alone the hijack would have been justified.

'Not too far now,' Leder said, gazing out of his window at some familiar landmarks.

'About another ten minutes,' Shaw replied. He was aware that Leder was trying to be particularly amiable. He had, in fact, throughout the entire operation, been obeying Shaw's orders without so much as a hint of question. He observed that Leder was more inclined to act pleasantly when Trauber was not present. It was as though he could not resist 'showing off' in front of Trauber whom he seemed to treat with almost idolising reverence.

An isolated farm worker's cottage loomed up in front of them and as they sped by a young woman in a flapping head-scarf was struggling to hang some billowing washing on a clothes-line that sagged over a sparse vegetable garden. She stopped what she was doing, took a clothes peg from her mouth and waved at them with a smile. Shaw turned in his cabin and waved back to the woman, and in that fleeting moment her face became another's . . .

*

. . . It was a lovely face with deep brown eyes that shone like a mischievous child's and a mouth that was perhaps a shade too large yet softly framed those perfect white teeth which contrasted so vividly with that near flawless light olive skin. A skin which was marred by a tiny crescent shaped scar on her right temple, the result of a tumble from a bike when she was very young, and which she sometimes managed to conceal by brushing her long hair over it, and, oh Christ, that hair, that golden-brown hair that flowed right down to her slight shoulders as proudly as a thoroughbred's mane. It was the hair that first captivated him, the way she tossed it like an impatient race horse rearing to flay the turf. He remembered that she did it when he first met her, threw her hair back as she leaned into the open window of his taxi and asked him in a low voice that had an edge of agitation, to take her to her home in Manor House.

He could see that she had been upset by something or someone and he wanted to start a conversation, but oddly enough — for he was a taxi driver and used to cheerful repartee — he found himself tongue-tied and the best he could manage was to mumble something about the weather. When he got to her home she got out of the cab quickly and searched through her handbag to pay the fare as tears began to fill he eyes. She told him that she did not have enough on her, but if he would wait she would go inside and get it for him. Shaw told her not to bother and there would be another time, but she absolutely insisted that he wait. After a few minutes she came down the steps with the money and a good tip which he felt strangely uncomfortable about accepting, and yet was too timid to refuse. He began to say something when she turned on her heel and ran up the stairs and even though he could only see her back, he knew that she was crying by the way she hung her head.

He did not see her again for many months, and that time it was not as a fare-paying passenger. He had gone with some pals up west to celebrate his twenty-third birthday, and after doing the usual tour of pubs, they wound up at their planned destination, the Astoria Dance Hall in the Charing Cross Road. That was where all the best-looking skirt hung out. The revolving mirrored light in the centre of the room reflected the magenta slide that indicated that a romantic set was to be played by the band, and a soft-voiced crooner broke into the verse of 'Whispering'. Shaw looked hastily around for a partner. He was full of confidence-giving liquor and was determined to show his pals that he was going to wind up with the prettiest girl in the place. And then he saw her! She was sitting with another girl, laughing at her companion's animated conversation. It was her all right, and suddenly his Dutch courage deserted him. Yet there was no one in the hall to compare with her. He walked over to her nervously and said, 'I know it's the oldest line in the world, but we have met somewhere before, and if you will have this dance with me I'll tell you where.'

'Ooh, Sylvia,' her friend giggled, and nudged her. 'What have you been up to?' Sylvia looked as though she recognised him, yet he knew she couldn't place the brief meeting although she was clearly intrigued, and with a warm smile she accepted his invitation . . .

*

Shaw changed the great gear lever furiously and felt it vibrate under his hand as, just in time, he remembered to double-declutch! His mind was far away. Hell! What the hell is it all about! He felt angry with God, with himself, with everything. He tried to recall the incident of Winkel in the road in the hope that he might regain his lost good humour, but all he kept seeing was that lovely face, while his ears rang with the words 'Bleedin' quisling!'

7

Dressed in a thin khaki vest and blue underpants, Harris shivered as he sat hunched and dejected on the rough board which served as a bunk, and gazed down at the stone floor. The small whitewashed cell he occupied was damp, cold and silent, the blank stillness broken only by an irregular drip of water that came from a corroding gutter outside the tiny barred window. But Harris did not hear it, he was listening to a different sound, one he had learned to dread. Faint at first, it became louder and louder as each approaching heavy footstep was heralded by the dull ring of metal studs echoing along the corridor which led to his cell. Suddenly the marching halted and the noisy rattling of a bunch of keys followed at once. Harris raised his head. There was a large bruise on the side of his cheek that nearly closed one eye, and blood that had come from his swollen nose had caked hard on his shoulder, staining the front of his vest. He stared at the door as he heard a key being slotted into the lock and the sound of a precise click as it turned to release the bolt. Instinctively he tried to bring his hands forward but only his shoulders responded to the mental command — his wrists were firmly cuffed behind him. He coughed painfully, stilled his shivering body and awaited their entrance.

The snowball guard, with a skin covered in freckles and a nose that lifted at the tip to expose his nostrils, flung the cell door wide open and moved to one side. A huge MP staff sergeant came in behind him, stood in the door frame and almost filled every part of it. He walked forward slowly, his flat face contorted with hatred as his grey eyes narrowed and seemed to bore into Harris like a dentist's drill.

The staff sergeant brought his stick down with a hefty smack into the palm of his massive hand. 'Where's Shaw?' he asked in a voice icy with menace. He turned to the snowball guard and nodded. The snowball guard closed the door, stood straddled against it on the inside and smirked at Harris sadistically. Harris threw him a look of sheer contempt and turned defiantly to the staff sergeant. 'He ain't one of ours,' Harris heard himself lisp between split lips.

'But you are, buddy,' the staff sergeant sneered and smacked the cane into his hand again. 'The Limeys want to know where he is, and we think you're going to tell us.' Harris dropped his eyes to the floor and made no reply.

'He doesn't know,' the staff sergeant repeated in the same tone. Harris looked at the fearsome duo, as they began their well-rehearsed routine and knew that he was powerless to avoid the inevitable outcome. Even if he had any idea where Shaw might be and he told them, they would still belt the daylights out of him because they'd got the taste of blood. He might just as well keep his mouth shut and save his friend.

'Maybe he does know,' the snowball guard continued in a derisory tone.

'Maybe — this is entirely possible,' the staff sergeant turned to his colleague as though they had just made a great discovery. 'Maybe the pissball doesn't tell us because he doesn't like us.'

Harris lifted his eyes again and a spark of failing spirit seemed to flutter across his battered face. The staff sergeant saw it, walked forward gleefully and stood just inches from where Harris sat.

'Could be he doesn't like his room here,' the snowball guard cooed, as though he were addressing a small child.

'Yeah, I guess it is a teensy weensy bit cramped,' the staff sergeant said, savouring the pleasure yet to come. 'Ya can hardly walk about without treading on somebody.' The staff sergeant took a step forward and ground his steel-capped heel down on Harris's naked toes twisting the boot as he did so. Harris screamed at the top of his voice, and the snowball guard leapt at him like a panther and crashed him behind the ear with his billy. There was a knife-like pain inside Harris's head and a jarring white flash burst from the back of his eyeballs . . .

A floating sensation came over him and in that indefinable space between consciousness and unconsciousness, he was a boy in a boat and his father was rowing, and he looked at the man he loved so much — he never could remember his mother, she had died when he was still a baby — and he felt really happy as his father winked at him . . .

But, Jesus, what the hell was he doing at the top of these stairs? Harris's head had cleared a little and he now realised he was again in the world of stark reality. The snowball guard and the staff sergeant flanked him at the top of a flight of bare stone stairs that led down to a basement in the cell block. Harris had his hands cuffed to his ankles and was balanced precariously on the topmost step. The snowball guard spun him round to face him and grabbed the straps of Harris's grimy singlet which he balled into his large fist, thus preventing him from falling back down the stairs. The staff sergeant toyed with a packet of Lucky Strikes as he turned to the snowball guard.

'Betcha our little Sheeny never believed them stories about prisoners falling down the stairs.' The staff sergeant flipped a cigarette from the pack and bent his head over to pick it up with his mouth. 'What d'ya say?'

'That's a terrible habit — gotta watch 'em the whole time,' the guard replied, clutching the blood-covered vest even closer. 'Some responsibility — we don't have no easy job!'

'Where's Shaw? the staff sergeant barked suddenly, as he removed the unlit cigarette from his lips.

'Where?' the snowball guard echoed at once.

'Shaw?'

'Where?'

'Shaw?'

'Where?'

Harris stared at the men as they continued the monosyllabic dialogue, leaning forward to yell in his ear in turn as they snapped the words like mad snarling dogs. Then, just as abruptly as he had begun, the staff sergeant stopped, replaced the cigarette in his mouth and turned to the snowball guard. 'Light me!'

The snowball straightened, fished in his pockets and pulled out a service lighter. Harris, suddenly released from the grip, toppled and seemed to balance for a split second, and then crashed backwards down the stone steps with dull sickening

87

thuds as he bounced off them, two and three at a time, until, completely insensible, he reached the bottom

The staff sergeant looked pleased with himself as he saw the lifeless form slumped at the base of the stairs, and leaned forward to light the cigarette from the flame of the snowball's lighter. He took a long puff and shook his head in wonder as he gazed down again at the crumpled Harris.

'Jeeze,' the staff sergeant turned to the snowball guard, 'take your eyes off 'em for a second! You gotta be a nurse-maid.'

The staff sergeant, followed by the snowball guard, began to make their way down the steps towards Harris.

'Gotta be a mother,' the snowball guard tut-tutted. Harris stirred slightly as the big hands grabbed him and started to drag him like a sack of potatoes up the steps again.

'Son of a bitch,' he muttered through a mouth thick with blood and stared with murderous eyes at the large flat face smiling at him evilly. The back of his head cracked against a jutting stone stair and once more he was plunged into a black velvet void.

＊

Shaw eyed the Germans as he sipped champagne from a tin mug. Trauber sat at the packing-case table with a pile of banknotes in front of him, intently adding a row of figures on a piece of torn paper with a silver pencil. Leder was leaning back in a chair leisurely cleaning a Luger, while Winkel was humming a tune to himself like a happy *Hausfrau* as he rinsed through the dishes of a recently finished meal. After some time, Trauber squeezed the bridge of his nose, threw his pencil at the paper and stretched his arms wide. 'Gentlemen, we have made near enough thirty-five thousand francs — that's from the sale of the petrol, the bowser and everything from the PX.'

'And the farm produce?' Leder frowned.

'Yes — that too,' Trauber replied flatly.

'Hardly worth nearly getting our heads blown off for, was it?' Shaw grumbled. He found it very depressing to learn that after all the risks they had taken he had less than 9,000 francs coming to him. Trauber shrugged philosophically, got up and, starting with Shaw, handed each man an equal bundle of notes. Shaw flicked through the thick wad, mentally counted it and finally folded the money and rammed it into the seat pocket of his trousers. Trauber sat down again and poured some champagne into a mug from a half-full bottle and fixed Shaw steadily in his gaze.

'According to Jacques,' Trauber began, and then realised the name meant nothing to Shaw. 'The fellow who took this from us,' Trauber waved his mug at the empty spot where the booty had stood, 'it is getting so dangerous in Liège now that Caminade has packed his bags and is lying low somewhere in the south of France.'

'Perhaps he told you that to try to keep the price down,' Leder said moodily.

'No, Martin, I don't think so. He is quitting himself, just as soon as he is able to get enough money together and he advised us to do the same. He is a very nervous man.'

Winkel had completed his chores and sat at the table listening attentively as he often did, but understanding precious little of the English conversation.

'Jacques said that the police are clamping down on the operators so hard,' Trauber went on, 'that if they catch anyone in possession of unaccounted-for merchandise, it's straight into prison and God help them if it's military stuff they're caught with!'

'But that doesn't make sense. I thought the big boys, like Caminade, had the Sureté Belge taped,' Shaw protested, knowing from his own dealings that the majority of the civilian police were on the 'take'.

'Well, not any more, it seems. The position has changed considerably of late. You know yourself how hot things are at the moment.'

Shaw nodded ruefully. He had had more close shaves with the military police in the last few weeks than he had had in all the months he'd been on the run put together. He also recalled the conversation with Françoise concerning the heavy hand of the SIB.

'All right — I'll grant you that the MPs are very active,' Shaw said with feeling, 'but the Gendarmerie have been taking graft for ages. I heard of one inspector who bought a mansion in Bruges that used to belong to someone in the Royal Family, just on the proceeds of the black market pay-offs!'

'I've no doubt that is true, but it is unlikely to happen again,' Trauber drank loudly, 'not in the present climate, anyway. It is the Military Police who have applied this pressure. You are aware, of course, that under the terms of war, they have far greater powers than the civilian police.'

'Yes, I know that,' Shaw realised his mug was empty and reached over to the champagne bottle to top it up, but only a couple of drops trickled from it. Disgusted he slammed it down on the table and saw Trauber turn to Winkel and ask him, in German, to get a fresh bottle from the cold-water bowl in the corner that contained two others. Winkel sprang up with a smile as Trauber spoke again in English.

'Now it seems the Military Police have instructed the Sureté to carry out an investigation into allegations of corruption among their ranks.' Shaw chuckled, 'Well, if it's an honest one, there won't even be a cop left for traffic duty. They'll all be in the clink.' Trauber grinned. 'Yes you're right, of course. They'll only go through the motions and it'll be a cover-up job, but, nevertheless, while its going on I'm afraid it'll put a stop to everyone's activities, and that, regrettably, includes us.'

Shaw nodded thoughtfully. Trauber's message was loud and clear. They had come to the end of the line as far as Liège was concerned, and he knew that a complete re-assessment of their situation had become imperative.

Trauber shifted his chair, clasped his hands together in front of him and leaned forward. 'I also understand that the orders to smash the entire black market operation in Belgium come from no less than the Allied Supreme Commander himself!'

'Why should he concern himself with the black market?' Leder queried, snapping a magazine into the Luger's butt.

'Oh, I can see why old Ike would do that all right,' Shaw responded, and almost leapt out of his seat as Winkel came behind him and uncorked the champagne bottle with a loud pop. Shaw looked over his shoulder, smiled at Winkel and lifted his mug to receive the foaming liquid. 'Rumour has it that there's so many Allied deserters in France and Belgium right now, they outnumber the Military Police by three to one.'

'Yes, but I still do not understand what that has to do with the black market.' Leder stared at Shaw with a bemused expression.

'Well, stands to reason, doesn't it? Without the *marché noir* to support him, how's a bloke on the run going to survive?' Shaw saw from the corner of his eye that Trauber was listening with an eager interest. 'Could we exist without it? 'Course not. No — you put a stop to the black market and a poor bastard deserter's got two chances — starve to death or give himself up.'

'Exactly!' Trauber sat upright. 'Apparently hundreds have done so already.'

Leder nodded thoughtfully. 'Yes, I see how that could be very effective. In my country of course desertion was never a real problem. We had an almost watertight method of preventing it.'

'Oh, what was that, then?' Shaw asked, but knew by the tone of Leder's voice he was about to hear something calculated to impress him.

'An order, issued by the Reichsführer SS Himmler,' Leder paused dramatically, 'declared that families of deserters will be summarily shot!'

'Christ! Is that true?' Shaw turned to Trauber and saw that his face became pinched as he nodded gravely.

'Don't you care?' Even a hardened man like Shaw was shaken.

'Of course,' Trauber said bitterly, 'but what the hell can we do?'

'Charming!' Shaw placed the mug to his lips, kept it there for a moment and then drank. He remembered that right at the beginning of their liaison Winkel had proudly shown him tattered snapshots of his family, and it dawned on Shaw, perhaps for the first time, that these Germans must have had very powerful motives for desertion. He noticed that Trauber was glaring pointedly at Leder, as though his reminder of the terrible revenge his country was empowered to take on its absentee soldiers was something they had agreed not to discuss.

'Here, I heard a weird story,' Shaw exclaimed brightly, anxious to dispel the sudden gloomy atmosphere. 'After we'd recaptured Paris, some bright spark at the War Department thought it would be a great idea to send over a couple of generals to decorate a group of hard nuts who'd fought in the French Resistance.'

'The so-called "maquis",' Leder sneered. 'Rabble!' Shaw ignored Leder's comments. 'Anyway, they laid on a big ceremony for them, full dress parade, brass band, the lot — in fact the only thing that was missing were most of the geezers they were going to give the medals to.'

'Really!' Trauber chuckled, and Leder listened with a detached interest as Shaw went on. 'Nearly all these blokes who'd been hand-picked as the bravest heroes of the Resistance movement were only British deserters from the First World War weren't they? They'd pissed off from places like Mons and that, into France, married French girls, looked more "froggy" than onion sellers, set up businesses. Some of 'em were even grandfathers. 'Course when it came for them to be presented with their gongs, you couldn't see their arses for dust. They thought their true identity would come out and they'd be hauled back and court-martialled. Bloody embarrassing for Whitehall, I should think that was.'

'Imagine living for what — er, twenty-six years,' Trauber shook his head sadly, 'and all the time the fear that you might be recaptured and most likely executed. That was the mandatory punishment on both sides for deserters in the fourteen-eighteen war.'

'Yeah, but it didn't apply to them,' Shaw drained his mug. 'They'd been granted an amnesty donkey's years before, but no one had told the poor buggers!'

'Look, this is all very fascinating,' Leder holstered his Luger irritably, 'but if things are getting as serious as Horst would lead us to believe, wouldn't it be better if you came up with a plan on what we should be doing, where we should be going— I mean it can only be a matter of time before they discover this place — and all this stupid talk of the past gets us nowhere, nowhere at all.' Shaw knew that Leder was right, but it did not stop him boiling over. He was only too aware that the nervy German had been looking for a target for his aggression all night. If it was a fight he wanted — Shaw was only too willing to oblige.

'Well, you've done your share of spouting, shit!' Shaw spun round on Leder heatedly. 'Instead of constantly knocking all the time, let's have a few constructive ideas from you.'

'You've adopted the mantle of leadership,' Leder said sneeringly, 'I leave that to you.'

'Yeah, well, the best idea I've had for a long time,' Shaw's temper was at snapping point, 'is to knock your fucking head off!'

He got up angrily, pushed his chair to one side and strode towards Leder. Immediately Leder sprang up from his seat and backed away. Trauber jumped between the two and raised a hand like a schoolmaster trying to curb an unruly class. 'Gentlemen, gentlemen! Look, there is no doubt we should have a sound alternative to staying here. But we will achieve absolutely nothing by quarrelling.'

Shaw burned inside for a few seconds, then grabbed his chair and sat down again. Part of his humour was restored by watching Winkel. The rotund little German, although not comprehending the cause of the argument, sensed that it was blowing into something far stormier. He attempted to quell it before it got completely out of control by twittering around with the champagne bottle like an overfed duck and ensuring that all the mugs were brimming to the top. Then, uncharacteristically for the usually reticent Winkel, he boldly questioned Trauber in German. Shaw knew just enough of the language to gather that he'd asked 'what the hell was going on?' Trauber quickly explained the position to him. Satisfied, Winkel sat down, cupped his elusive chin in his hands and studied Shaw as though he expected him to announce an immediate solution. Shaw was compelled to respond to the questioning eyes, and although he knew Winkel was unlikely to understand a word, he addressed his remark to him.

'I think we should pool our money and get some civvy clothes. A set of good idents each, and see if we can operate in Brussels for a while.'

'But surely that will be going from the frying pan into the fire!' Trauber frowned at the suggestion.

'Well, it's a much bigger set-up than Liège. It could be safer for us to hide out there,' Shaw continued, but he was aware that the champagne had begun to dull his thinking.

'In that case, why not Paris?' Leder said sullenly.

'Well, Berlin is even bigger,' Shaw could not resist the temptation to bait him, 'fancy that, do you?'

'Very funny,' Leder answered without smiling.

They sat silently for a while, all occupied with their own thoughts. Shaw wondered where Harris might be now. He'd seen him run. Knowing Les, he was sure he must have got away. Nikki had taken a fancy to him. She'd hide him. He smiled to himself as a mental picture of Harris mounting the tall Nikki flashed across his mind. Yes, he'd be all right — old Les would always be all right!

*

When Harris regained consciousness in his cell, he was aware of the presence of other people around him. He tried to raise himself from his bunk, but sharp pains knifed across his chest and held him back. He attempted to open his eyes, but the lids resisted as though they had been glued. Eventually, he managed to force them apart and through the blur he saw two faces staring at him. 'Oh, God! Not again,' he thought as the memory of his attackers came rushing back. He'd hoped he was dead, perhaps he was, and he was in Hell. He knew he'd wind up there one day. His Aunt Sophie used to yell at him: 'You're just a no-good waster like your good-for-nothing father, God rest his soul — although I don't think God would want his soul. Somewhere else he's gone! And that's where you're heading!' So maybe that's where he was, and Hell was just being dragged up stone steps and knocked down 'em again — and yet those faces were different. They looked — dare he believe it? — as though they were concerned. He attempted to sit up, but the agony of the first effort frightened him.

'Easy, soldier,' a firm but soft voice uttered. Harris blinked the man into focus. He was wearing a stethoscope over his captain's tunic. At his side stood a grave-faced young snowball lieutenant, and just behind them a snowball corporal.

'They're animals!' the doctor rounded on the lieutenant. 'They talk about Nazi atrocities — these are our own men they're doing this to!'

The lieutenant licked his lips. 'Staff Sergeant Varley and p.f.c. Forster have been relieved of all duties pending an enquiry over this incident, sir.'

'Incident! Is that what you call it, lieutenant?' The captain did not hide his disgust. 'I want this man removed to the infirmary immediately. He is to be in my care. I want a full report on how this happened, and I want it on my desk in the morning — is that understood?'

'I don't see that I can interfere with the official enquiry, sir.'

'OK, lieutenant, as General Harmon's personal physician I may be able to speed things up.'

'It'll be on your desk in the morning, sir.'

'Atta boy, captain. Up your ass, lootenant. Varley, you fuck, you gotta die.' Harris saw the staff sergeant's face in his mind. It was grinning grotesquely. Harris was smashing his gun butt into the face turning it into one red raw pulp.

*

Several hours later, after falling into a stupefied slumber in the chair, the aroma of brewing coffee awakened Shaw. He stared across the room and saw that Trauber had taken the pot from the oil stove and was pouring the steaming black liquid into a mug. Shaw arose, stretched and felt as stiff as a freshly blancoed belt. His head seemed to contain a hundred tiny hammers that would only stop tapping when they had succeeded in knocking his eyeballs from their sockets, and his mouth tasted as though a careless chippy had used it to dump waste sawdust and surplus french polish. Champagne was not his favourite drink!

'Could use a gallon of that,' Shaw yawned and nodded to Trauber.

'Help yourself — just made,' Trauber smiled pleasantly.

'Did we get anywhere last night?' Shaw asked, and filled a mug that still smelled of flat champagne with the strong dark coffee.

'I don't think we did,' Trauber replied.

Shaw warmed his hands on the mug and sipped the coffee slowly. 'Ah, that's lovely.' He took a jug of hot water that stood on the stove and poured some into a porcelain basin that rested on a packing crate under a chipped mirror. He picked up a brush, soap and razor that lay nearby and lathered his face. He gazed over to the far end of the cellar and saw that Winkel was curled up under a blanket that was surmounted by a schutze's thick greatcoat and was snoring like a motor bike ascending a hill.

Shaw grinned at the slumbering Winkel and turned to Trauber. 'Where's Leder?'

'I think Martin is suffering more than any of us,' Trauber said good-humouredly. 'He felt a little sick and has gone for some air.'

Shaw nodded and a moment later cursed under his breath as he nicked himself with the razor and saw the faint red tick on his cheek spread into a crimson blob. He finished shaving quickly, dried his face on a frayed yellow towel, and hunted for a piece of paper to cover the steadily dripping wound.

'Here, try this,' Trauber said helpfully, observing Shaw's predicament and producing a white banknote from his wallet. He tore a small corner off the note and handed it to Shaw. Shaw washed the blood away again and placed the tissue-thin fragment on it. 'Ta!' Shaw grimaced as the paper adhered to the cut. 'That's a fiver, isn't it?'

'Yes,' Trauber unfolded the note for Shaw to see more clearly, 'a British five-pound note.'

Shaw took it and held it lovingly. 'Too true it is. Seems a bloody age since I've had one of these. Christ! How I'd like a big fat bundle of 'em.'

'Not those, you wouldn't — it's made in Germany.'

'Never!' Shaw examined it closely, studying every detail as he held it against the light of the bright oil flame. At last he shook his head. 'I don't believe it.'

Trauber chuckled. 'Yes — a forgery.'

Shaw looked at the note again, repeating the process of scrutinising it in front of the lamp and saw the flickering light through its transparent flimsiness.

'Look, mate, I've seen forgeries, but I've never seen one like this. You could take it to . . . the Bank of England.'

'Yes, you could. A perfect forgery,' Trauber was plainly amused by Shaw's disbelieving expression. 'It was made in a con —— er — a labour camp. I'll tell you about it. At times I find it hard to believe myself.'

Shaw sat down and listened, wide-eyed as a child, as Trauber recounted an amazing story. Shaw heard how, under the personal direction of SS Reichführer Himmler a team of top SS officers, including Reinhard Heydrich, Head of the Security Police, and Ernst Kaltenbrunner, had been given the task of perpetrating a plan, approved by Hitler, to organise what was to be the biggest counterfeiting operation of all time. The main objective of the scheme was to flood neutral countries with tens of millions of pounds' worth of forged British currency, thus totally undermining the value of British sterling and causing economic havoc on the money markets of the free world. However, although this was to remain the prime objective of the plan, the forged banknotes were to have other widespread uses, and these, later, ranged from financing virtually the entire 'Fifth column' network which permeated both occupied and unoccupied territories, to purchasing arms from countries who were openly hostile to the Nazi cause, and were under the firm conviction that the couriers carrying the British money were buying the weapons solely for Allied use. Shaw learned of the birth of the idea and how, with typical Teutonic thoroughness, the team delegated SS Oberstaführer Bernhardt Kruger, then Head of the German Special Services,

Bank of England

Promise to pay the Bearer on Demand the Sum of Five Pounds

1944 June 26 London 26 June 1944

For the Gov. and Comp. of the
BANK of ENGLAND.

J 55 070516

J 55 070516

J 55 070516

Chief Cashier.

97

and forgery expert Alfred Naujocks to produce the 'perfect' British banknotes. Kruger and Naujocks set up a department in Berlin and systematically rounded up all the top master engravers and printers in the Nazi-held lands of Czechoslovakia, Poland, Holland, France and Denmark. These men, most of whom were Jewish, were placed in two selected cell blocks that contained living quarters, administrative offices and a newly built section which housed a workshop, printing plant, and bank, all of which were enclosed within the isolated confines of a concentration camp near Oranienburg. The area set aside from the rest of the camp and known simply as Blocks 18 and 19 originally accommodated about forty men, but later the strength was increased to one hundred and forty.

At first there were many problems encountered in producing the perfect forged notes, not the least of the headaches being trying to discover the correct paper. But after a great deal of trial and error, even this formidable obstacle was overcome as it was found that the flax imported from Turkey had first to be woven into a rough cloth, then used in industry until it became soiled rags, and only then could the material be converted into that unique type of paper. The plates had been ready some time before and were faultless copies of the ones in use by the Bank of England at their own printing house. When all the snags had been finally sorted out and they felt confident to start production, they decided to subject the money to one more crucial test. A small quantity of notes were printed, made dirty by handling, and given to a German envoy posing as a Swedish businessman to take to the director of a prominent bank in Switzerland. The 'businessman' explained that he had been paid the money by a client, but had subsequently begun to suspect that the notes may be counterfeit. He then asked if the banker would use his good offices to have the money checked by the Bank of England. The Swiss bank obliged at once, and dispatched the notes to London with a letter of explanation. It was only three days later that the money was returned, accompanied by a letter on Bank of England notepaper, stating in positive terms that the notes were authentic British issue, and 'undoubtedly genuine'. For good measure this letter also gave the issue date of the currency based on the serial numbers of the notes. Himmler and his staff were overjoyed and instructed Bernhardt Kruger to commence 'Operation Bernhardt', the code word for the plan named in his honour, at once.

Shaw listened enthralled as Trauber casually stated that that meant manufacturing one million British banknotes a month in £5 to £50 denominations. Trauber added that at any given time the vault at Sachsenhausen never contained less than a £5-million reserve.

Shaw was greatly impressed. He tasted his coffee and realised it had gone stone cold. He had been so absorbed by Trauber's account that he was only partially aware that Leder, looking white as a sheet, had returned, and that Winkel was quietly getting dressed.

'One thing you mentioned,' Shaw probed, 'the serial numbers, that's a dead give-away.'

'The numbers used were always those already issued by the Bank of England,' Trauber answered easily.

'But if two turn up with the same number you know you've got a dud,' Shaw smiled.

Trauber returned the smile. 'It is just possible that somewhere in the world, some day, a man will hold a genuine five-pound note in one hand and a Bernhardt fiver in the other.' Trauber paused, 'As you say, he will know then that one of them is forgery. He will never ever find out which of them is forged. Neither will your Bank of England be able to tell him.'

'You crafty bastards,' Shaw could not hide his admiration.

'Horst, this is *Geheime Reichssache*,' Leder scowled at Trauber.

'What?' Shaw said as he saw Leder use sign language to Trauber to keep his mouth shut.

'Reich top secret.' Trauber shrugged and then addressed Leder. 'What the hell does it matter now?'

'It matters,' Leder prickled. 'The war is not yet done.'

'Oh, don't give us any old cobblers about a fourth Reich, will you!' Shaw had not forgotten Leder's animosity the previous evening, and nor, it seemed, had Leder. The rift between the two of them was still very evident.

'Talk big, Shaw,' Leder said bitterly. 'One day you may see.'

'You're hardly the new hope of Germany, mate,' Shaw retorted cuttingly. 'I don't pretend I'm anything but a deserter, and you shouldn't kid yourself you're any different.'

Leder looked as though he was going to vomit. With an angry gesture, he turned on his heels and left.

As the trapdoor slammed and the sound echoed throughout the cellar, Shaw turned to Trauber, furious as hell. 'I'm getting sick and tired of that bloody prima donna.'

Trauber looked at Shaw but made no comment.

'Can't stomach the plain truth, that's all,' Shaw was fuming.

'Look, Wally, none of us deserted just because we wanted to,' Trauber said eventually. 'You had your reasons. We had ours. For Martin it was finished for him when his friend was killed.'

'Friend?'

'Yes,' Trauber's steely grey eyes displayed that look of compassion Shaw had noted on other occasions.

'He's a "Brown hatter"?' Shaw uttered, but it was more of a statement than a question. Trauber seemed puzzled at the phrase. Shaw flapped his wrist effeminately. There was no derision implied in the gesture, merely a way of emphasising his point. 'A pansy — likes blokes?'

'Oh, I see, yes.' Trauber took a deep breath and paused. 'You know of course that homosexual behaviour in the SS is regarded as a capital offence?'

'No, I didn't. That's a bit off, isn't it?'

'Martin was awaiting trial when an air raid blew the prison apart. Along with a few other survivors he managed to escape and finished up in Belgium. I met him in a café when he was trying to pass himself off as a Pole. He's not such a bad fellow — a little mixed up, I grant you, but very loyal.'

'Oh, yeah.' Shaw looked doubtful.

'No, I assure you, once he has settled on a course of action— as with our set-up for example — he will honour it to the last breath.'

Shaw picked up the five-pound note and toyed with it. 'What about you, then?' Shaw stared at Trauber pointedly.

'Pardon?'

'Are you and Martin — like . . . you know . . . together?'

Trauber looked at Shaw quizzically for a moment, then the penny dropped. Trauber threw back his head and roared with laughter. Without uttering a word, his face still creased in smiles he unbuttoned the flap of his tunic pocket and produced a small antique tinder box. 'I deserted for love, yes, but she was all woman. What a woman!' Trauber's eyes shone with mirth as he lifted the lid of the tinder box. 'Unfortunately she was also the wife of the general of my division. I may say she did nothing to dissuade me and we had a very interesting affair until an ambitious brother officer denounced us.'

'A good friend, eh?' Shaw rubbed the piece of paper on his cut chin absentmindedly.

'Well, I thought so, till then,' Trauber replied without a trace of malice. 'Anyway, they didn't want a scandal so I was transferred to an administrative post at Sachsenhausen Concentration Camp where I saw . . . well . . . I repeatedly applied for another posting and in the end I got it. I was switched from Totenkopf to Waffen SS, demoted to the rank of sergeant and ordered to the Russian front. As you are aware, I did not go.' Trauber emptied the tinder box on to the table. A tiny bunch of brown hair tied together with a minuscule pink ribbon spilled out. 'Meet the general's wife!'

Shaw picked it up and examined it closely. 'I thought German girls had blonde hair.'

'She had,' Trauber paused, the laughter still in his eyes, 'on her head!'

Shaw grinned, stroked the pubic hair memento with his fingertips and handed it back to Trauber. He then picked up the five-pound note and studied it again, shaking his head in admiration as he gazed at it. Trauber observed the fascination the banknote had for Shaw. 'One of the better ideas to come from the SS,' Trauber said ruefully. Shaw looked at him steadily and his eyes seemed to penetrate the German's mind. Perhaps it was telepathy, or perhaps just a linking of common thought streams, but Trauber proceeded to answer Shaw's unasked question.

'What made us join the SS? What makes intelligent and basically decent men become part of a force that encourages the use of terror tactics to achieve its goal?' Trauber shrugged. 'I've asked myself this question a few times, I can tell you. With the benefit of hindsight we can all be wise, of course.'

'Yeah, well I expect you had good reasons at the time,' Shaw's voice was not convincing. The whole world had been made aware of the murderous brutality that had become synonymous with the name of the SS.

'Oh, we all had our reasons. You have to remember it was considered a great honour to be accepted. It was no "Foreign Legion" you understand. It was an élite corps.' Trauber walked over to the coffee pot and filled his mug. He beckoned with the pot to Shaw. Shaw nodded and Trauber returned to top up Shaw's mug, emptying the pot in the process.

'Yes, you would really have to have been part of that Germany to fully appreciate the excitement that prevailed. There were the rallies, the flags, the drums, the uniforms and above all, of course, our great leader telling us how marvellous we were; restoring our battered pride — that was very important to all of us.' Trauber sat down. He was in an expansive mood, but Shaw was only half listening. His mind was beginning to formulate an idea. At this stage it was not a whole concept, just a series of disjointed thoughts. Shaw noticed Winkel hovering in the background and turned towards him as Trauber glanced in his direction. He was anxious not to interrupt Trauber's flow but was obviously waiting to talk to him. In hushed tones he addressed Trauber in German.

'*Ja, ja,*' Trauber replied when Winkel had finished. He gave a little jerk of his head first to Shaw, then to Trauber, and made a hasty exit.

'He said the jeep has been giving a spot of bother and he feels he should check it,' Trauber explained.

'Good idea,' Shaw replied.

'You take Martin for example,' Trauber returned to the track of his discussion. 'His father was a plumber, unemployed more often than not. He was a drunk and a bully, constantly taunting Martin for his unmanly ways. His wife had left him for another chap when the boy was only a few months old.'

Shaw sipped his coffee and made a pretence of being very interested, but his thoughts were a long way from the cellar.

'So Martin was brought up by his sister, Ursula. He absolutely worshipped her — mother figure, I suppose,' Trauber went on. 'One day he comes home early from school and finds his father and sister in bed together. Young mother figure for the father too, it would seem. Anyway he was horrified, and he ran away.'

Shaw nodded and picked up the five-pound note again. 'He had nowhere to go so he called in to see his father's brother, his Uncle Wilhelm. Now his father he always saw clad in dirty overalls,' Trauber gulped down some coffee. 'His uncle had just joined the SS. There he stood, resplendent in a black SS uniform, with the death's head insignia, the leather trappings, the jackboots, the Luger. Well, the boy pictures his father and his uncle side by side, and he asks himself this question: "Do I want to grow up to be an oaf like my father or a conquering hero like my uncle?" Quite obvious what he will decide, yes?'

Shaw realised that he was required to make a comment, but hadn't been fully aware of the question, and rather than ask Trauber to repeat it, he nodded sagely, giving an impression of intelligent understanding.

'Exactly,' Trauber continued, 'Well, he begged his uncle to enlist him in the SS. He was far too young, of course, but he was able to join the Hitler Youth and live in a home with other boys. There he learned he was a member of a "super" race and he found an identity of sorts. Do you know the first thing he did when he was enrolled in the Hitler Youth?'

'Comb his hair forward and grow a little moustache,' Shaw replied dryly. Trauber smiled. 'No, he told his commander that his father was a Communist, and had him committed to a labour camp.'

'What a nice little bloke — and you reckon you can trust him?'

'Implicitly. And in a strange way, he admires you immensely too.'

'Could have fooled me,' Shaw grunted. 'Why did you join, then?' It was a question Shaw felt he had no right to ask. They had an unwritten agreement to leave the past buried, but his curiosity had got the better of him.

'Me? . . . Oh . . . in a word— boredom, I suppose.' Trauber regarded Shaw with just a touch of suspicion, then he seemed to realise there was no ulterior motive in the query and he leaned forward in the confidential manner Shaw had often seen him adopt whenever he engaged in an earnest conversation. Trauber cleared his throat and continued. 'I was a medical student. A lot of us undergraduates would spend our evenings in the Bierkellers around Munich. Oh, we used to get drunk, I can tell you!' Shaw winced good-humouredly. His own hangover had not departed. 'As well as the beer, there were girls of course and also these fanatical fellows who used to congregate and make speeches about the new order that would one day take over, National Socialism.' Trauber stretched his long legs in front of him. 'At first, of course, we used to shout them down. It was good rowdy fun. But after a while we began to listen, especially to those who spoke passionately of the way we had been betrayed by our own leaders after the First World War. All of Germany's economic problems, the poverty that was everywhere, were mainly due to that stab in the back. It was true, of course.'

Shaw began to wish that he had never posed the question. It wasn't that he was no longer interested, it was simply that the seeds of his idea had begun to germinate. However, he knew he must let Trauber sound forth now he had got into his stride, and he pushed the notion to the back of his mind.

'Well, I became very interested in the New Order. I spent more time distributing pamphlets than I did at my studies. Inevitably, I failed my exams. I was sent down and I took a job in my father's ship-broking business.' Trauber sighed. 'Of course I was not in the least bit interested in following in the old man's footsteps and when the SS were formed, without his knowledge I enrolled. Because of my earlier work for the party, my background, etc. I was recommended for a commission. My parents were mortified.' Trauber looked over at Shaw to try to gauge his reaction, but Shaw maintained an impassive expression.

Trauber continued in a more philosophical tone. 'You cannot imagine how exciting it all was then. I don't just mean the rallies and the ballyhoo and all that. Obviously that was part of it. But we sincerely believed we were men of destiny — a destiny that was principally to protect Europe against the tyranny of Communism and other evil influences. We were the legion of the new Rome. We would rule for a thousand years.' Trauber shrugged his rounded shoulders. 'A thousand years! Some hopes eh? Look, I'm not trying to justify my actions. What's done is done. But if I am to be perfectly truthful, had I not been indiscreet, I would still be a willing participant, disillusioned, perhaps, but still part of it all.'

Shaw was impressed with Trauber's frankness. There was a no-nonsense honesty about the man that had revealed itself from their first encounter. There was also a lot, Shaw felt, that Trauber had glibly and conveniently skated over. Never once had there been any mention of the murder of thousands of innocent women and children. Never once a hint of the atrocities he'd heard about as the Allies liberated town after town, and terrorised people who looked as though they'd just escaped the clutches of Satan himself. No, it was all too smooth an explanation for Shaw's liking. However, that did not lessen the respect Shaw had for the man. At least he had not entirely sidestepped the issue, and Trauber had given him a fleeting glimpse into the mind of a member of the SS.

104

They were both silent for a while. Suddenly Shaw stood up and picked up the five-pound note. 'Listen, Horst, I've been thinking about what you were saying.' Trauber seemed slightly edgy. 'What about — Martin? Me? The SS?'

'No, not exactly,' Shaw replied. Trauber detected an air of intrigue in Shaw's manner. He scrutinised the note yet again. 'This place, Sax . . . what do you call it?'

'Sachsenhausen?'

'Yeah. How do you know so much about the set-up?'

'Well, I told you, I was there for six months. I had access to the secret correspondence file, and I could observe things for myself. Why?'

Shaw measured his words carefully. 'Listen, what's stopping us raiding it, and nicking all that money?' Trauber sat up as though an arrow had pierced his behind. 'You're joking, of course?' He looked at Shaw's grim, set features. 'No, you're not joking. We could never get in there!'

'Why not?' Shaw asked steadily.

'Wally, do you realise,' Trauber blustered, 'it's . . . it's a concentration camp, designed in every way to prevent escape.'

'Exactly, but is it designed to keep anyone out?' Shaw smiled as he saw Trauber's brow knit into a deep frown.

'But, surely, it's the same thing?'

'Not at all, mate!' The adrenalin was beginning to surge through Shaw's veins. The feeling that he was on the verge of something big and exciting was reflected in the confidence of his voice. 'Look, you just said yourself the camps were built to stop the poor buggers escaping, but who would expect anyone but a madman would want to get in? Now, we're all trained squaddies, and we've cracked some pretty tight places since we've been together . . .'

'But . . .'

'Wait, let me finish. We've been risking our necks here for what? A lousy few thousand francs. Trying to flog gear people are too scared to handle. OK, maybe we get shot — it's good odds we get shot anyway. But look at the prize. How much did you say was there at any one time?'

'Five million pounds,' Trauber replied flatly.

'Five million quid,' Shaw repeated the amount slowly almost making it sound as though the money could be seen and touched. If we make it, we could sod off to Sweden, all of us bloody millionaires!'

'If we don't?' Trauber said weakly.

'We're dead,' Shaw replied unemotionally, 'but that's a risk the front-line soldier takes daily for thirty bob a week.'

Trauber nodded, and a faint smile played across his lips. 'We would need all kinds of papers, authoritative documents, passes . . .'

'Yank I know forges anything — great.'

'In German?'

'In Hindubloodystani if need be!'

Trauber seemed to linger on the edge of Shaw's infectious enthusiasm for a split second, then Shaw saw the momentary excitement in his face fade away.

'No, no, it's preposterous,' Trauber shook his head vehemently. 'Wally, you don't realise what you are suggesting. Sachsenhausen. No, no, my friend.'

'Five million pounds.' Shaw had got the bit between his teeth — he had no intention of letting go.

'I'd like time to think about it.' Trauber was using delaying tactics, hoping Shaw would eventually cool. But Shaw would have none of it.

'What time? We don't have any more time. About the only thing Leder said that made sense was that we've got to get out. But where to? Wherever we go there's going to be danger. For Christ's sake, man, if what you are telling me is true, all we have to do is plan very carefully — ' Shaw paused, then like a solo player producing the ace of trumps '— and there's a vast fortune just waiting to be picked up!'

Trauber squeezed the bridge of his nose as though the action would let the air into his brain and he would be able to find a conclusive and damning fact that would make Shaw's wild scheme totally impossible. But he could find nothing. After what seemed an age, he looked at Shaw and made his last wavering stand.

'I'd put our chances as a good deal less than fifty-fifty.'

'That's bloody good odds, these days.'

Trauber nodded gravely. 'Where is your American?'

'Harris? Oh, I'll find him — he's in Liège somewhere.'

'Right, you do that, and I'll search every corner of my memory and draw up the complete layout of Sachsenhausen. I'll also put Leder and Winkel in the picture. They may not, of course, wish to have any part of it, and I wouldn't blame them, but if they do, they'll be more than useful. Martin has almost photographic mind as far as documentation and details are concerned.'

Shaw grinned widely. Trauber gazed at him, then with a play-acted irritability he stood up. 'Well, what are you wasting valuable time for? Go and find this fellow Harris!'

Shaw shot to his feet and chuckled. 'Right away— partner!'

8

Shaw stood with his back to the fireplace in the Cordiers'
comfortable living-room, smoking a cheroot. The fire at his
rear crackled and warmed him in its friendly glow. He was
dressed in a tweed sports jacket, open-neck shirt and grey
flannel trousers, silhouetted against the yellow flames leaping
from the newly placed coal. Max approached with a ballooned
brandy glass and handed it to him, stepping back expectantly
as Shaw took it and gazed at the burnished gold liquid that
rested contentedly at the bottom.

'Thank you, Max,' Shaw allowed some of the cognac to
dwell on his tongue before he grudgingly let it slip down his
throat. It tasted as smooth as the touch of warm velvet. 'Ah,
that is rather special!'

Max nodded, clearly proud that his guest appreciated such a
fine liqueur. 'Bonaparte would have given up Josephine for
that,' Shaw grinned, and looked to the door as Henriette's
presence was announced by the tinkling of egg-shell china
cups as she carried a tray of steaming coffee into the room.

Shaw sniffed the pungent smell. 'Real coffee, eh?'

Henriette smiled an acknowledgement.

'What a meal,' Shaw said admiringly, 'I haven't eaten like
that since I last ate here.' His hosts laughed. Max took a sip of
brandy and became more serious. 'We may as well enjoy it
while we can — if the Boche get back we've all had it!'

Henriette placed the tray on the table and stared up at
Shaw.

'What do you think? Do you think that is possible?' Shaw

saw the concern on her face.

'Well, all I've heard is the same as you— just that a couple of days ago the Krauts launched a big counter-attack around Bastogne.'

'And everyone predicted it would all be over by Christmas!' Max said sadly. 'And with only a week to go that is not very likely.'

'No, not very.' Shaw looked pensive. He was only too aware of how the Germans could dig in. From what he had learned, Hitler had thrown everything into his last desperate bid. In the few hours prior to his dining with the Cordiers, he had called at several old haunts in an attempt to locate Harris, but no one had seen him for days, and all the buzzing conversation centred around the German offensive. It seemed that several Panzer divisions had crossed over the border, completely cut off the town of Bastogne, and were advancing towards the middle of the Ardennes. No one was really certain what was happening, as when the attack was launched a couple of days earlier on the 16th December, there was so much fog and cloud about that it was impossible to send up any Allied reconnaissance planes, and everyone was very vague about the precise strength and position of the advancing German army. All reports seemed to agree about one thing, however. The enemy were not the low-calibre late recruits the Allies had encountered in recent months. They were tough, experienced fighting men and there were a lot of them. Even in the short space of time Shaw had spent in Liège that day, he had seen a staggering amount of activity as Allied armed convoys rumbled along the main streets on their way to the front. He thanked his lucky stars that he had decided to wear civilian clothes as redcaps and snowballs were everywhere, rounding up reluctant warriors and hustling them into 'Pongo' waggons. He was more than relieved to get to the safety of the Cordiers' home, and to be cosseted by their hospitality. He had not yet evaluated whether this sudden turnabout in the war could help or hinder his plan. It was something he would have to consider when the true position became clearer. Whatever the case, his first priority was to try to discover Harris's whereabouts.

'Wally.' Shaw suddenly realised that Henriette had been talking to him. She stood at his side holding the delicate cup that contained the piping-hot coffee.

'I'm sorry.' Shaw smiled apologetically as he placed his

empty brandy glass on the mantelpiece and took the offering from Henriette: 'Miles away!'

'I can see that, *chéri*,' Henriette chided him. 'Where were you — in England or with one of your girls?'

'I was thinking about Les,' Shaw sighed. Realising that his cigar had gone out he turned and threw it on the fire. It spluttered like a Chinese cracker as a flame curled its way around it. 'Look, Max, you've no idea where they took him?'

Max squinted at Shaw through his frosty spectacles. 'Wally, I don't even know that it is him. All I can tell you is what I heard. Simply that his girl — oh, what's her name?' Max turned to Henriette: 'You know the one with the big . . .' Max arched his hands around his chest.

'Jacqueline?' Henriette offered uncertainly.

'Yes, I think so. Anyway, she came in for a skirt with this friend of hers who lives with a snowdrop . . .'

'Snowball,' Shaw corrected.

'I don't know how it came up, but it seems that he was due for a promotion, so he'd given this girl some extra spending money —— '

'Oh, doesn't he have a terrible way of dragging things out?' Henriette interrupted impatiently, 'Get to the point.'

'Ssh, be quiet, woman, I'm trying to think.' Max held up a hand. 'Yes, that's right, he was to get a stripe because he had personally captured a habitual deserter who had given them a great deal of trouble.'

'Well, they reckon that about all of us,' Shaw grunted.

'Mmm, but as I mentioned over dinner, what made me prick my ears up was that the girl said the GI they picked up made such good passes that no one could tell them from the real thing. I thought at once, "Mon Dieu, Leslie!" '

Shaw nodded, grim-faced. 'That's gotta be Les. I couldn't get any joy when I asked around the usual places. No one had seen him. You hadn't seen him. Gotta be Les!'

Henriette smiled at Shaw sadly. 'You know this girl he's talking about?'

'Yeah, I know Jacqueline anyway. She fits Max's description. Funnily enough, I never saw either of them tonight.'

'Maybe they will be there now, or later. You know what time these girls go in.'

Shaw glanced at his watch and nodded. He lifted the cup and took his coffee down in one gulp. He placed the fragile cup and saucer on the table and shook Max's hand firmly. He then moved to Henriette, took her in his arms and glided a few dance steps around the carpeted floor, hugging her tightly to him. He turned to Max gravely as he held her close. 'Max, I think I should tell you I'm madly in love with your wife, and I intend to run off with her the moment your back is turned!'

'What, with all those pretty girls around?' Henriette giggled coquettishly. Shaw winked. 'We had to learn a poem at school once which went something like this:

> This, fair maiden, I hold to be true.
> Kissing don't last, but cookery do.'

*

Harris sat up in the bed. A brilliant light shining on his mis-shapen face made him blink. The nursing orderly stood at his side with a breakfast tray. 'Jeeze, whadya do, buddy?' the nursing orderly said, almost flinching at the sight of Harris's swollen countenance.

'Fuck-all.' Harris's voice seemed to come through his nose as his lips hardly moved.

'Well, I'd hate to imagine what you'd look like if you had done something.' The nursing orderly shook his head and placed the tray on the bedrest. 'Try and get some of this down you, Mac. Make you feel a whole lot better.' The nursing orderly left, still shaking his head. Harris looked round the ward. On either side of him were empty beds. Directly oppo-site, propped up against a large pillow, lay a Negro whose head was almost entirely swathed in bandages. When he saw Harris gaze in his direction, he raised a hand in greeting. Then, without a word, he picked up a book, balanced it on his bent knees, and started to read. Harris saw that further along the ward on his left-hand side two men were playing checkers on a small table in the centre of the room, and that two sets of crutches leaned against their chairs. In another bed an innocent-faced young guy was writing furiously on a note pad. And still further down the ward a couple of heaps were sleep-ing soundly. Harris's eyes dropped to the contents of the tray. A fried egg with a hardened yolk sat on top of a pile of baked beans, and a couple of thick slices of bread and butter hung over an adjacent plate. He picked up a slice and tried to get it into his mouth but his jaws hardly opened and he replaced it on the plate. He lifted the coffee cup but the liquid scalded his lips. He pushed the bedrest with the tray away from him irritably and closed his eyes. Every bone in his body ached as though it had been broken, and if he breathed other than very gently it felt as though his ribs would pierce his lungs.

'OK. Pay attention. Officer approaching.' A non-commissioned snowball guard bellowed at the door. Harris opened his eyes. No one in the ward gave the entering lieutenant more than a cursory glance as he strode across the ward. He stopped in the middle of the room and looked around. Suddenly he spotted Harris and walked quickly towards him.

'How do you feel now, soldier?' the lieutenant said brightly as he leaned over the bed. Harris looked up at the lieutenant and noticed his shoulder flashes. He had the Seventh Army red and yellow pyramid encompassed by a blue triangle, above which was the provost tag of the 75th Infantry. Across his chest was a faded double row of fruit salad. He was only a small guy for a snowball, Harris thought, but he looked as tough as a steel spring and had obviously seen plenty of action. Harris was sure he'd seen the man before. There was something familiar about that taut expression and those deep-set penetrating eyes. Then he remembered. This was the officer whom he'd seen in that haze in the cell, the man who'd been as wide-eyed as Little Orphan Annie when the army doctor had torn his ass.

'Can you hear me?' the lieutenant's initial breeziness had gone.

'Sir!' Harris lisped between his blood-caked lips.

'I asked you a question. I said, "How are you feeling?"'

'Dever feld bedder!'

'Now, look, soldier, I'm not going to beat about the bush,' the lieutenant said in a voice of controlled fury. 'In my book you're scum! Men like Staff Sergeant Varley and young Forster are worth a hundred of you. They know what this man's war is all about. They were holed up at Omaha and saw their buddies floating in pieces all round 'em. It's no wonder they hate the guts of people like you, vermin who live on the misfortune of others.'

Harris could have told him that he was in the Normandy landings too, and it wasn't exactly a picnic at Utah, but what the hell! The lieutenant was on the boil and wouldn't have listened anyway.

'The British Military Police have asked us to assist them in trying to establish the whereabouts of one of their most wanted deserters,' the lieutenant continued, 'a man with a criminal record called Shaw. A man we know full well is a friend of yours!

If those bastards had got nothing out of him, Harris thought, *what chance do you think you got, lootenant?* If that's why he'd made this visit, he was wasting his time. He wasn't too keen on his bedside manner, anyway.

'Now I'm not going to say that I entirely approve of the methods of questioning that Staff Sergeant Varley adopted,' the lieutenant softened a shade. 'No, that is not the way we like to do things in the Provost Corps.'

Your ass it ain't, Harris burned inside, *it's the only way you like to do things.* His only wish was to get strong enough quickly enough to be able to get that Varley in a dark corner and cut slices off him!

'But,' the lieutenant jutted out his chin to make the point, 'sometimes force is the only language rabble like you understand.'

Harris stared at him. How he'd like to push those teeth down that leathery throat and stop that Adam's apple going up and down like a fucking yo-yo!

'I have had to waste valuable time preparing a report on your interrogation because some soft-bellied Hebrew doctor with high-up connections decided that one of his tribe had been pushed around a little too much for his liking.'

I'll go to synagogue as soon as I'm well — I promise you, God! Harris was enjoying seeing this West Point jerk squirm.

'Now, in my report I stated that under questioning you became violent and you had to be restrained.' The lieutenant glared at Harris as though he'd crawled out of a piece of rotting meat. 'That, we know, may not be strictly true, but let me put this to you. Who is a military tribunal going to believe? A man who has spent more time over the hump than he has in his unit, a black marketeer who broke loose to avoid a court martial? A man whose pre-war career included forgery, confidence tricks and a whole string of felonies? Or two veteran soldiers with clean service records, eh? You're a gambling man — who's your money on?'

OK, if it's so cut and dried, Harris thought, *why the visit?* He was soon to find out.

'Last week the American Army executed its first deserter since the Civil War. You may have heard about it. Private Slovik was shot for desertion in the face of the enemy. Compared to chicken-shit like you, he was a hero.'

Harris had heard all right. The army had made an example of the poor slob. Slovik was a badly trained, uneducated replacement brought in like many other former rejects to bolster up Ike's leagues of truant soldiers— men like himself who had opted for the sweet life in France and Belgium. His comrades had written home about it and there was a row going on as to why Ike had not rescinded the execution order.

'A loudmouth senator who knows nothing of what is happening out here is building himself a dubious political reputation stirring up the case . . . as if that could bring the boy back to life.'

All right, get to it, lootenant. Harris was getting tired of the man's monotonous droning.

'Now he's decided to investigate so-called army brutality.'

AH! Now you got to it! Harris saw that the lieutenant was beginning to sweat.

'This . . . doctor . . . has threatened to write to him about your little incident.'

Whoopee, I'll deliver the letter by hand. Harris became very interested again.

'What I'm saying is that he is going to have nothing to write about.' The lieutenant put on that menacing glint again. 'Because you're going to agree with every word of that report, you're going to sign a voluntary statement saying that the report contains the unvarnished truth and that you are prepared to accept the punishment meted out to you by court martial for your recent spell of AWOL.'

The hell I am! What kind of a prize prick do you take me for, lootenant? Harris's eyes blazed their defiance.

'Now in consideration of your behaving exactly as I've outlined, I'm prepared to see that you only get a first offence sentence— no more than ten days in the stockade. After that, it'll be back to your unit and if there's any scrap of decency left in you, you may yet pull yourself round to becoming a soldier. It's not too late, even for you!'

Oh, lootenant, you're so good to me — you make me want to cry.

114

'Well what do you say?' The lieutenant was actually smiling.

There was such a lot he wanted to say, but all that came out was: 'I'll dink aboud id, sir.'

'Yeah, you do that, and quick too — and remember this. If you don't play it our way and this crap head senator finds that the public have got tired of his stupid bleatings and he's gotten on to another hobby-horse, we'll still have you . . . and believe me, soldier, you'll wish every second of every hour that you could change places with Private Slovik.' The lieutenant jutted his chin, paused for a second, then spun on his heel and marched briskly out of the ward.

'Hey!'

Harris looked up across the room as the black chin and mouth under the bandages addressed him.

'Yeah?'

'The way that loo was bending yo' ear, seemed like yo' boyfriend, or somethin'.' The Kentucky drawl came through the thick bluish lips.

'He is,' Harris said. 'Cabe to dell me he was bregnant and we gotta get barried right away!'

A minstrel-like chuckle came through the dazzling white teeth . . .

9

Shaw shifted to a more comfortable position on the lumpy cushion of the fireside chair and listened to the rain percussion against the window, noting the variation in tone as the heavens opened and the downpour increased in intensity. The room seemed quite a bit smaller than he remembered, but then, he recalled, he'd only ever been in it when he was half-cut or in danger of capture. If it were the former, he was usually rolling in the sheets with one of the *poules*. If the latter, he was boxed up in that hellhole of a trick mattress, and after stepping out of that, everything seemed large! Now, viewing the room from this angle he could see it was of claustrophobic proportions. Its furnishings were sparse and its faded wallpaper damp and peeling. Yet, for all its seediness, there was something warm and friendly about the place. Perhaps all the love-making it had witnessed, however shallow and fleeting the passion, had permeated the walls themselves and created a sexual ambience that lingered within its confines and gave the room an ever present feeling of erotic expectation.

A gathering wind had joined the lashing rain and Shaw was glad to be near the heat of a single-bar electric fire that stood in a grate that had not seen coal for a long time. For several months coal had been the one commodity exclusively handled by the black market. It was absolutely impossible for anyone to obtain as much as a single piece of the fuel unless it was purchased on the *marché noir*. It was this factor, more than any other, that had initially made the Belgian Gendarmerie merely pay lip service to the Military Police in their efforts to

116

smash black-market dealings. Sitting around cold and draughty stations was understandably not a very attractive prospect for them, however keen they were to uphold the letter of the law. In return for being left alone to conduct their business, many operators would send a sack of coal as a gift to the personnel of a police station who, far from being concerned with the rights or wrongs of the bribe, were only too delighted to accept it. Shaw recollected a black-market dealer telling him that he made more profit out of selling a few hundredweight of coal a week than he did out of the earnings of a whole 'stable' of tarts. But, he admitted with a gold-toothed grin, it was not half so much fun!

Shaw did not know how long he had been waiting for Jacqueline — maybe two or three hours. When Shaw had finally tracked Jacqueline down and asked her to see if she could find out where Harris had been taken, she had given him a key and told him to go and wait in the room she used for 'business'. Jacqueline had explained that she would have to visit her friend, Claudette, and try to persuade her to get her snowball boyfriend to talk. Shaw was very grateful and promised her, in addition to some extra cash, several bars of her favourite chocolate if she could obtain the information. Then Shaw had wearily climbed the stairs, entered the room and flopped into the chair in front of the fire. He realised that he must have dropped off to sleep almost at once. All the good food he'd eaten at the Cordiers' and the quantity of drink he'd had subsequently, drifting in and out of an assortment of bars in his search for Jacqueline, had taken their toll. It was ironic, he thought, that his trying to hunt Jacqueline down among all the rowdy establishments of the rue de la Casquette had been a waste of time and money, because, as he later discovered when he returned to Antoinette's, foot-weary and well-oiled, she'd arrived only a few minutes after he'd left. When he spotted her she was about to go upstairs with a worse-for-wear Canuck airman. Shaw had got rid of the man by the simple expedient of whispering in his ear, in that peculiar bonhomie that bonds the inebriated into a blurred brotherhood, that the girl on his arm was known around town as 'Syphilis Sal'! No one sobered up quicker, no one took off faster than the grateful Canadian. Jacqueline angrily asked him what he'd told her client, and Shaw had said that the airman had to report back to his base at once as they needed him on a very important bombing mission over Hamburg. Jacqueline calmed down after the explanation, but it inwardly amused Shaw because, like most of the *poules,* whilst she had no qualms about being screwed by *les déserteurs,* she was also starry-eyed about the brave servicemen who were fighting the hated Hun. Shaw also knew full well that under the German occupation, she was a very willing collaborator in the only way a girl with her kind of looks is required to collaborate — with open legs. He told himself that he shouldn't be so cynical, the girl had to earn a living, and with her background she was hardly cut out to be a Florence Nightingale. Yet, in her own way, she was providing an equally essential service for the troops and he should be the last one to knock it.

Shaw was aware that she liked him a lot. She'd even said she loved him, and whilst Shaw realised that for her love meant sleeping with the same bloke twice in a week, he felt that she was fond of him and would, within reason, do his bidding. There was certainly something he felt for her too. It was not just her prettiness that appealed to him, or the fact that she was an enthusiastic filly in the rumpo stakes. So many of the *poules* just lay spreadeagled whilst they puffed a fag, or looked at their wristwatches impatiently, resenting the time it took their clients to get their money's worth. It was simply her laughter — it had a lovely fluid melodious ring. Her eyes would shine and she seemed to light up from inside. It was almost impossible not to be captivated by her infectious gaiety. But there was another mannerism she had, an almost precocious tilt of the head whenever she asked a question that poignantly awakened memories in Shaw that he had believed to be so deeply buried that they would never come to the surface again. They were so far down now, he was not even sure that they had ever occurred. It was as if he were an intruder gazing on a scene that was very private and did not remotely concern him. His heart throbbed as the soft lovely face became more and more vivid. It was a crisp, dry winter, just as it was now, and he was bursting with a joy he could hardly contain. He had driven her in his taxi away from the smoke-filled sky of London to the open country and there, walking hand in hand along a tree-bordered oval green under a ceiling of drifting cloud, he'd spoken of his dreams of the future. As she listened attentively, occasionally tilting her head and looking up at him with eyes that were as misty as that forgotten meadow, the uneven grass danced in the wind, and a grey squirrel daringly rushed across their path and was half-way up a tree before he felt safe enough to stare down at them. Shaw remembered how she laughed, and how irritated he felt at being interrupted in the middle of outlining his exciting plans one day to own the biggest fleet of cabs in London! He remembered the touch of her tiny finger on his lips silencing him, and then the warm softness of her mouth on his, and her husky voice whispering lovely, foolish things as she snuggled close to him. Oh, Sylvia, why in God's name were you taken from me? Shaw stood up, breathing angrily, his face twisting with grief.

The door handle rattled noisily and broke through his painful evocation. A second later Jacqueline entered the room. She shook her dripping umbrella outside the door and turned to Shaw as she removed her headscarf and took the umbrella to stand in the sink.

'*Mon Dieu,* what a filthy night,' Jacqueline said breathlessly, as she unbuttoned a cerise-coloured raincoat and threw it carelessly on the chair. She kicked off her shoes and reached up to Shaw to give him an affectionate kiss on the cheek.

'So, what did you find out?' Shaw prompted her at once.

'You are right. The *police militaire* have him.'

Jacqueline lowered her eyes. 'They've beaten him very badly to try to get information on you.'

Shaw stiffened. 'How do you know that?'

Jacqueline stared at her stockinged feet. 'This snowball who stay with Claudette told me. We get him very zig-zag. He started to boast. Claudette is a good friend, she didn't mind.'

'Didn't mind what?' Shaw scowled.

Jacqueline flushed a little. 'That we all go to bed together. It was what he wanted.' Shaw nodded. He didn't know why he should, but he resented the idea of this snowball screwing her.

'Did he tell you where they've got him?'

'Yes, they have him in a new stockade twenty kilometres from Liège. I know it. There is a farm nearby where we buy eggs.'

'Does it have a name?'

'Well, I do not know if the stockade has, but the village is called Saeffelen.'

'Good girl.' Shaw's attitude relaxed as he looked at the girl standing in front of him. For all her worldliness, she seemed strangely vulnerable, like a colourful moth with a broken wing. He moved towards her, unbuttoning his fly. 'Come on, then,' he said, and let his eyes roam over the firm little body cocooned in a bright green silky dress.

'No,' Jacqueline bit her bottom lip.

'Eh?' Shaw froze in his tracks.

'Volly, I'm too sore,' Jacqueline could not look him in the eyes. 'You want me to find out things. That snowball is a very big pervert. He does not use his *petit frère* like other man. He wants me to have up bottle, while he go with Claudette and watch me.'

Shaw sighed philosophically and shrugged as he did his buttons up. 'War is hell!'

'Pardon?'

'Never mind. I'll get you some nice chocolate, some soap and stockings. You did well.'

'Oh, thank you, Volly,' Jacqueline reached up to kiss him again.

'Yeah, yeah,' Shaw grunted, and thought about the snowball. He gets all his kicks and I gotta pay for it!

Shaw peeled off his jacket from the back of the chair, adjusted his tie, swept back his hair with a flat hand and started to think about what uniforms and equipment they would need before they could make the next move. Depositing a couple of notes on the bed, he winked at Jacqueline, smacked her bottom playfully, and took his leave.

10

The thin afternoon sun lit the imposing square of the place de la République Française as the jeep made a slow circuit and stopped in front of the magnificently pillared Opera House. Shaw sat stiff as a frozen shirt in the back of the jeep, wearing the uniform of a full colonel of the Corps of Military Police. His hair was tinted grey to match his false moustache, and to round off his disguise he wore a pair of steel-rimmed spectacles that made him squint. Trauber sat at his side, emulating his 'superior officer's' erectness and displaying the three stripes and shoulder flashes of a sergeant of the British 120 Provost Company. Winkel was in his now familiar role of driver, but this time impeccably turned out as an MP. Leder, who was similarly dressed but with the addition of the single stripe of a lance corporal, was demonstrating from his position on the front seat, how a sitting man could appear to be at rigid attention.

A young GI, one of many with a thirty-six hour pass roaming the historic streets of Liège, stood admiringly in front of the Opera House, hungrily snapping the old building from a variety of angles with a well-used box camera. Shaw smiled at the sight, rather as a big game hunter does when his prey comes into view. He nodded briefly to Trauber who leapt over the webbing safety strap at the side of the jeep and in a few strides was at the soldier's side. Shaw watched, amused, as the astonished photographer, having been told he had been arrested, walked weakly towards them.

'Know why you've been detained, soldier?' Shaw barked at

the weedy youth who shook from head to toe at the door of the jeep.

'N . . . no, sir,' the ashen-faced GI stammered.

'That's what they all say when they've been caught red-handed, what!' Shaw turned to Trauber. Shaw was clearly enjoying the masquerade he felt it wise to have as a little rehearsal before appearing at the main theatre of operation.

'Yes, sir!' Trauber screamed in reply.

'Sites of military significance, contrary to prohibited areas, photographing of,' Shaw could barely continue as he saw Trauber turn away trying to suppress his laughter, and the back of Leder's shoulders were moving up and down. 'Allied War Zone, Europe, Belgium, 1944 — clear enough, what?'

'I . . . er . . . I'd no idea, sir. I was only shooting the Opera House,' the bewildered soldier muttered almost inaudibly.

'Yes, that's what they all say,' Shaw grumbled. 'Chuck him in the jalopy — got to be on our way.'

'Sir!' Trauber bellowed and pushed the unfortunate GI into the front of the jeep with Winkel and Leder.

'Well, get the deuced camera orf him — that's our evidence, man.' Shaw scowled at Trauber as though he was an idiot. Trauber's moody response indicated that he felt the 'colonel' was getting just a little too carried away with the part, but nevertheless he removed the camera from the luckless prisoner and jumped in beside Shaw.

The jeep slowed and ground to a halt on the gravelled entrance drive. Shaw glanced at the sign outside the main gate and the grim message which read: 'U.S. Armed Forces Detention Camp IV'. There was a depressing atmosphere about the whole place. He cast his eyes quickly over the stockade and saw the rows of orderly hutments which led to a large administration block. Just behind the buildings was a spotless parade ground and, towering above and enclosing it all, was a double barbed-wire fence which rose a menacing twenty feet into the air. Shaw saw the sombre expressions on the faces of his companions and knew just what they were thinking.

One of the two armed sentries casually left the gate house and strode almost languidly towards the jeep. He suddenly recognised the value of Shaw's red tabs, straightened up at once and saluted smartly. Shaw returned the salute by touching the peak of his red-banded cap with his swagger stick in a deliberate off-hand manner.

'Colonel Crawford taken charge here yet?' Shaw looked the sentry up and down as though he were on a full-dress parade. The sentry shifted uneasily. 'Colonel Lowry is commanding, sir.'

'My other jeep in here yet?' Shaw squinted hard at the sentry and noted his pallid complexion, and the long nose with the rounded tip that moved like a rabbit's when he spoke.

'Beg pardon, sir?' The sentry cleared his throat.

'My adjutant, has he gawn in?' Shaw snapped.

'Not to my knowledge, sir.' The sentry looked over to his companion hoping to gain assistance, but the other man had also spotted Shaw's rank and decided to stand stiffly to attention, stare glassy-eyed in front of him, and keep well out of it.

Shaw frowned at the sentry. 'When he comes, send him over to me at admin block. Where is it?'

'Just back of the guard house, sir,' the sentry directed, and stood at the side of the jeep waiting. Shaw knew the sentry was expecting to see a pass.

'Well, open the gate, man,' Shaw rumbled like a bad-tempered walrus. 'I can't drive through it.' The sentry paused for a second, glanced once more at his motionless buddy, and concluded that all decisions rested on his own frail shoulders. Clearly this Limey redcap officer was not one to be kept waiting. He hurried to the gate, pressed an electric button and stood back as the wire doors swung open. Winkel did not hesitate, he had driven the jeep into the compound almost before the gates had completed their slow-sweeping arc, and brought the vehicle to a halt outside the admin block.

'Right-ho, let's have him,' Shaw nodded to Trauber who grabbed the GI by the arm and ushered him roughly out of the jeep. Shaw followed quickly, and saw from the corner of his eye the horror on the young soldier's face as he realised he was being conducted to the guard house.

Leder and Winkel stood rigidly by the jeep, as Shaw ambled leisurely up the steps of the guard house. He clutched a bulky brown leather briefcase, which had been badly scuffed, in one hand, and pushed the door open with the point of his swagger stick which he held in the other. The provost lieutenant was just receiving a telephone message from the gate and was half expecting to see Shaw as he walked in. Two snowballs sitting behind desks sprang to attention as Shaw entered, followed by Trauber and the shaking GI. The lieutenant slammed down the phone, rushed round his desk and nearly knocked over a wooden filing cabinet in his haste to confront Shaw. He quickly regained his composure and gave Shaw a crisp salute. Shaw returned the salute lazily, dumped his briefcase on a nearby desk and stared over his spectacles at the lieutenant. 'Told my other jeep hasn't arrived. What's going on, lieutenant?'

'We had no information, sir,' the lieutenant licked his lips, 'in fact, we didn't even know you were ——'

'What a bloody cock-up,' Shaw cut across him. 'All right, see him meself. Oh, before we get to it, caught this laddy of yours getting up to no-good with his box of tricks.' The lieutenant threw a puzzled glance at the stunned GI. 'Yes,' Shaw continued belligerently, 'warrant you'll find classified info on that roll of film.' Shaw nodded sternly to Trauber who stiffly handed the camera to the bemused lieutenant. 'Look into that right away, will you!'

The lieutenant gave a silent order to one of the snowballs and the luckless prisoner was marched out of the guard room and into an adjoining one for questioning. But Shaw's plan to confuse the lieutenant completely had only just begun. The innocent dupe of a GI was merely the 'hors d'oeuvre'.

'Now then, down to business.' Shaw folded his arms and squinted at the provost officer. 'Opened up yet, has he? Got this Shaw fellow pinpointed, have we?'

'I don't quite follow you, sir,' the lieutenant looked very unhappy.

'Great God, man!' Shaw thundered, 'you've had a signal?'

'Well, I guess . . .' the lieutenant said lamely, becoming more miserable by the second.

'Harris, Harris . . .' Shaw had summed up the lieutenant very quickly. He was convinced the domineering approach he'd adopted would be the best way to get results, but was aware he had to soften a little to make his character totally believable. He undid his briefcase and took out an imposing bundle of papers. He waved them fanlike in front of the lieutenant. 'Leslie Harris, 35th Infantry wallah — you have got him, haven't you?'

'Oh, him, yes sir,' the lieutenant croaked as realisation dawned.

'Good, good, well, what have you learned?' Shaw's eyes bored into the lieutenant like a gimlet.

'I — I don't believe he's told us too much, sir,' the lieutenant replied, clearing his throat.

'Hasn't he, by George. All right, let's not waste any more time, take me to him.' Shaw stroked his moustache and to his consternation felt part of it becoming detached. He held his finger to his lips as though he were in deep thought, and unobtrusively tried to stick it back. 'Yes, well, we'll get the beggar to talk, eh? Lead on, MacDuff!'

He dropped his eyes to the papers and made a pretence of studying them. He could feel the lieutenant hesitating. Shaw looked up at him sharply: 'Well?'

'It's just, sir, that perhaps I should check with er . . .'

'I wish you'd telephone General Bradley directly if you have any doubts, young man,' Shaw glowered at him, and saw the last inkling of resistance drain from the lieutenant's face as he swiftly considered his career. He moved at once to a desk drawer and brought out a large bunch of keys. Silently he walked to the door. Shaw followed at his heels and turned to Trauber before he left the room. 'You stand by here, Hardcastle.' Shaw almost froze as Trauber instinctively clicked his heels at the order, but fortunately only Shaw had noticed the Prussian salute. He shot an acid look at the embarrassed Trauber, the meaning of which clearly stated 'Wait till I get you home!'

The wide stone corridor rang with their steps as they walked briskly between the rows of heavy plain iron doors that sealed the cells. Shaw's head was buried in the folder of documents, but his eyes darted from left to right as they progressed and he missed nothing. The lieutenant stopped abruptly, selected a key from the bunch on the ring and unlocked the door in front of him. Shaw looked over the lieutenant's shoulder and saw Harris sitting on his bunk staring down at the laceless sneakers. He showed no interest as the door opened. He was lost in his own thoughts and looking as white and still as though he was cast in plaster. The lieutenant prodded him with his billy, hard in the shoulder. 'Right! Up, you!' he snarled. Shaw's hand dived into the document case and quickly came out holding a pistol. With a lightning swiftness, he brought the gun butt down on the back of the unsuspecting lieutenant's head. He folded and fell without a sound like a khaki blanket dropping off a clothes line.

'Right — up you, too, lootenant.' Harris grinned and looked

down at the crumpled form at his feet. Shaw removed his steel spectacles and studied Harris's swollen features. 'Who's been a naughty boy, then?'

'You should'a seen me before I came up from the infirmary.'

Shaw took a length of cord from the document case, and tossed it to Harris. 'Tie him up.'

Harris shook his head 'Aw, come on Wally — great to se ya, and I appreciate the visit, but I ain't gonna bust out.'

'Why the hell not?' Shaw exclaimed.

'See, they gotta kind of enquiry going on about yours truly, and if I keep my nose clean they say they'll let me return to the unit and wipe out my record.'

'Balls!'

'No, really! I gotta doc on my side and he's rootin' for me.' Harris seemed pleased with himself. Shaw did not have the time or the inclination to argue with Harris at this point. He could be an obstinate cuss and only extreme action would get the man shifted. Shaw delved into his document case and rapidly pulled out three pieces of a Sten gun, which he expertly proceeded to assemble. He rammed a magazine home and handed it to Harris, who was now showing more than a passing interest.

'Wh. . .what's this for?' Harris said uncertainly.

'Stick this in my back and let's get out of here. We got work to do,' Shaw ordered in a businesslike voice.

'Yeah, what?' Harris eyed Shaw suspiciously.

'This is big, Les,' Shaw replied quickly, 'really big.'

Harris examined Shaw's face. He could see Shaw was sincere, but it did not dispel his doubts. 'Just you and me?'

'Yeah — practically,' Shaw lied unconvincingly. 'Yeah, you and me.'

'And those craphead Krauts of yours?' Harris handed the Sten back in disgust. 'Forget it. No, buddy boy, I'm staying here. Ain't nothin' worse can happen to me now.'

'Listen — there's millions in this. Millions of pounds — no bullshit, Les.' Shaw stared straight into Harris's eyes.

Harris lowered his head and spoke firmly, 'No!'

Shaw moved quickly to the door and listened for any warning sound. All was still and quiet. He returned to Harris. There was a no-nonsense manner in Shaw's bearing as well as in his voice.

126

'You've got as long as it takes for me to tell you this. When I go I'll lock this door and they'll bloody shoot you for beating up this officer.'

'He's only had a tap,' Harris retorted, 'he knows it wasn't me that did it.'

Shaw lifted the unconscious officer and propped him up against the whitewashed cell wall. His head lolled to one side. Shaw backhanded him fiercely across his mouth, and then repeated the action, almost seeming to knock his head from his shoulders.

'You tell them you didn't do that while he was lying there?' Harris looked decidedly nervous.

'Want me to give him some more?' Shaw stared hard at Harris and poised his clenched fist at the oblivious lieutenant's jaw.

Harris resignedly snatched the Sten from Shaw. Shaw smiled and raised his hands. Harris looked at the officer slumped against the wall.

'Well, now, if I'm gonna get the blame . . .' Harris struck the lieutenant so hard across his chin it stung his fingers and sent the man sprawling face down on the floor. 'Just a sample of what I'm going to do to Varley if ever I see the sonofabitch,' he muttered grimly and pushed Shaw ahead of him with the gun.

At the wall of iron bars which cut across the cell block corridor, the guard on the other side threw a leisurely glance at the sound of approaching footsteps, returned his gaze to the Hollywood 'cheesecake' magazine he was absorbed in, then a second later sprang up, hardly daring to trust his eyes. Harris was at the iron division armlocking Shaw by the neck, pointing the Sten at his temple. Shaw was acting the 'victim' with wide-eyed terror. Instinctively the guard reached up to press the alarm bell.

'You do, and he gets it,' Harris screamed, observing the movement. The guard's hand froze in mid air.

'Pass the keys through or I'll shoot this bastard, then you,' Harris said savagely. The guard looked uncertainly at Shaw.

'Do as he says, soldier,' Shaw chokingly gasped through the stranglehold Harris had on him. 'I'll take full responsibility.'

The guard gingerly took the keys from their position in a small cupboard and handed them through the bars. Harris grabbed them from him, holding the gun so that it swayed dangerously, found the key for the barrier lock, undid it, and with an urgent tilt of his head summoned the guard to move to their side. Harris quickly perused the cell numbers on the keys and unlocked the nearest one to him. The inmate, a huge Negro wearing the same kind of faded blue denims as Harris, stood at the door, thoroughly perplexed by what was taking place. Harris prodded the guard into the cell and saw the Negro's frightened expression. 'What you in for,buddy?' Harris stared up at the big Negro who padded towards him, trepidation showing in his every step.

'They said it was larceny,' the Negro replied sadly.

'What do you say it was?' Harris asked.

'I say it was stupidity,' the Negro boomed, 'stupidity for getting caught!'

'Amen, brother!' Harris retorted with feeling. 'You want out?'

'Yo' sweet ass I do.'

Shaw tapped Harris's hand to release him from his grip, and when he did so Shaw walked briskly into the cell to face the astonished guard, and roughly grabbed the service revolver from his holster. He spun on his heel, strode out of the cell and heard the door click as he closed it gently behind him. The Negro was still looking very wary and his eyes were firmly fixed on Shaw's red tabs.

Shaw smiled, patted him on his arm and handed him the revolver. The Negro relaxed and broke into an ivory grin. 'Thanks, general,' the giant said as he took the gun.

'Now, listen, Mac,' Harris addressed the Negro in clipped sentences. 'We gotta create one hell of a riot. That way we all gotta chance. But you let us get to the gates before you start using that piece, huh? It'll be bad enough facing them bums, we don't need you shooting at our tails, OK?'

The Negro nodded slowly. Harris tossed the keys to him. 'Right, get busy. Open them cages and let 'em out.' The Negro seemed hesitant.

'Go, man!' Harris yelled impatiently.

'Some of these is better in here,' the Negro said in a doleful baritone voice. Harris nodded, comprehending at once.

'Then just let the fuckin' niggers out,' Harris growled, 'but shift your ass.'

The Negro beamed and waved at the retreating men, then he immediately started to go about his task, looking into each cell through the spy hole before opening it up . . .

The small trickle of emerging prisoners grew steadily into a mingling throng as the bewildered men started to gather in the corridor. By the time Shaw and Harris, walking stealthily, had reached the main cell block, the Negroes had formed into some sort of order, and led by the big man with the revolver were no more than thirty or forty feet behind them.

As Shaw and Harris got to the main cell block door, Shaw turned round and signalled for absolute silence. They froze into a petrified black forest. Harris hammered on the iron partition and waited for the observation panel to slide open. As it did so, Harris thrust his Sten barrel through the opening and aimed it menacingly at the three startled guards. Before they could make a move for their guns Harris audibly unlocked the safety clip on the Sten and stared down at the snowball trio with narrowed eyes that spelt out instant execution for any untoward action they may have contemplated.

'OK, now I'll say this once only,' Harris breathed in a voice as cold as steel. 'Drop your guns very slowly on the deck . . .' The snowballs knew he meant business and morosely did as they were ordered. 'All right, you,' Harris eyed the guard closest to the door, 'unlock this door.' The guard, just for a second stared back at Harris defiantly. Shaw could feel the stomach-knotting tightness as the guard weighed up the dubious advantages of being a dead hero. A tense moment later the guard wisely deferred his decision for another day, and sullenly unbolted the door. In an instant Harris sprang through, legs astride, pointing the Sten so that in one sweep, had he wished, he could have cut all three guards in half. Shaw casually bent down to retrieve the revolvers from the floor, and to the snowballs' utter amazement threw the weapons to the Negro prisoners who had now come in behind them. 'When we reach the gate,' Shaw addressed the big Negro, 'you lot come out blasting.' The Negro flashed a toothy affirmation. 'You'd better silence these mutts first,' Shaw nodded at the guards who, prompted by Harris, stood facing the wall with their hands held high. As he undid the main door with Harris armlocking his neck again, he heard the sound of three successive pistol whips and muffled gasps as bodies hit the floor.

It was the captain who saw them first. He looked up from a folder of papers he had taken from the filing cabinet and was about to close the drawer when he cast a casual glance through the guard house window. There, crunching their way across the rough gravel towards them was a British officer being held in a tight stranglehold by a prisoner waving a machine gun.

'Corporal of the guards,' the captain beckoned urgently to the snowball NCO, who was busily typing a report at his desk. The corporal jumped up at once, saw what the captain was staring at in disbelief, reached back to his desk to grab a white helmet, placed it on his head and was undoing his holster flap when Harris's shrill voice resounded round the parade ground.

'Now, hear this! The Limey gets his unless I get clear out of here!' Harris paused a moment, then getting no response moved nearer the guard house towards the goal of the still distant gates. Shaw felt the razor's edge of tension as Harris, holding him tighter than was necessary, shoved him roughly forward.

The captain quickly assessed the situation and gave a hurried order to the MPs inside the guard house. The snowballs unholstered their revolvers and, led by the corporal who was holding his at the ready, they moved cautiously to the guard house entrance. Trauber and Leder waited nervously by the jeep and Winkel's fingers were at the starter switch, itching impatiently to kick it into motion.

The corporal dropped on one knee and whispered from the safety of the door frame something to Trauber which he could not quite hear, but he gathered it was an order to keep their position and let the snowballs do the rest. Trauber acknowledged his understanding by a surreptitious wave of the hand. Shaw and Harris moved closer and closer to the guard house, and with each step their hearts beat louder. Silently, another snowball had inched the guard house window open and rested the tip of a Browning automatic rifle on the ledge. He held his breath and trained the gun on Harris, fixing him tightly in his sights. The captain, diving low under the window frame, came to his side and peered over his shoulder, getting the same view of Harris.

'Let's get him a little closer, son,' the captain breathed in the snowball's ear. 'Wait.'

Shaw sensed that all was not well, and from the corner of his eye observed the BAR at the window. Between stilled lips he whispered to Harris that they had him in range from the guard house. Harris looked up and saw the weapon aimed at him.

Grabbing Shaw so that he almost bent him over backwards, and jamming the Sten into his kidney area, he shouted up at the window. 'Throw that gun out, or I splatter this bum all over your nice clean square!'

There was no reaction from the guard house. Harris took the gun from Shaw's side and with one hand ripped off a short burst, which threw up a shower of gravel close to the guard house and caused some of the smaller pebbles to rattle against the glass in the window.

'I said now!' Harris screamed like a maniac.

The captain grimly considered the position. To have to explain the murder of a British colonel was something he did not exactly relish. His mind had already leapt into the future and to the court of enquiry that might strip him for a reckless and irresponsible action. How could the prevention of the escape of one lousy piece of scum be worth the life of a high ranking Allied officer?

'OK, do as he says,' he muttered bitterly to the snowball. The BAR fell with a clatter to the ground outside, and whilst all eyes were watching the next move Harris might make, Trauber had edged to the jeep and, with Leder, had pulled aside a tarpaulin which covered the space between the rear and front seats. He cast a hasty eye over the contents, and seemed satisfied that all was intact and ready. Harris, holding Shaw to him, close as a Siamese twin, raced in the direction of the jeep.

'Don't mind me, men,' Shaw shouted up at the guard house in a choking voice, 'shoot to kill!'

The shock of Shaw's utterance almost caused Harris to release his grip on him. 'What are you saying?' he hissed in Shaw's ear.

'Realism, mate!' Shaw chuckled, as they came alongside the jeep and heard it roar into life. Suddenly there were other noises at the end of the parade ground. Pistol shots, followed by a wild cheering. Like a swarm of migrating blackbirds the Negro prisoners poured out of the cell block yelling and firing. In a flash Shaw jumped into the jeep beside Winkel, while the three others bounded over the vehicle into the back. A snowball rushed from the door and tried to reach the BAR from the gravel path. He almost got it in his grasp, but Trauber had anticipated the move and as the jeep began to turn, he snatched his tommy gun from the floor and fired at the snowball's chest. The smack of the bullets thudding into him spun him round and lifted him bodily into the air. A moment later he was on his back gaping glassy-eyed up at the sky.

Almost before the jeep had completed a tight circle and headed in the direction of the gates, the entire area was in an uproar of noise. Shots from Thompson machine guns, automatic rifles, and hand guns cracked out in the echoing square above the voices of shouting, running men. Gravel was being hurled by kicking bullets in all directions. Bullets whined round the jeep as it sped towards the already alerted gate guards, who, bent on one knee, were taking careful aim with their revolvers at the fast oncoming vehicle, confident that as the heavy wire gates were fully shut, there was no way out for it. About twenty yards from the gates Shaw held the bazooka which he had lifted from the space at the back of his seat, and holding it as steadily as the bumpy ride would allow, sighted the base of the gates and fired. With a mighty bang the projectile found its mark and the gates blew into thousands of pieces. Winkel, bent over the wheel like a racing driver, headed straight for the smouldering opening. There was no visible sign of the guards as he screeched towards it. Suddenly, cutting through the air was a sound like a kid running a stick against railings, and a line of bullets came up behind the jeep and right through it. Winkel stiffened in his seat and crashed face down onto the instrument panel. The jeep, with no driver's foot on its clutch, juddered to a crazy halt. Shaw lifted Winkel's head back by the hair and felt an unaccountable anguish as he saw the vacant staring eyes in the mushy red face. With his boot and hands, he pushed Winkel out onto the gravel and got behind the wheel. In the back seat Harris, Leder and Trauber were firing light machine guns at an advancing group of MPs who already seemed to have quelled the break-out of the prisoners, and were now coming dangerously close. Shaw pushed the ignition button on the jeep. It coughed, spluttered, and refused to start. He desperately repeated the action. Still it would not respond. A cold sweat broke out all over him. He made one more frantic attempt, tugging the throttle out as far as it would go. This time the engine, weakly at first, started to tick over. Shaw slipped the lever into gear and eased one foot on the clutch and the other onto the accelerator with the finesse of a cathedral organist, dreading that the engine might stall again. It did not. Slowly and smoothly the jeep moved forward, increasing in speed, towards the mangled opening. Shaw gripped the wheel hard and felt the jolt as they crunched over the jumble of wire wreckage and raced off.

11

The tiny two-roomed apartment Shaw had rented through a contact was on the seamy side of Malmédy and had cost a small fortune. They had taken the place for two weeks, but the preparation for the break-out of Harris from the stockade had taken five days, and the purchase and setting-up of all the equipment they would need to get into Germany had taken another three days. That left them only six days to prepare for the raid on Sachsenhausen. Not a lot of time, Shaw ruminated, to organise what would be, if successful, the greatest robbery of all time. He was also acutely aware that most of their financial resources had been used up in obtaining the very necessary apparatus to carry out the raid; a newly stolen jeep, uniforms, guns, mostly acquired from active service men with an eye for some ready cash. Then there was food, ammunition, petrol, obtainable on the black market at prices, Shaw had said with feeling, that 'squeezed your balls so hard they made your eyes water'. But now they had got virtually everything they needed. The only commodity they couldn't buy was luck, and that, as Trauber reflected, would decide the issue not of just whether they could pull the job off, but quite simply whether they lived or died.

Harris had been impressed with the painstaking care that had gone into the plotting of the robbery. Shaw had taken a good deal of time, after the hair-raising escape they had made getting Harris out of the stockade, filling him in on the overall plan. Shaw had deliberately left out the finer details until the following morning when they would have all been refreshed from a good night's sleep. Harris had, however, insisted on examining the 'Bernhardt' note. This was to be, for him, the deciding factor on whether or not he would participate in the mission. When Trauber produced it for inspection Harris was staggered and studied it for a long time. There was no doubt in his mind about the undetectable quality of the counterfeit money. His one misgiving, as he was at great odds to point out to Shaw, was his genuine abhorrence of working with 'lousy Krauts'.

However, although Harris did not exactly extend the olive branch when he was formally introduced to the Germans, at least he maintained a surface, cool politeness, and for this alone Shaw was grateful. Too much money had been invested already to destroy all their well-laid plans before they had even got off the ground, and Harris's part in the operation was vital. Without an expert forger on hand, it would be impossible to go ahead.

The fragrance of the Camp coffee Trauber was brewing on the gas ring aroused Shaw from a deep sleep. He had slept on the settee, whilst Trauber and Harris had curled up under a bundle of greatcoats on the frayed carpet. Possibly because of the uncomfortable sleeping arrangements, Harris and Trauber had risen early, and when Shaw stirred Harris looked as if he had been up for some time and had even shaved. Shaw got out of bed and yawned loudly. He walked over to Harris who was holding up the 'Bernhardt' note to the window. He turned to Shaw, sensing someone was peering over his shoulder. 'It's beautiful,' Harris kissed the note. 'Wally, beautiful!' Shaw nodded, happy to see his friend's excitement. Harris chortled like a schoolboy who had discovered the corner sweetshop had been left unlocked. He could not take his eyes off the note. 'When do we move?'

Shaw leaned over Harris and lifted a neat little stack of stiff brown cardboard booklets off a table near the window, and handed them to Harris. 'Soon as you get these British paybooks looking the real McCoy, we get our arses up to the Rhine bridgehead.'

Harris frowned as he flicked through them. 'You mean the British are going to pay us for doing this?' Shaw threw Harris an old-fashioned look. 'Come on, Les, Yanks have ident cards, British have paybooks.'

'Yeah, yeah, I was forgettin' that's what you call 'em.' Shaw smiled, Harris was already lost in study as he picked up a magnifying glass from the table and ran it over the pages. 'We're going to need good photos, of course.'

Trauber came up with a mug of coffee in one hand and an expensive-looking camera in the other. He handed the camera to Harris and placed the mug of coffee near him on the table. Harris ignored the coffee but held the camera up admiringly. 'Hey, a Leica. I lika!'

'I should hope so,' Shaw said good-humouredly, 'it cost a bomb. We've even got developer, fixer and trays, the bloody lot, mate!'

'You guys seem to have thought of everything,' Harris voiced his approval.

'Yes, we hope so,' Trauber said and moved round Harris to the window table. He picked up a folded map and spread it out. Leder came wandering in, holding a steaming cup of coffee, and poked his head in the space between Shaw and Harris. There was a hushed silence as Trauber pointed at the map with his gold pencil. 'We are here — ' Trauber flicked at the dot marked 'Malmédy' —'We have heard that all along this line there is fierce fighting. It is at its most intense here —' Trauber indicated the town of Bastogne — 'It now seems that this area is entirely surrounded by German Panzer divisions.'

'You're not suggesting we try to cross there?' Harris's face was a picture of worry.

'No, of course not,' Trauber replied patiently, 'but we must look as though we are part of the British reinforcements coming close to this point. Now, along here'— Trauber poked his pencil to a spot on a spidery blue line — 'there are several places where the Allies are likely to cross. We have seen convoys going constantly in that direction. It cannot be long now before they attempt to cross the Rhine. When they do, we shall be with them.'

Harris nodded slowly. 'Assuming we all make it in one piece, what then?'

Trauber's eyes twinkled impishly. 'That's when we use our experience to blend in with the German countryside, don our Wehrmacht uniforms and proceed, as planned, to Berlin!' Harris blanched visibly. 'Berlin!' he croaked.

Shaw saw the fear in Harris's face and jumped in quickly. 'See, Les, Horst has got this contact in Berlin, and to fake a genuine-looking authorisation to enter the camp we must

136

have the right blank paper and seals.'

'And most important,' Trauber interjected, 'we need a sample of Kaltenbrunner's signature.'

Harris still looked unhappy as he addressed Trauber. 'Listen, this contact of yours — how do you know he'll still be around?'

Trauber appeared for a moment to share Harris's concern. 'It's a "she" actually. A lady to whom I am very attached. If she is not, as you say, around, it will make life more difficult for us. We may then have to wait until there is an Allied air raid, then stage a little break-in at the Reichssicherheitshauptamt offices.' The name meant nothing to Harris: 'Is that going to be tough?'

Leder sniggered. Harris turned on him hotly, 'What's so goddam funny?' Leder's smile faded at once, and a contemptuous expression replaced it.

'It's only a contingency plan,' Trauber said more reassuringly. 'I have every reason to believe that my Irene is still very much around!'

Harris shot a nervy glance at Shaw, then turned with as pleasant a smile as he could muster to Trauber. 'Say, listen, I ain't had a lot of time to talk to my buddy here about er——'

'I understand. I am sure you must wish to discuss it before you make up your mind,' Trauber said affably. 'Come on, Martin, let's sort through the uniforms and weapons. It will save time later.'

Harris waited until the Germans had gone into the adjoining small bedroom, then dropped his voice as he hissed at Shaw. 'Now, listen, you louse — you didn't say nuttin' about Berlin!'

'I said Germany,' Shaw tried to sound calmly detached. 'What's the difference?'

'What's the difference!' Harris was almost apoplectic. 'Hell, man, Berlin is the capital, that's where Hitler runs the whole damn ballgame.' Harris lowered his voice to a whisper as he observed that Leder was staring at him through the open door of the bedroom. 'Don't you realise the place'll be crawling with armed Krauts. Jesus, Wally, it's fuckin' *hara kiri*!'

'No, it won't be as bad as that, mate,' Shaw said.

'Well, 'ow bad will it be, mate?' Harris badly mimicked a cockney accent. He was very distraught. Shaw understood Harris well. With Les in one of his edgy moods, only a friendly, logical and cool approach would restore his equilibrium.

'Les, I'll give it to you straight.' Shaw stared steadily at Harris. 'We've hocked ourselves up to here,' Shaw held his hand under his chin. Harris started to speak, but Shaw stopped him. 'Look, there's no way we can stop now. Sure as hell, if we hang around here the MPs will nab us.'

Harris tried to speak again. Shaw held up his hand to stop him. 'Let me finish,' Shaw continued evenly. 'You don't owe me nothing, Les. If you want out of this it's OK. We'll miss you but we'll manage. But what you'll miss is about the only bloody chance you'll ever have of being a millionaire!'

Harris scratched at his freshly shaved yet still stubbly chin, and slowly broke into an easy grin. It made him look suddenly younger. 'Then we shift the bundle over to Sweden, you said last night?'

'Oh, I see you remembered that part all right,' Shaw returned the grin. 'Yeah, sod off over the border to Sweden and sit what's left of the war out, with a few million quid to help us. Lovely!'

'OK — so what are we waiting for!' Harris checked the camera, adjusted the lens and gazed into the viewfinder. 'I think we'll have to take them by this window here for maximum light.'

'I'll get the others in, they'll be ——' Shaw halted in midsentence as, with dismay, he observed Harris bending over the camera with a gold Star of David dangling from his neckchain above it. The pendant had slipped above his singlet and hung out through his open-neck shirt. It would have been clearly visibly to the Germans even from the next room had they been looking in his direction. Shaw moved in front of Harris at once, shielding him from their view, and made a pretence of showing a startled Harris something on the camera with one hand while with the other he swiftly thrust the Judaic symbol inside Harris's shirt, out of sight. 'Take that bloody thing off,' Shaw gritted between clenched teeth.

Harris was taken aback for a second by Shaw's action. Then, as realisation dawned, he leisurely straightened his singlet and buttoned his shirt. He looked at Shaw purposefully: 'This stays on. I'm working with them only for the kind of payday you're talking about — but this stays on!' Harris's brown eyes burned. 'And don't be surprised if there's two more dead Krauts at the end of this caper, buddy.'

138

'You do what you like when we've finished this job, son, but in the meantime keep that out of the way,' Shaw said sharply. 'If I see you flash it again I'll rip it off meself. All right?'

'OK, OK.' Harris smiled, shrugged his shoulders like a caricature Jew, made a final adjustment to the camera, and shouted to Trauber and Leder in the next room, 'OK, you two, let's get these photos took!'

Trauber came in at once, Leder a moment later.

'I gather you have decided to remain with us,' Trauber extended his hand in friendship. Harris made no move to take it. Instead, he looked into the viewfinder. 'All right, who's first? You, Wally, over there, watch the birdie!'

12

The wintry air, blackened with the smoke of burning vehicles, the dust of crumbling houses, the acrid eye-stinging odour of cordite and the stink of rotting bodies, human and animal, assailed Shaw's nostrils as the jeep, now tailed by a bouncing, equipment-laden trailer, churned its way along the cratered outskirts of the little Rhine town. Troops were everywhere. Convoys moved at a snail's pace towards the bridgehead and a constant stream of GIs and Tommies marched warily over the battered highway. Above all the clamour of great grinding vehicles, tanks, coaxial guns and lorries, was the sound of men's voices; NCOs screaming orders, officers briskly snapping out commands.

Interspersed through the continuous noise were the deafening explosions of heavy gunfire. All along the Rhine the Germans had built up an almost impenetrable wall of defence, desperately trying to fend off the relentless Allied onslaught which was now on the very doorstep of their beloved Fatherland. The jeep moved slowly into all the chaos. Harris was at the wheel, Shaw at his side. Trauber and Leder in the rear. All of them were in the uniforms of the Royal Signal Corps. Shaw with his three stripes looked every inch in command of the small unit as he guided Harris in and out of huge vehicles that had come to a sudden halt. Harris, weaving an effective course and apparently oblivious to the grim scenario being enacted all around, unexpectedly broke into song. In an unmelodious voice, and in an accent he fondly imagined to be British, he started singing the jingoistic 'We're gonna hang out the washing on the Siegfried line'. Harris's performance aroused a quiet fury in Leder, an air of total indifference in Trauber, and one of restrained amusement in Shaw. A tin-hatted REME major emerged from a group of engineers who were working like beavers trying to get equipment off a shell-crippled AVRE and transferring it to another vehicle that was parked parallel and completely blocking the road.

Shaw bellowed in Harris's ear for him to stop and, more important, to shut up as the major came towards them and waved them down with a pipe he had removed from between his clenched teeth. 'And where are you wallahs off to, eh?' the major hollered above a series of earth-shaking bangs.

Shaw saluted smartly. 'Communications party, sah!' Shaw eyed the officer and noted that his outward calm belied a near-the-surface look of utter confusion. The major wearily returned the salute. 'Yes, well, leave your buggy here. We shan't be through for a good half-hour at least. Take what you need and report to Captain Sayers at the bridge. Chop, chop, carry on!'

The major wandered back to his engineers but kept a firm eye on the jeep. It was not that he was particularly interested in the activities of this Signals Corps party, it was really the boredom of waiting for his men to finish their task that kept his unwanted attention on Shaw and the three others.

'Christ, we can't leave this lot behind,' Harris hissed at Shaw. 'He said take what we want, didn't he?' Shaw replied testily. 'Let's park the jeep safe as we can, take what we can carry and come back later for the rest. Come on, shift it— he's watching.' Harris swung the jeep into the only space available and Shaw, Leder and Trauber scrambled out and started to raise the tarpaulin from the trailer. They removed four Sten guns, some knapsacks containing food, and several rounds of ammunition. It was all they could take with them at this stage without arousing suspicion. Nevertheless, they had come prepared to look as though they were the genuine article, and when Harris joined them they hauled over the side of the trailer a heavy and quite useless reel of cable which, in a half-loping crouch, they proceeded to roll up the street. The major smiled at them good-naturedly as they went past him, replaced the pipe in his mouth, stuck his finger in the bowl and seemed surprised to find it had gone out.

The fighting was at its heaviest at the approach to the

141

bridge. Rubble filled the streets and was added to constantly by cascading buildings. Shaw turned to Harris, who was puffing like a train with the effort, and was about to speak when a succession of blinding white lights flashed over them. A moment later there was a thunderous crash, followed by another and another. Shaw looked back for a second and watched in awe as the section of street they had just come from disintegrated under a barrage of mortar fire. As yet another mortar bomb descended even closer, Shaw ducked low and dived, with the others at his heels, through the gaping doorframe of a miraculously still standing house. Breathless, they slumped against the wall and sat down on a plaster-strewn floor. Ear-shattering crashes rattled them back and forth like dice in a cup, then all at once the ferocity of the attack, though unabated, changed direction.

Trauber spoke first. 'Our jeep went up in that lot, didn't it? He addressed his question to all of them.

'Yeah,' Shaw replied flatly.

'Our German guns and uniforms were in there,' Leder said dejectedly.

'That's right.' Harris turned to Shaw. 'What do we do now, sarge?'

Shaw smiled grimly at Harris. 'Just say after me: Our Father who art in Heaven . . .' Trauber saw the funny side at once, and chuckled softly. Leder sat moodily silent. Harris seemed almost relieved. It would seem they would be unable to cross the Rhine on this trip. But Shaw, although despondent, was not beaten.

'Look, all we've lost are the Jerry uniforms and guns. We're just going to have to use a few commando tactics and get some more when we get into Germany. We can't turn back now — agreed?'

'Agreed,' Trauber grunted thoughtfully. Harris and Leder nodded together in affirmation. Harris took a pack of gum from his battledress blouse and handed it around. They all accepted a stick.

'I once heard a Limey spout a beautiful poem that I think very appropriate for such an occasion,' Harris said with mock seriousness.

'Don't keep it to yourself, son,' Shaw uttered encouragingly, as he tore the wrapper from his gum.

'You're right. This is an example of the poet's art which

142

should be expressed at a memorable moment like this.' Harris cleared his throat loudly.

> When your balls touch your bum
> And they rattle when you run
> And you fart like a gun,
> You're a man, my son!

Harris pushed a stick of gum into his mouth and winked broadly at Leder who responded with a weak smile, not really comprehending whether Harris was being serious. Trauber was in no doubt. He threw back his head and roared with laughter. Shaw had that strange feeling that most people experience at some time or other that he'd seen the whole scene before. Perhaps it was just a similar occasion that gave it a familiarity. He'd been in other places like this, where the company clown had come into his own, reeling off funny jokes, anecdotes or bawdy rhymes. Anything to relieve the tension of a situation which, in a fateful second, could bring about horrifying death or injuries. These barrackroom humorists rarely won medals for bravery, but every soldier remembered them with affection long after the heroics were forgotten.

Shaw shook his head and tut-tutted like a vicar who had found some rude words in the Bible underlined in ink by mischievous choirboys. 'Why we let your ancestors keep a nice place like America, I'll never know.'

The momentum of the attack they were sheltering from began to diminish, and soon they noticed there were quite long lulls between each bombardment. Shaw waited for such a respite and crawled to the glassless window. He gingerly peered out of it. He assessed the position and decided it was time to take their leave. He went to the door, bowed low like a flunkey, and ushered his three assorted comrades with a sweeping arm gesture to the doorway. 'Gentlemen, shall we rejoin the army?'

With Shaw at the head of the small line, and using the outer wall of the house to shield them, they moved forward, guns at the ready, crouching low, faces set. Soon hey had joined groups of Tommies, all of them cautiously approaching the bridgehead. Instinctively Shaw grabbed Harris and threw him to the ground — another thunder-clapping battery of gunfire had opened up from the opposite bank.

Shells screamed over their heads and blew a convoy of waiting trucks into a broken skeletal line of burning hulks. The sky seemed to be on fire as the pounding of the German eighty-eights continued relentlessly. Shaw glanced to his side and saw Trauber and Leder had taken shelter behind an overturned British tank. He waited until they lifted their heads and looked in his direction, and then waved them forward. Shaw led just a few paces in front and they formed into a moving party again.

Although they were only a few yards from the west bank of the Rhine, it was a nightmarish journey to reach it. Every step forward seemed to take them closer into the jaws of hell. Shaw had no idea how much time they had spent trying to negotiate the last few feet of the bank, but when they finally arrived at the river and rolled exhaustedly into a protective shell crater, he realised that night had overtaken day. That dusk had descended and had not been immediately apparent was due to the incredible illumination of warfare, which had held the darkness at bay. They sat in the hole for a few seconds, looking at each other without speaking. Trauber was the first to move. Carefully he edged his way up to the lip of the crater and stared out to survey the scene eastwards. Finally, he slid through the mud back down the incline. He gazed at Shaw gravely. 'It could be ages before they take that bridge.'

Shaw climbed up and saw that Leder had followed him. A moment later, so had Harris. The brightly lit view made it easy to inspect almost the entire length of the bridge.

'It'll be days before enough men and equipment are moving over it to cover our crossing,' Leder whispered gloomily. But Shaw was not listening, he had spotted something that had riveted his attention.

'Hey, have a butcher's at this lot,' he said as Trauber scrambled up beside him and looked in the direction of Shaw's pointing finger. Drawn up on a shady section of the river bank were a number of rubber assault boats, and Trauber knew immediately what Shaw had in mind.

'Shouldn't we wait until the attack is less intense?' he queried anxiously.

'Not 'alf,' Shaw replied with a wry grin.

Harris worked the slide of his Sten. 'Well, while we're waiting, we might as well look as though we're winning the war.' His gun started to blaze almost before he finished speaking. Shaw was aware that Harris had opened fire mainly to

144

needle Leder. On that score, he reckoned, studying Leder's tight-lipped face, he had succeeded.

Shaw heard the shell coming. He glanced for a split second at the faces of the others and knew they'd heard it too. As one man they threw themselves face-down into the muddy earth, and covered the sides of their heads with raised arms. A rush of wind seemed to part the air above them. The blast of the explosion sent splinters humming past their ears. The noise seemed to be trapped in their heads for a moment, before it rattled round inside their skulls and jarred their mouths open to let it out. Harris coughed harshly and spat the dirt from his mouth. 'Jesus! That was close.'

Shaw looked at the mud-stained faces of Leder and Trauber, then turned to the still spitting Harris. 'If they come any closer, you got nothing to worry about!'

'What we gonna do — hang about till they do?' Harris grunted, clearly shaken.

'No — we're off to fight the Hun, my son,' Shaw replied, and nearly bit his tongue off at the *faux pas* as he caught the anything but friendly reaction of Trauber and Leder. Clutching his Sten, Shaw groped his way up to the top of the crater, slid over and belly-crawled his way towards the lower section of the bank, where the rubber boats were haphazardly moored. Shaw quickly inspected the first one and observed that it had two paddles lying in the bottom. He motioned to the others to assist him as they quietly came up behind him and pushed the boat down the silty mud into the black water.

Wading silently in behind the boat, the men clambered aboard one by one. Harris and Leder grabbed a paddle each and Shaw and Trauber crouched, Stens at the ready, keeping watch fore and aft. After an uncertain start, when the boat began to circle, Harris and Leder developed a fairly even rhythm with their dipping paddles, and the frail craft proceeded crabwise upstream towards the German east bank.

Shaw gazed up at the sky which had changed from a stark magnesium brightness into a dull orange glow and saw the nail-clipping of a moon peer apologetically from behind a thin wisp of cloud. It seemed to sense it was no match for the display of fiery dazzling lights that intermittently flashed beneath it, and ducked behind a larger, darker cloud and vanished again. There was a moment's panic when suddenly the boat seemed to be swept into a surging current that made the paddling efforts of Harris and Leder seem completely useless, until they realised that they were being pulled rapidly upstream, as though assisted by a powerful unseen hand, towards their destination.

Two helmeted heads rose up above a covering of branches that sprouted from a river-bank bush. The German soldiers had both spotted the approaching boat. One of the soldiers turned to the other and shrugged his shoulders as if to say, 'Is this how they intend to invade us?' The other shook his head, equally puzzled. But it was clear to both of them that these sitting ducks, who presented such an easy target, would, if captured alive, no doubt have a mine of information on Allied troop movements, information that would be greatly appreciated when extracted by the 'experts' at High Command. Perhaps this was the chance to gain one of those Iron Crosses the Führer was now throwing out like confetti.

When the boat was within a few yards of the bank the Germans raised their rifles simultaneously, worked the bolts in unison and fired off a single round each. The shots cracked out and reverberated through the naked trees that lined the bank. One of the bullets found its mark with pin-point accuracy. It ripped through the rubber skin of the boat, punctured a buoyancy chamber and sent a stream of air bubbling out beneath the water line.

'Oh, that's bleeding delightful, that is,' Shaw uttered in dismay as he saw one side of the boat sag limply and watched helplessly as water started to slosh over the gunwale.

Trauber stood up unsteadily and shouted wildly in German to the soldiers at the top of his voice.

'Germans, we are Germans— stop firing.' Harris and Leder paddled frantically as they desperately tried to get the fast-sinking boat to the safety of the land. Then, just as it seemed the boat would get no further, Shaw felt that the wallowing craft had reached the shallows and had grounded. Trauber turned hastily to Shaw and addressed him in a low whisper: 'I'll keep them talking. You do the rest!'

Shaw did not even have time to reply when Trauber jumped over the side and with hands raised splashed through the water to the edge of the bank where the two soldiers were waiting with their rifles steadily aimed. Shaw led Harris and Leder over the side and, with hands held high, walked in the icy river a few feet behind Trauber. Shaw heard Trauber's haughty voice barking in German as he traversed the last few feet and came onto dry land to confront the German soldiers.

'We are a special scouting party — 'night wolf' — returning from the west bank. Waffen SS.' Trauber's superior attitude could be detected by Shaw, even though he only understood a few words.

The thicker-set of the two German soldiers moved forward in his bulky greatcoat, suspicion clearly visible in his narrowing eyes. 'Show me your identity papers.' Trauber stood truculently in front of the soldiers and held their attention while Shaw, Harris and Leder came to his side, trying to look as inconspicuous as possible.

'We are carrying British paybooks,' Trauber snapped impatiently, as though having to explain his actions to these two soldiers was far beneath his dignity.

'Why?' the thick-set German soldier questioned. He believed only what he could see. Here were four British soldiers and he and his comrade had captured them, and Iron Crosses were something to boast about to the kids. Trauber became extremely angry. 'What did you expect, you numbskull? For us to carry German papers? Direct me at once to your Field Headquarters!'

The German was jolted out of his stride by the outburst. This man certainly acted like a German officer. He turned to his comrade who shrugged as he had done when he first saw the boat approaching.

'Am I talking to myself?' Trauber shrieked.

The second German soldier lowered his gun and turned to point northwards. Unlikely story it might be, but he knew that the SS were capable of any lunatic suicide mission, and he wasn't looking for trouble. His companion, the sturdier one, followed his gaze. Who wants a bloody Iron Cross anyway! *'Zwei hundert meters unt . . .'* His words were cut off in a strangled cry as Shaw and Harris slipped cheese wires over their heads with the striking speed of a brace of black hawks, and pulled the simple but deadly weapons as tight as they could. Shaw heard his victim's larynx snap as the face became a gruesome ruby colour, his eyes bulged as though they would fall from their sockets at any second, and a great length of tongue rolled from his gaping mouth. A moment later Shaw was holding the limp weight of the dead German by the wire that had cut into the skin of his thick neck. He released his grip, and the soldier slumped to the ground like a grey sack. He turned to Harris who was still crazily tightening the cheese wire around the throat of the other soldier, although the spirit of the German had departed several seconds earlier. Shaw nudged Harris gently. Harris came out of his frenzied stupor at once, and let the soldier crumple at his feet. Shaw watched Harris gawping down at the corpse, saw his ashen, stunned expression, and expected him to vomit over the body at any moment. Instead, Harris turned away and took a long, deep breath.

Trauber and Leder, wearing the field grey jackets and greatcoats taken from the dead German soldiers, looked like a couple of crane birds as they bent over the river edge with incongruously exposed bare legs, and washed the trousers they had recovered from the soldiers in the freezing water.

Just behind them, on a grass verge, Harris was seated with his head between his knees. Shaw chewed a blade of grass and sat at his side.

'Keep your head down,' Shaw muttered sympathetically, 'you'll feel better.'

'Yeah.' Harris looked up. 'Honest to God, I never thought it would be like that!'

Shaw leaned over and pushed Harris's head forcibly between his knees again. 'Down,' Shaw commanded.

'Three years in this man's army and I never killed anybody.' Harris's muffled voice came from below his legs. 'Christ! The smell!'

Harris looked up and followed Shaw's gaze as he quietly studied Trauber and Leder puffing and blowing with cold as they wrung the water from the freshly rinsed trousers.

'Blokes get killed like that — they're entitled to shit themselves,' Shaw said woodenly. 'You heard of the stink of battle, boy? That's it!'

He remembered only too clearly when he had felt like Harris. He was leading a small platoon, jogging alongside the tank. He could see it now. The cherry-faced corporal in the turret, he could even recall the tank markings: 'E' Squadron, with the bright red letters 'Snow White' under a Disney cartoon. Just as they were approaching the outskirts of an Italian village, a salvo of shells fell on them, bringing a holocaust of death and destruction. Only three of his platoon of eight were still left, and the shrieks that he heard from the blazing tank as its occupants roasted alive he would never be able to forget. He had rushed to try to get near the tank, but the flames beat him back. Later, as the fire burned out, he tried again, this time to salvage what was left of the charred bodies. With the help of the three remaining members of his platoon, he lifted the slumped corporal from the turret. He was just black skin and bone. As they hauled him out and over, they saw that his trousers had ballooned with the melted fat of his body that had got trapped between his boots and gaiters. When they laid him on the ground, the still warm liquid fat gushed out as his trousers shifted with the move. The human fat poured over Shaw's boots and surrounded his ankles. He could smell it now! He decided he would not go back for the other two men inside the tank. Yes, Shaw knew how Harris felt, all right.

13

It suddenly dawned on Shaw that for the first time since the
war began he was on enemy soil. He was in Germany. As he
trod wearily over a rough forest road with Harris plodding
silently at his side, the irony of the situation hit him. He'd
fought the Italians, the Germans, then later the Allies — well,
the Provosts anyway, and evaded capture by all of them. Now,
here he was, hands on head, dressed as a British Tommy, a
voluntary prisoner, walking into the lions' den as though it
were an evening stroll through the park. It did not help his
state of mind to know that Trauber and Leder, dressed in the
uniforms of the dead German soldiers, and who now carried
all the guns as they shuffled behind Harris and himself, were
only play-acting. He was convinced that, should the situation
be put to the test, the play-acting might be transformed into a
stark reality. It was a sobering thought.

Great black trees skirted their path, and the quarter-moon
was now visible again, providing a steady, if faint, light. Just
below a hill, a shadowy clutch of cottages came into view. It
appeared to be a small slumbering village. Harris threw a
hurried glance over his shoulder at Trauber and Leder, who
were engaged in earnest conversation, and stepped in closer so
that he could speak quietly to Shaw. 'Reckon we can trust
those two bastards with all the guns?' Shaw had wondered
how long it would be before Harris had felt the same uneasi-
ness as himself, but knowing what a highly strung bugger he
could be, he was certainly not going to be the first to mention
it.

'I dunno,' Shaw replied, eventually, 'Got any better ideas?'

Harris thought for a while, and then shook his head. 'No!'

Shaw smiled grimly to himself as they walked towards the village. A cold drop of water fell on his nose from an overhanging branch, and a slow drizzling rain commenced. They withdrew their heads miserably into their greatcoats.

'Hold it!' They heard Trauber's voice right behind. Shaw and Harris turned towards him. 'I think it unwise to go into the village,' Trauber's face showed concern. 'Martin and I believe it is possible there could be a small garrison nearby, and we don't need that problem.'

'True.' Shaw nodded in agreement.

'I've noticed that on the other side of that hill there's a stream,' Trauber said, pointing beyond the forest perimeter.

'So?' Harris queried.

'Well,' Trauber replied, studying his compass, 'if we follow the course of the stream, at least we shall still be heading in the direction of Berlin, without the danger of taking undue risks on main highways.'

'I'll buy that,' Harris grunted irritably.

The party re-formed as before, and trudged on. Soon they were approaching a little stone bridge — a shimmering shape that was just visible in the thin moonlight. Trauber and Leder rushed quickly round in front of Harris and Shaw. 'Stay here,' Trauber panted, 'while Martin and I have a look around.'

Shaw and Harris stood concealed in the shadows while Trauber and Leder approached the bridge and checked the situation, looking, as far as visibility would allow, in both directions, and straining their ears for any sound of activity. Fatigue and the cold were beginning to get through to Shaw, and he could see that Harris was suffering similarly. He nodded to him encouragingly, but Harris made no attempt to respond. He was in a sullen mood and was obviously very concerned with the way events were shaping.

Shaw stamped his feet miserably to bring some life back into them and heard the squelching sound of water in his boots. After a few minutes Leder returned breathlessly on his own. Shaw wondered for a second if anything was amiss, but his fears were soon dispelled. 'It is not guarded. We can go on,' Leder said, sucking in deep breaths. He turned to Harris and pointed to the bridge. 'Follow Trauber up there.'

'Don't give me orders, buddy,' Harris swung on Leder

hotly. 'Les!' Shaw shot Harris a fiercely warning glance. Harris paused defiantly for a moment, then marched on sulkily to where Leder had directed. Shaw spaced himself strategically between Leder and Harris, and all three silently made their way over the bridge towards Trauber. Trauber was kneeling in a soft earth ditch, just a short distance from the other side of the bridge. As they got closer to him they saw that he was bent over a map and was studying it intently in the bamboo-thin beam of a pen torch.

'How far are we from Berlin?' Shaw asked, coming up behind Trauber and peering over his shoulder.

'Four hundred and sixty kilometres,' Trauber replied, standing up and brushing the mud from his knees. He switched off the torch and refolded the map.

'We gonna walk there?' Harris grumbled, still plainly hostile. Shaw saw Leder give Harris a look of contempt, and then turn to Trauber whom he addressed softly in German: *'Könnten wir riskieren, einen Zug zu nehmen?'*

Harris erupted. 'Why doesn't this squarehead talk English?' Leder stared icily at Harris. Shaw had seen that look before — it spelt trouble, and there was no doubt Harris was doing his level best to stir it up. What a bloody time to start goading Leder, Shaw thought angrily, here in Germany when he and Harris were both unarmed. Shaw was about to round on Harris and admonish him when Trauber, anticipating that there could be a flare-up, placed a hand gently but firmly on Leder's arm and cautioned him with a look of almost serene calmness. It seemed to work. The hatred drained out of Leder as though an evil spirit had been exorcised.

Trauber addressed Harris: 'Martin simply asked if I thought that getting on a train would be too dangerous for us.' Harris grunted something barely audible in reply, but slowly regained his composure. Trauber included Shaw in his next remark. 'I think it would be decidedly risky, with you two having no German.'

'Well, we're going to need some kind of transport,' Shaw said, stamping his numbed feet.

'Yes,' Trauber agreed. 'Martin and I will go back up on the bridge, and hope we can stop something suitable.'

Shaw settled down on a nearby bank, plunged his hand into his greatcoat pocket and produced a tin of corned beef. From his tunic pocket he removed a steel clasp knife. 'Could be a long wait,' Shaw murmured glumly, and drove the blade hard into the can of meat.

Trauber made no reply, but silently beckoned Leder to follow him as he climbed the bank. Then, as an afterthought, slid back down to Shaw and Harris, and smiling amiably, left the two Stens with them. With long-legged strides, he clambered hastily up the bank again to join Leder who stood at the top waiting for him, legs astride, his left hand placed firmly on his hip, while the fingers of his right hand drummed impatiently on his rifle. In a few seconds they were both approaching the hump of the bank and could only just be seen as two shadowy figures in the distance.

Harris picked up a Sten and made a pretence of fixing Leder in his sights. 'Boy, would I love to empty this up that goddam Kraut's butt,' he said glaring along the barrel of the gun as he watched Leder, just behind Trauber, vanishing over the small rise.

'He might like it,' Shaw said, chewing on a piece of corned beef.

'Yeah.' Harris placed the gun at his feet in disgust. 'I thought they didn't allow fags in the SS.'

Shaw offered Harris a chunk of corned beef which Harris declined. 'They're not supposed to,' Shaw said, and spat out a large piece of gristle. 'Old Adolf's had loads of SS shot before the war for being fairies.'

'So, how do you reckon she's got away with it, then?'

'Give us a kiss and I'll tell you!'

'Yeah, If my old man, God rest his soul, had known I'd be going out with a Gentile boy, he'd have had the lot off when I was circumcised.' Harris smiled grimly.

'Good job he never knew, then,' Shaw remarked with a grin, and putting the half-eaten tin of beef back in his pocket, he wiped the clasp-knife blade on the damp grass. 'You're going to need all you got in Sweden. Nobody needs it more often than a millionaire!'

Harris took off his steel helmet and using it as a pillow, laid his head on it and closed his eyes. Shaw's last words rang pleasantly in his ears and his thoughts changed to the happy, sunny days of the future. His imagination suddenly took over and he was in Sweden, surrounded by beautiful blondes, driving expensive cars — a continuous orgy of love, laughter and champagne. He'd live wildly, spend madly, die young. His

153

excursion into a hedonistic dream world pushed aside the fears he had of the present, and helped stave off the boredom of the long wait . . .

. . . And Shaw was only too right. It was a very long wait. In the painfully slow lapse of time the rain had increased from a steady drizzle to a flooding downpour. Trauber and Leder sat huddled in their soaking greatcoats, vainly trying to protect themselves against the icy needles that fell from the sky. Now and again they would brighten a little, as they heard the faint sound of a vehicle in the distance, but it would only get louder for a moment and then fade away as it turned off to take a bypassing road. Once again they heard the whisper of an engine far away, and, despite their previous disappointments, they straightened themselves in readiness. This time the sound of the car did not decrease, but got stronger as it rapidly came closer. There was no doubt, a vehicle was coming their way.

The soldier driving the small scout car peered through his mud-splashed windscreen with difficulty. His wipers were doing precious little to clear his vision, and his half-hooded headlights were quite useless against the torrential rain. In a way he was almost relieved to see the two sentries who were waving him down on the bridge just ahead. Perhaps they knew a road that could get him speedily to his destination, for over the last few miles he had become convinced that he was lost as he had recognised no landmarks he had been told to watch out for. His co-driver, the Oberschütze, was no damn help, as usual! He was spark out and the only utterance he had made in the last half-hour or so was a noise like a zip being pulled up and down, as he slumped, with his head against the window, sound asleep.

Trauber waited impatiently for the Kübelwagen to draw to a halt, and as it slowed down he quickly approached the driver and leaned into the open window out of the rain. Leder, unobserved, went round the rear and came alongside the slumbering co-driver's door. The driver, who was waiting for Trauber to speak, hadn't quite grasped why this sentry should now be pointing his rifle at him, and tried to act as though it wasn't there.

'*Guten Abend*,' he said pleasantly.

'Shut up and get out,' Trauber addressed him curtly in German, making sure there could be no doubt that he meant business by poking the rifle hard into his ribcage. The driver did not need prompting twice. He unlocked the door and scrambled out. 'What's going on?' he asked feebly.

'I said "shut up",' Trauber snapped and worked the bolt of his rifle to emphasise the point. Leder opened the co-driver's door, and a second later the toppling man, suddenly awakened by his collision with the muddy ground, rose to his feet, still in a state of semi-unconsciousness, and wondered why he should be gazing down the barrel of the sentry's gun. Leder ushered him wordlessly to the side of the driver. In a staccato voice Trauber made his intentions very clear, and it was soon a race between the driver and the co-driver as to who could shed their uniforms first.

In the back, under the canvas top, a third man gently stirred. With infinite care he eased himself silently to his Erma sub-machine gun which lay on the floor and then, grasping it firmly, he cautiously raised a fraction of the canvas flap to stare out at the scene in the road. He saw his two companions sitting down in the mud in their underwear, and struggling to take off their boots, as Trauber urgently motioned them to hurry up with his rifle. The German soldier carefully inched along the seat and almost soundlessly eased the rear door open. He looked out, eyes alert, and stared straight into the muzzle of Shaw's Sten. 'Boo!' Shaw said flatly, as he watched, with barely concealed amusement, the expression of utter astonishment on the German's face. A few moments earlier he and Harris had heard the car slow down, and had decided to take an unobstrusive look at what was going on. Shaw crept up on the scout car and had just heard the faint shifting noise coming from inside the back. He realised at once that there could be at least one more passenger.

Trauber was delighted by Shaw's quick thinking, and told him so as they headed east along the glassy surface of the road towards Berlin. They were now all dressed in Wehrmacht uniforms, but Harris was having trouble with an over-large helmet. Whatever way he tried to adjust it, it still gave the impression that a giant tortoise had crawled up on his shoulders and bitten his head off. Despite himself, for he knew how bad Harris must feel about being attired in a German uniform, Shaw could not contain his laughter. Trauber, too, was quick to see the funny side, even though he only observed Harris in the driver's mirror, as he was concentrating hard to keep the car under control on the treacherous road. Leder made no bones about it. He roared with laughter at the odd spectacle Harris presented, and Shaw was aware that Leder's mirth had a particularly spiteful edge to it. Harris, who, as Shaw knew, was a bloke who could normally take a joke, did not see the humour of the situation at all, and was slowly coming to the boil. Trauber reached over to a small shelf to the right of the wheel and removed a pair of gloves from the top of a forage cap. Still smiling, but less so than before, he tossed the cap back to Harris, and swerved to avoid a sharp corner. Harris waited until the car straightened, took off the helmet and placed the forage cap on his head. Although it was a slightly better fit, it still slid over his eyes and bent his cold red ears outwards. Leder turned to look at him and collapsed with laughter.

'Go and piss up your kilt,' Harris snarled at Leder, 'and play with the steam!'

Trauber had been driving through the undulating, wooded country for about an hour while the others dozed. Suddenly Shaw awoke as the car reduced speed noticeably. He shook away the sleep and saw that Trauber was scanning the road ahead very carefully.

'What's up?' Shaw said, leaning forward from his seat in the back. Trauber half turned and Shaw saw his face wore a puzzled look.

'I don't know— something!' Trauber gradually brought the car to a halt. The stopping of the car's motion soon aroused Leder in the front. Harris, in the back, shot bolt upright with a dry-mouthed 'Wassa matter?'

Trauber pointed out some charred bushes that were just visible in the moonlight. It had not been raining for quite some time now, and the headlights, although fixed with regulation covers, still picked out quite clearly an area ahead which was plastered with a pattern of recent craters. More scorched bushes lined an irregular path in front of them and fresh mounds of earth had been thrown up alongside the country road.

'There's been a lot of bombing here,' Trauber's voice was full of curiosity. 'Why bomb here, open country?'

Shaw thought for a while. 'Some plane — jettisoned its load?' Even though he had uttered the comment, he didn't feel it was very likely. Trauber's eyes wandered over the terrain again.

156

'Perhaps,' Trauber paused thoughtfully, 'or perhaps there's something here — something we can't see right now.'

'Troops maybe,' Harris volunteered. 'We'd better be careful.'

Trauber shook his head. 'It's unlikely this far inland — well, not in any number anyway.'

'An airfield?' Leder posed the question excitedly.

'Now that could be very interesting,' Shaw said, becoming more enthusiastic.

'Yes, it could, couldn't it!' Trauber measured his words carefully. 'I think we had better take a look.' Trauber put the car in gear and moved off slowly. Shaw saw he was heading for a gap in the cindered hedgerow, and felt the bumps as the car lurched across the uneven ground. Trauber sought a spot by a clump of trees which blocked out the hazy moonlight and threw a shadow across the car. Shaw got out first, followed almost immediately by the others. Shaw dug his hands deep into the pockets of the German greatcoat, and had mixed feelings about the fact that the German coat was thicker, longer and warmer than the British equivalent. Trauber had taken the lead and was following the path of the bomb craters like a bloodhound trying to pick up a scent.

The starkness of the fields with the grey moonlight casting long dark shadows on to the zig-zag line of craters made the area resemble a site of an archaeological dig that had been hastily abandoned because of some indefinable evil that hung over it. Without knowing anything about the place, Shaw was filled with a strange and unpleasant sensation, a sixth sense seemed to tell him that a lot of people had been killed there. He felt that resentful souls deprived of their full lifespan were all around and closing in on him. He hoped it was only the bitterly cold night that was making the flesh at the back of his neck crawl, and he found he was shivering violently. He could see that the others had picked up the eerie atmosphere too. Their faces were taut and their silence said a lot more than words. The burnt-out remnants of the odd cottage could be seen here and there. It was now becoming obvious that a whole village had been wiped out in an attempt to get to a target. A few moments later Shaw was the first to see what that target was. Leder's guess had been accurate. Bounded by a huddled group of blacked-out buildings was a small airfield. They moved stealthily forward to get a closer look over an open stretch that preceded the wired perimeter fence. Shaw could clearly make out the shapes of two wireless vans, some service trucks that were grouped near a repair hangar, and a neat line of grey prefabricated huts. Two aircraft stood silently on the apron. Others which were badly wrecked had been towed to form an untidy heap nearby.

'You're crazy,' Harris whispered cheerlessly, reading the others' unsaid thoughts. 'So who can fly one of those?'

'Well, fortunately I have a pretty good idea of how to navigate, even if I am unable to fly the machine,' Trauber said softly.

'Anyway, let's worry about that if, and when, we get aboard,' Shaw whispered dryly.

A guard with his rifle slung over his shoulder tramped into view, walking his beat inside the wire fence and singing softly to himself. Four heads flattened at once into the damp earth. Eight eyes followed the guard's ambling gait until he disappeared behind the buildings.

'Tunnel?' Shaw asked Trauber quietly. Trauber nodded and removed his helmet. He started to dig in the soft earth with his bayonet, scooping up the dirt with his helmet. Shaw and Leder followed his example. Harris, not having a helmet, took charge of depositing the earth a short way behind them. After about five minutes, the strains of an old German drinking song were heard again, and the guard returned along his well-trodden path. Shaw and the others froze, hardly daring to breathe, until, still singing, the guard strolled along the airfield perimeter and disappeared again in the darkness.

This digging and ducking routine continued, on and off, for nearly an hour, by which time the hole was large enough for them to slip under the wire one at a time. Once on the other side they waited in the shadows until the guard passed by again. Then Trauber, signalling to the others to follow, sprinted low towards a pile of huge concrete sewer pipes that lay stacked about twenty yards behind the repair hangar. Harris and Leder followed close on his heels. Shaw looked at the freshly made dug-out and was not happy to leave it gaping and exposed. He slid back inside and started to draw some surrounding bracken over the hole to screen it from view. He had nearly completed his task and was about to emerge, when he heard the guard returning, walking much faster this time. As the footsteps crunched nearer, Shaw quickly ducked back into the hole. He held his breath, waiting. Suddenly, the heavy trudging came to a halt and Shaw could see the toecaps of the guard's boots just above him, only inches from his face. He prayed that the guard had not spotted him. For all he knew the guard was pointing a rifle at him this very moment! He contemplated grabbing the guard swiftly by the ankles, pulling him into the hole and thrusting a bayonet through his ribs. His hand moved silently towards his bayonet scabbard.

From their position behind the sewer pipes, Trauber, Leder and Harris were gazing on the scene, fearful and tense. Harris gently laid down his Sten, silently took the rifle from Trauber and worked the bolt under the cover of his greatcoat to deaden the noise. He raised the gun carefully and fixed the guard in his sights.

The guard, unaware of how close he was to meeting his maker, opened his greatcoat, braced his legs, farted like a foghorn at Millwall Docks, and a moment later was sending down a steaming stream of yellow water through the undergrowth on to the unseen crown of Shaw's helmet.

Cheerfully relieved, the guard rebuttoned his flies, folded his greatcoat over, adjusted his rifle strap to a more comfortable position, and began to sing softly again as he marched off to patrol his beat.

Harris slumped back against the concrete sewer pipe, and clutched his ribs in an effort to suppress what he knew would be a bout of hysterical laughter. Trauber and Leder also had great difficulty controlling their mirth. Harris quickly made his way into one of the larger sewer pipes, where he moved up to the end, allowing Trauber and Leder to join him.

A moment later Shaw's face appeared at the mouth of the pipe. His splashed helmet was still dripping on to the shoulders of his coat. The moonlight illuminated a segment of the pipe just sufficiently for Shaw to catch sight of Harris's grinning features. Trauber and Leder were also trying, unsuccessfully, to appear as though they had not witnessed the incident. Shaw slid inside the pipe next to Trauber and waved a naked bayonet at the three seated men.

'First one to say a word,' Shaw said firmly and jabbed the bayonet up to the top of the pipe, 'cops this right up the jacksie!'

His threats were greeted with a respectful silence. Shaw turned up his sticky, wet collar and settled down to get some sleep. Trauber whispered in his ear, '*Guten nacht!*'

'Goodnight,' Shaw replied with eyes closed. A faint wheez-
ing sound, half stifled, coming from the end of the concrete
pipe made Shaw chuckle softly to himself. Harris had at least
temporarily regained his lost humour!

14

'About goddam time, too,' Harris grumbled as, with the other occupants of the sewer pipe, he watched a fuel bowser, seating two mechanics, skirt along the airfield apron and turn off towards the airstrip where two Junkers 88 fighter bombers stood perched like a pair of stuffed prehistoric birds, 'I think I've got a permanent curvature of the spine,' Harris continued miserably, as he awkwardly tried to straighten his back in the limited confines of the rounded pipe.

'Sssh!' Shaw silenced him as he observed with mounting interest the activity taking place outside. The bowser swung to the side of one of the planes and screeched to a noisy halt. A moment later the two mechanics had leapt out onto the rock-hard ground. A weak sun had only just started to warm the early day, and Shaw could clearly see the men's frosty breath linger in the cold air as they wrapped their coats round their ears and dutifully set about their work. Whilst one of the mechanics started to refuel the aircraft, the other meticulously checked the wheels and fuselage for any sign of damage. Satisfied that all was in order on the outside, he clambered inside the plane to continue his check-up there. Trauber nudged Shaw and pointed towards two men who had just emerged from one of the huts each carrying a large black can of film under their arm. All the eyes in the sewer pipe followed their progress as the two men headed towards the plane, first at a leisurely pace, then more briskly, and finally at an even jog. When they reached the JU88, the men nodded a brief greeting to the mechanic who was still refuelling the plane, and immediately started to load the film into the wing cameras.

'Good,' Trauber nodded approvingly.

'Feldauf-Flügzeug,' Leder whispered.

'What?' Shaw frowned as he stared at the activity by the JU88.

'A plane for taking photographs only,' Trauber replied.

'Right, first things first,' said Shaw raising his eyebrows casually. 'Number one: we gotta get on board without being spotted. Number two: we gotta take it over in mid-air. Number three: we have to get the pilot to land us near enough where we need to be and at the same time not be seen, like in a nice wide open field somewhere. Any questions?'

The men were silent, aware that Shaw's glib orders were going to be dangerously difficult to carry out.

'Kinda like hijacking, only with an airplane,' Harris said nervously.

'Yeah, I suppose so,' Shaw replied, not too certain of the term.

'Whoever heard of anybody doing a dumb thing like that!' Harris shook his head more convinced than ever that continuing their journey by plane was a stupid idea.

'You did! Just now!' Shaw replied grimly, his eyes firmly fixed on the Junkers.

'Shit, man! I get sick in airplanes,' Harris murmured gloomily.

'You'll get a bloody sight sicker if you stop here,' Shaw grunted tersely. Then he broke into a humourless smile: 'We've got to get on the thing first. You might be dead before that happens. That's a marvellous cure for air-sickness, that is!' No one seated in the pipe thought the utterance funny. They sombrely checked their weapons and prepared for a further wait.

The mechanic working inside the plane emerged, dropped to the ground, blew into his numbed cupped hands, and was joined almost at once by his companion. The two ground crew had also finished their work and the four men huddled into a small group as they animatedly chatted. Then three of them set off together, walking towards the inviting warmth of the huts and the tantalising aroma of freshly brewed coffee that wafted their way, while the other climbed into the bowser's cabin and drove the truck slowly behind them, honking loudly

162

on the horn for them to get out of his way, his broad grin showing that he was highly amused by the obscene gestures and comments he got for his trouble. Soon the men had gone into the hut for their early breakfast, and the aerodrome went quiet again.

Shaw, Leder, Trauber and Harris were keyed up and alert, impatiently waiting for this moment.

'Now! Let's go!' Shaw breathed urgently and sprinted towards the JU88, taking advantage of every scrap of cover, but gambling everything on speed. Leder was right by his side. Shaw's mind flashed back to his running days. He would have had trouble with this one. Leder had a natural flowing stride, and he reached the plane first and wrenched the access door open and jumped in. One by one the others followed him and hurled themselves inside the fuselage. Trauber, the last one in, quickly pulled the door behind him. They squatted on the bare deck, panting, but holding their guns at the ready, listening intently for any sounds that might signal that they had been seen. But outside all remained still and silent. They kept their positions for some moments, then relaxed with brief self-congratulatory smiles and set about the task of hiding themselves in the dark spaces at the rear of the aircraft. Shaw sniffed the air inside the fuselage. Enemy plane it might be, but that smell of fuel, paint, dope and canvas was all too familiar. It brought back that bellyful-of-butterflies feeling he had had when he made his first jump from a Whitley bomber. He'd had countless jumps since then, been promoted to lance jack, full corporal, sergeant-instructor, done it the hard way, broken his ankle twice, once on a training drop from a balloon. But it was always the first real jump from a moving plane that remained firmly planted in the mind. The rush of cold wind, the spinning world, the feeling of power yet utter helplessness until the tug at the back informed you that once again you'd cheated gravity and would float gently to the ground. It was a bit like the first woman you'd made love to, he thought. You'd be sick with excitement, yet fumbling and nervous at the same time. There would be many others, and you'd learn something new from each one, until, eventually, the pupil would become the teacher — but that maiden drop you never forget.

The roar of an approaching vehicle's engine alerted Shaw and the three others. They became rigid, dry-mouthed with tension.

'Stay put,' Shaw hissed, and lifted his head a fraction to the rear gunner's perspex window to look at the scene outside. A generator truck came alongside and went out of view. A moment later they felt the plane tilt as a mechanic hooked a power line to its nose section. Shaw watched for any further activity, and then observed a small car with four Luftwaffe aircrew in full flying kit racing directly towards the plane.

'Freeze!' Shaw whispered urgently to Leder, and to Harris whom he heard shuffling about.

Shaw saw the door open and a carpet of sunlight heralded the entrance of the four aircrew. He could just see the boots of the pilot and co-pilot ascend the short ladder to the cockpit. The two gunners followed behind, and walked right by Shaw's huddled form, conversing among themselves, as they settled into their take-off positions on the deck.

Shaw lurched forward a little as with a cold cough and whine, first one and then the other engine turned over and warmed up. Outside the ground crew dragged the chocks clear and the aircraft began to roll slowly forward off the tarmac on to the damp grass of the airfield, turning downwind to taxi to its take-off position.

Shaw wondered about Harris's state of mind. Earlier he had caught a glimpse of him, miserable and shaking at the prospect of the imminent flight, gritting his teeth as the engines revved, and grimacing as the airframe strained forward against the pull of the brakes. He knew how wretched he must feel, but he also knew that Harris had guts, lots of 'em, and in a crisis he was a darn sight cooler than many a so-called veteran.

As the brakes were eased off, Shaw felt the aircraft rumble faster and faster along the uneven surface of the runway, and then a sudden sinking in his stomach as the plane lifted off into the grey sky. Soon the aircraft had attained its set height and began to level off and maintain a comfortable cruising speed. With the plane comparatively steady, the two air gunners got to their feet, one of them intending to go forward and take his seat behind the nose gun. He never made it. A crack on the back of his head from Shaw's rifle butt sent him to oblivion instead. His companion accompanied him a split second later, helped along by a similar gesture from Trauber. Leder and Harris pounced upon the unconscious aircrew, ripped the intercom leads from them and secured their hands behind their backs with some surplus webbing they had found.

In the cockpit the pilot and co-pilot settled back in their seats. Both men were experienced ex-fighter pilots and having earned their spurs in the Messerschmidts of Goering's now almost totally defunct Luftwaffe, had been virtually put out to graze on these comparatively uneventful reconnaissance missions. The pilot switched on his intercom, his polished German diction distorted as it went through his mouthpiece: 'Report your positions.' The pilot waited, then frowned as he repeated his order. 'Pilot to nose gunner; pilot to rear gunner.' The puzzled voice crackled down the wires to unhearing ears. 'Report your positions.' The long silence that followed gave him that feeling of foreboding that this was not to be just another ordinary trip. He turned to his co-pilot and spoke in clipped words through his intercom. 'Go below and check. See what the hell's the matter with them!' The co-pilot nodded, unstrapped himself from his seat, descended the cockpit ladder, and walked straight into the baseball-bat-like swing of Shaw's rifle butt, which came up out of the shadows and struck the unsuspecting airman square on the jaw. He keeled over and entered a carefree world of blackness.

The pilot turned expectantly to the familiar flying-helmeted figure that he believed to be his co-pilot ascending the steps into the cockpit. But his eyes widened with surprise when he saw that the face inside the helmet was that of Trauber, and that he was aiming a Luger level with his head. Trauber, still keeping the gun pointed menacingly at the pilot, settled into the co-pilot's seat and plugged into the lead of the headset intercom. Shaw followed Trauber into the cockpit almost at once, and coming up behind the pilot thrust his Sten gun firmly into his ribs. Ignoring the pilot's startled expression, Shaw turned to Trauber and indicated with a tight-lipped nod that all was in hand below, then glancing at the instrument panel a sudden panic seized him. 'Take out the wireless,' he shouted to Trauber over the loud drone of the engines. Trauber, unable to hear Shaw's voice, lip-read the order. He reversed his grip on the Luger and smashed the butt of the automatic several times against the front of the radio turner unit. He reached his hand inside the broken panel and ripped out all the wires. Then, in crisp German, he spoke to the pilot through the headset microphone. 'Turn back onto 085 and climb,' Trauber demanded curtly. The pilot leaned forward instinctively as though to obey the command, then changed his mind and sat back, shaking his head defiantly as he realised that these armed intruders were incapable of flying the aircraft without his aid.

Shaw jabbed the Sten into the pilot's flesh and saw him wince with pain. Trauber bellowed into the intercom, 'We have your crew. If you value their lives you'll do precisely what we say.' The pilot threw a hostile glance at Trauber and stubbornly refused to do as he was bid. Trauber worked the slide of his Luger. 'Very well, perhaps we can help you make up your mind. We shall dump a man from the plane every thirty seconds, starting with your rear gunner.' Trauber paused ominously, and then added, 'They will be dropped without their parachutes.' Trauber then stood up as though intending to make good his threat, but the pilot quickly bade him sit down again. He inched forward the throttles, slowly banked the plane to starboard and pulled back on the stick. Trauber gave Shaw a relieved grin as the aircraft, now on its new course east, climbed steadily above the dark clouds.

In the main fuselage space below, Harris sat limply on the deck and gripped a stanchion with both hands; his knuckles were white, his face whiter. Leder sat opposite, sneering silently at his predicament. Harris caught Leder's look of disgust as a stomach-racking spasm caused him to double over in pain. Harris wasn't sure whether it was the pleasure of seeing Leder's sneer being wiped off his face and a look of absolute horror take its place as a stream of vomit narrowly missed him, or whether it was due to the relief that normally accompanies the aftermath of throwing up. Whatever it was, he felt a damn sight better.

Shaw's mind began to race. The original idea of getting an aircraft to bring them closer to Berlin had at first seemed sound, but he now began to realise it was fraught with danger. Even if, as they had discussed earlier, they could make the pilot land in some reasonably obscure open country, the chances of their being seen were still very considerable. Whereas a parachute drop was unlikely to be spotted so easily, especially if the present stormy weather continued and the cloud formation got denser. There were four parachutes on board. It was too good an opportunity to miss. He moved across to Trauber, lifted the flap of his helmet so that he could speak directly into his ear and, still keeping his gun trained on the pilot, he outlined his plan. Trauber nodded gravely. He, too, was becoming concerned about finding a place to land, and also by the fact that the aircraft, which was not in radio contact with any ground base, might already be arousing suspicion. Shaw leaned across to the pilot and indicated with the help of the Sten that he was to remove his parachute. Trauber inexpertly tried to steady the control column as Shaw, none too gently, helped the pilot out of his parachute harness. The operation completed, the pilot, to the relief of all, took charge again and the plane resumed its course more smoothly.

Harris was mortified. 'Now I know you've flipped your trolley,' he exclaimed when Shaw had finished telling him and Leder of his intentions.

'It's the only way,' Shaw argued. 'Look, even if we get this crate down in one piece, it's on the cards we'll have a bloody reception committee to greet us when we land.'

'Well, for Chrissake, why the hell didn't you think of that before we got on the goddam thing?' Harris blurted out angrily. 'You know how much I hated the idea!'

'Look, Les, it was a good move to make the rest of the journey this way,' Shaw answered flatly. 'Four hundred miles is a lot of distance to cover on the ground, and we could have been picked up anywhere on the way — you know that.'

Harris started to protest again, but saw that Leder had already removed a parachute from one of the still unconscious crew and was trying to put it on. Shaw went to his side and expertly demonstrated, using the one he was wearing as an example, how the straps should be buckled, and the pack positioned. From the corner of his eye Shaw watched Harris roll over the rear gunner and unfasten the webbing straps of the 'chute. He could not help smiling to himself as he heard the torrent of abuse that Harris was muttering under his breath as he carried out the task. Shaw helped Harris on with the 'chute and tightened the harness for him.

'Now this is all very simple,' Shaw said, facing Harris and Leder who sat on the steel deck. For a moment Shaw was back at Aldershot lecturing a bunch of fresh-faced kids who were about to make their first jump, a leap from a ten-foot wall onto a row of mattresses. He showed Harris and Leder the D'ring of the rip cord, told them how important it was to see that they had no loose outer clothing that might catch on the plane, explained that they should step out, not leap or dive, and that they should step out as quickly behind each other as possible.

Only then would they be sure of landing close together. Shaw said that on leaving the plane, they should give a slow five seconds' count before firmly pulling the D ring, and that they should not be scared if it looked as though the tail plane would decapitate them. It was merely an optical illusion. He finished his brief instruction by telling them how to roll forward the moment their boots touched the ground and that if they remembered just those few points, there would be absolutely nothing to worry about. His voice had the confidence of an expert enthusing on his subject, and he knew that he had impressed Leder, and, in some small way, allayed Harris's fears. It was, by necessity, a very fundamental covering of the principals of parachuting and he was aware that they would need a large slice of luck to get them down without a few twisted limbs, or worse, broken bones, but he was certainly not going to mention that!

Shaw bent down to unfasten the straps of the last remaining parachute that was on the back of the crumpled co-pilot. Grabbing it quickly he climbed the steps into the cockpit. He looked out of the window and through a gap in the clouds saw a stretch of open country ahead. He whispered urgently into Trauber's ear again, who translated his orders into staccato German commands: 'Turn to 145 and hold course. Throttle back. We are going to jump.'

The pilot moved the throttle back a little. Shaw gazed over his shoulder at the airspeed, at the clouds, and at the ground. 'Too fast,' Shaw yelled at Trauber. Trauber leaned over and rapped the pilot's knuckles with the Luger, as he barked into the intercom, 'Slower!' The pilot responded at once, and Trauber turned to Shaw to await his approval.

'All right,' Shaw shouted above the drone, 'let's go!' He turned to descend the ladder down to the fuselage space and saw that Trauber was standing up and putting on the parachute Shaw had brought for him.

'You be very careful,' Trauber said menacingly to the pilot through the still attached intercom. 'I shall be the last to leave. If you make any untoward move you will pay for it with your life!' He undid his flying helmet and tossed it onto the co-pilot's seat. Then, giving a final prodding caution with his Luger and still keeping a watchful eye on the pilot, he descended the stairs to join the others.

Harris's face was white with fear as he saw Leder braced by

the open door and felt the great rush of wind howling though the fuselage. 'I can't, Wally,' he said shamefacedly to Shaw.

'You bloody well can!' Shaw shouted and made a final adjustment to the buckles of Harris's harness before turning away to stand at Leder's side. Shaw tapped Leder's wrist to get his attention, knowing that any words would be completely lost in the rushing wind, and Leder indicated that he was ready for the go-ahead to jump. Shaw gazed down at the ground through the trembling frame of the open door until he was satisfied that they were right on course for the fields that spread out far beneath them. He motioned in a sweeping gesture for Leder to jump. With a quick wave of his hand to Shaw, Leder stepped out. Trauber, who was standing on one of the rungs of the short staircase came forward to the door at once. Shaw checked that his harness was tight and gave him a gently push out. 'Come on, Les,' Shaw shouted across to Harris. Harris gripped the stanchion miserably and shook his head. Shaw reached awkwardly to the back of his collar and pulled out his old standby grenade. He made certain Harris saw it, wrenched the pin from its locking holes, and rolled the hissing grenade along the forward section of the fuselage. In almost the same instant he tumbled out of the plane. With a tortured 'Oi, vay!' Harris rushed to the open door and with a terrified look on his face he stepped out into the rushing slipstream.

Shaw looked up to see the grey bundle that was Harris some hundred feet above him. The clouds spun crazily as he watched him fall. By judgement rather than counting, for veteran paratroopers rarely bothered with the five-second rule, Shaw tugged the D ring. With a mighty jerk that almost crushed his testicles, and a hefty pull at his back, there was a crack like a sail in the wind, and his revolving world straightened.

Harris prayed hard as he got to the five seconds' count and pulled. There was a mighty explosion above him and Harris ducked his head uselessly as a million pieces of burning metal descended. Harris was frozen with fear, and it was a good few seconds later that he realised that his billowing parachute was taking him gently and safely down to the earth below.

15

'Lightning, I think,' Shaw murmured when Trauber, with obvious displeasure, confronted him on what had happened to the aircraft. Leder and Trauber both eyed Shaw suspiciously, totally unconvinced by his almost flippant reply. But if they had a comment to make, neither felt it worth making and nothing further was said on the subject. Harris, unseen by the Germans, gave Shaw a sly smile.

To Shaw's great surprise they had made the jump without so much as a scratch between them and, more important, it seemed that not a soul had seen their descent. Harris had, in fact, been quite elated by the experience and vowed that he wouldn't mind doing it again at some future time. His voice, Shaw felt however, had more relief than the ring of conviction in it.

After hurriedly hiding their parachutes, Trauber, using his compass and the now well-battered map, fixed their position at somewhere just outside the small community of Marzahne, about twenty kilometres from the capital. They set off on the walk briskly enough, but slowly the long journey on foot began to take its toll, and conversation between them, which at first had been quite animated, had now virtually dried up. To the casual onlooker they were just another party of dusty battle-fatigued German soldiers back on a brief spell of leave.

As they marched in step through the narrow streets on the outskirts of Berlin, small children came out of the doorways of the little houses to greet them. A couple of scruffy boys 'fired' make-believe guns as they passed by, and a little girl rushed up to Shaw and kissed him, and said something to which Trauber hastily replied. When Shaw asked what she had said, Trauber told him that she had just wanted to know if he had seen her 'Papa'.

Shaw was becoming very tired and hungry, and he could see by the expression on the faces of the others that the pangs were getting to them too. 'I think we should take a rest somewhere — I'm knackered,' he said with a sigh. Trauber nodded his approval at once, relieved that Shaw had taken the initiative as, like Harris and Leder, he had not wished to be the first to complain. Trauber quickly consulted his map again. 'Well, look, if we could push on just another kilometre in this direction, we'll be out in the open again and . . .' Trauber broke off as the whining, rising and falling sound of an air raid siren began to fill the air. At first it was merely a handful of people who came out of their houses in response to the warning. But in a few moments the numbers had swelled to a crowd of rush hour proportions. Old men hobbled, young women walked, sure of foot, and children hopped and skipped past them in an ordered, and by now well-practised, drill of getting to the safety of the underground shelters as speedily as possible. As the overhead drone of RAF Lancaster bombers came nearer, Trauber suggested that it might be a good idea if they were to join the masses descending into the bowels of the earth. Shaw at first was undecided, and with Harris at his shoulder gazed up in fascination at an afternoon sky darkened by an incredible number of British aeroplanes, and lightened at the same time by a barrage of flak that was being sent up by pounding anti-aircraft guns. But a five hundred-pound bomb, which demolished a cinema before their eyes less than a few hundred yards from where they stood, had Shaw readily agreeing with Trauber that taking shelter was a bloody good idea.

In the crowded shelter, men too old and infirm to fight, and women with faces lined by the worry of bringing up a family with no husbands and very little food and money, treated them like conquering heroes. Leder and Trauber did a lot of answering of questions, while Shaw and Harris nodded seriously, and smiled amiably when they thought it appropriate. Although the group of people with whom they sat had precious little of anything themselves, Shaw and Harris were both impressed by the measure of hospitality they were shown. They were given black bread and cold garlic sausage, and a resourceful

171

young mother, who had filled some baby's bottles with hot ersatz coffee, passed one of them over with a shy smile. An old man spent ten minutes rolling a cigarette from fragments of tobacco, which, when completed, he offered to Shaw. It was a pitiful effort, but Shaw could not refuse it without greatly upsetting the old boy. It was his way of saying 'thank you' to the brave soldiers who were defending the country. Shaw puffed at it and watched Harris who, he was sure, had very similar thoughts to himself. These people were pretty much the same as anywhere else. The sadness was that they had been greatly misguided, even hypnotised perhaps, by a ruthless gang of politicians who had promised them a paradise on earth, but had given them a hell instead.

After the All Clear had sounded, and they had shaken many hands and kissed a few kids and pretty women, they came up to the surface to find that dusk had fallen and the streets were full of noise. The bells and sirens of ambulances and fire appliances urgently ringing could be heard everywhere. Rescue workers were shouting hoarsely at each other as they frantically dug deeper into the still smoking debris. One of the men, haggard, drawn and dust-covered, turned towards Shaw and the others as they walked nearby. He stared at them for a moment and tilted his head towards the mound of bricks beneath him, silently beseeching them to help him. Tears filled his eyes as he cradled in his arms what looked like a broken doll, but was in reality the lifeless form of a small child. He shook his head from side to side, his hollow face expressing more than words ever could his stunned disbelief at man's inhumanity to man as he clasped the pathetic little victim to him and uselessly rocked it to and fro. Something in Shaw snapped. He broke away from the others and, with an angry cry, he bounded up to where the man stood. In a wild frenzy he began to burrow under the rubble like a crazed mole, clawing his way below ground. Trauber and Leder watched him with wide-mouthed astonishment as he hurled bricks all around him in his fervent attempt to clear the pile of debris at break-neck speed.

'Has he gone mad?' Leder addressed Harris, the shock of the sight of the normally cool Shaw acting in this way still registering on his thin face. Trauber was silent, but looked at Harris waiting for an answer.

'There was a direct hit on his own house. His wife and kid

were inside,' Harris said grimly. 'When the raid started she'd gone to the shelter, like she always did, but the kid was hollering for some pet dog they'd left behind, so she ups and goes back to the house with him.'

'And they were killed immediately?' Trauber questioned softly.

'Well, no, that's the thing,' Harris continued, 'they were under a staircase, just about alive, maybe they could've been saved. See, they suffocated.' Harris paused, then went on, 'But they didn't find that out till much later. If they'd known they were down there under all that rubble, who knows!'

Trauber nodded sympathetically, and looked at Shaw's sweating features as he stood astride the mound of debris, feverishly tearing into it.

'Yeah,' Harris said solemnly, 'the poor bastard was fighting at Salerno when it happened. They gave him three lousy days' compassionate. He spent all of 'em searching round what was left of the house.'

'What for?' Leder questioned coldly.

'I dunno,' Harris answered. 'I never asked him.'

'Well, this is idiotic,' Leder shrugged impatiently. 'He will draw attention to all of us if he carries on like that. The Wehrmacht do not behave in this undignified manner. I will tell him to come down at once.'

'I wouldn't if I were you, buddy,' Harris glared at Leder fiercely.

Leder turned to Trauber for support, but none was forthcoming.

'I think that is sound advice,' Trauber said softly. 'In fact, I think we should all assist.' He swung away from Leder and, climbing over a sliding pile of bricks, starting excavating. Harris threw Leder a triumphant look, and a moment later he, too, had joined in the work. The man holding the dead child was still in a state of shock, and had not moved. But two other rescue workers had gently taken the tiny corpse from him wrapped it in a blanket and crunched down the slope of bricks and masonry to the wide open doors of a waiting ambulance. Leder watched the scene dispassionately and dug his hands into his pockets while he moodily kicked some fallen, dust-covered clothing back into a pile at the kerbside.

It was Harris who discovered her. He thought he heard a faint moan and quickly lifted away a crushed kitchen table to expose the slender white fingers of an otherwise buried hand. The fingers moved fractionally. Harris was about to yell with excitement but stopped himself in time, and rushed to Trauber. He tugged urgently at his sleeve and pointed to his 'find'. Trauber rattled off a series of orders to the surrounding workers, and, led by Shaw, they soon got the woman clear of the debris. Shaw gazed at the barely alive plaster-covered woman, and felt the tears welling up uncontrollably inside him. He turned away and brushed his eyes roughly with his sleeve, unaware that Harris was watching him, deeply moved by his friend's torment.

16

Shaw observed the anticipated pleasure on Trauber's face as he bounded up the steps that led into the building with almost juvenile agility. The façade of the block of apartments, a once elegant example of modern architecture, was now fire-scorched and shrapnel-pitted. Most of the ground floor windows were either missing or had been boarded up. The centrepiece, a large stone fountain in the forecourt, displaying a leaping dolphin from whose open mouth a sparkling jet of water would, in more halcyon days, once have gushed continuously, was now badly chipped and dry; the semi-circular basin beneath it, slimy with a stagnant and stinking moss-green deposit. In the entrance hall itself an aged night porter in steel helmet and *Volksturm* armband, gazed at them with no more than a passing interest. Trauber approached him and explained that they had been sent by Fräulein Keisel to remove some heavy furniture which was to be taken to the Reichssicherheitsdienst. Shaw could see by the contemptuous expression on the old man's face as they ascended the flight of stairs that he thought that was about all the motley bunch were good for — moving furniture!

In the corridor outside the apartment's entrance, all was quiet. Trauber reached up to the door frame and smiled as his fingers touched the key he was looking for. He held it up for all to see and winked at Shaw.

Shaw, Harris and Leder flopped wearily down into the deep, comfortable armchairs, luxuriating in the comparative safety of the spacious apartment. The lounge was a big room all right, Shaw thought, expensively and tastefully furnished. This lady obviously had a 'few bob'. Shaw took off his boots and wriggled his toes, not convinced until he saw them move, that they were still part of him. He then loosened his gun belt and looked over at Trauber who, with a happy smile on his face, was standing at a mahogany sideboard, gazing at a silver-framed photograph. 'She still loves me,' Trauber said proudly, and Shaw saw his eyes were shining with good humour as he handed the picture to Shaw. Shaw sat up with interest and nodded approvingly at the photograph of the fresh-faced young couple who smiled back at him. It showed a youthful Trauber with his arm around a slim and beautiful blonde. While Shaw was looking at the photograph, Trauber had gone to a small drinks cabinet and poured out four large measures of Schnapps. He returned to where Shaw sat and exchanged one of the glasses for the photograph.

'That's a nice piece of grumble you got there,' Shaw said, full of genuine admiration as he sipped his drink. Trauber looked puzzled by the term. 'Pretty girl,' Shaw explained, 'very pretty. You're a lucky bloke.'

'Oh,' Trauber smiled modestly.

Harris was next to study the photograph, but not before he'd half choked himself by downing the Schnapps as though it were a drug-store soda. 'I second that,' he said between fits of coughing.

Trauber finally passed the photograph to Leder who smiled, nodded politely, and returned it almost at once without comment.

'What time she get back?' Harris asked, clearing his throat.

'When she finishes her work,' Trauber replied. Then as an afterthought, 'Six, seven, even later sometimes.'

'Work near here, does she?' Shaw vaguely remembered asking Trauber this question before, but could not recall the answer.

'Yes, the Reichssicherheitshauptamt is quite near here,' Trauber finished his drink.

'What did you say that name was again?' Harris asked.

'Translated, it simply means the Central Security Department.' Trauber lovingly polished the silver frame with his coat sleeve and carefully replaced it on the sideboard. 'I'm sure there will be something to eat in the kitchen. While I investigate,' Trauber announced, obviously happy to be back in

176

these familiar surroundings, 'help yourselves to another drink.'

The bread, butter and the cheese were of first-class quality and no doubt better than that enjoyed in the majority of Berliners' homes, Shaw reflected, as he drained his ice-cold stein. The SS apparently still had the best of what little was available in the besieged capital of the Fatherland. Shaw felt more than satisfied with what was now becoming only too rare an experience in these last few weeks — a full stomach and a comfortable inner warmth. He eased himself contentedly back in his chair. What would have rounded the meal off nicely for him would have been a good cigar, but he knew the others didn't have any, and he imagined that Irene didn't stock them.

Harris looked over to where Trauber was sitting, holding a glass of Schnapps, while he leaned back in his favourite arm-chair, dangling a long leg over the side.

'Say, listen, I've had a crazy thought,' Harris said 'Your broad . . . er . . . your fiancée, you say she's gonna get us all the notepaper and other stuff we need to fake up our permits and authorisation, right?'

'Right,' Trauber replied amiably.

'Well, supposin' she don't agree,' Harris grunted uneasily.

Shaw shot a glance in Trauber's direction and studied his reaction. Deep down the thought had occurred to Shaw as well. After all, Trauber had not seen the girl for some time, and what she would have remembered was an attractive, virile, ambitious young SS officer, not a weary-looking deserter.

'Irene will agree,' Trauber answered quietly, 'she loves expensive things, and when I have explained our plan,' Trauber smiled thoughtfully, 'she will agree. I know how to get round my Irene. Anyway, there is nothing for her to lose, what with the Russians nearly on our doorstep.' Trauber's voice sounded confident, and whilst not entirely dispelling Shaw's and Harris's doubts, at least it made them feel that Trauber had not been blissfully unaware that there might be difficulties, and, indeed, had decided how to tackle the prob-lem, should it arise.

'Somethin' else,' Harris sat up suddenly. Christ, thought Shaw, Les could be such a pain in the arse sometimes. 'OK, so supposin' she gets the papers. Where the hell are we going to get these SS uniforms — at the local "five and ten"?'

Leder, who had been quietly and steadily drinking, and was now getting progressively more intoxicated, straightened in his chair. 'A military tailor, near the Adlon,' he slurred. 'I saw it as we came by. I pointed it out to Horst.' He lifted his glass up to Trauber who was holding the Schnapps bottle. Trauber was reluctant to pour any more into Leder's glass, but thought better of it, and filled it to about half way. He then topped up Shaw's and Harris's empty glasses, and replaced the bottle on the sideboard. 'Yes, Martin is right, it is still in business. Now, if we can rely on your RAF to provide the cover we need after dark,' Trauber squeezed the bridge of his nose, 'and I think, weather permitting, it is certain they will, we should be able to loot the store and take what we need.'

'If the buggers don't blow us up in the attempt,' Shaw grunted.

'I could die with pride,' Leder gulped his drink and stared ahead, misty-eyed, 'if I were again in the uniform of the SS.'

An embarrassed silence followed Leder's drunken outburst, with no one quite knowing what to say. Harris bristled. 'Well, bully for you ol' buddy boy,' he said eventually. Leder stood up, tottering slightly and looking more absurd with every gesture. 'To die well! It is important! You have never seen an SS funeral.'

'Just another one of life's little pleasures that has passed me by,' Harris quipped sarcastically.

Leder was now becoming quite carried away, and slowly goose-stepped over the carpet as he spoke. 'The banners, the muffled drums, and the singing of the *Horst Wessel* song! Splendid! Inspiring!'

Shaw could see that Harris was getting needled, and knew that even though Leder presented a comical spectacle, Harris, a little under the influence himself, was in no mood to appreciate it. At any moment now Harris could blow a fuse. Trauber, for once, was at a loss to know what to do. He could certainly feel a tense situation developing between Harris and Leder, but the only solution he could think of was to stop giving Leder any more to drink. It could ruin everything if there were an ugly scene in Irene's apartment. Leder now stood still, gazing down over his imaginary coffin and shot his arm out in a Nazi salute. That was it! Harris sprang up, murder in his eyes. Shaw leapt in at once and grabbed him firmly by his arm. 'He's pissed out of his head, Les,' Shaw grunted as he almost crushed Harris's arm in his grip. 'Don't nause it all now.'

'Yeah, well maybe I'll give him the chance to have his funeral a lot sooner that he expects,' Harris sneered. The pain in his arm was excruciating, but it brought him to his senses. Shaw released his hold and Harris turned to Trauber: 'Listen, pal, where's the bathroom? This guy makes me want to puke, and I'd hate to throw up over your girl's fancy carpet.'

Trauber, relieved that the explosiveness of the situation had been somewhat dampened, hastily guided Harris out of the room, along the apartment's passage, where he pointed to the bathroom door. Shaw glanced over to Leder. He was still standing to attention, holding his arm stiffly out in front of him, his mind far away in some macabre fantasy world of military glory.

17

The old night porter wagged his head from side to side as he walked along the once splendid corridor to the apartment. He was trying to explain to the beautiful, long-legged girl who walked at his side frowning, why he had let those four scruffy soldiers go up to her apartment without requesting some form of authority.

'They said you'd sent them to get some furniture, *fräulein*,' the porter uttered. 'They seemed genuine enough.' The girl said nothing but signalled for the porter to stay where he was while she searched the door frame for her latch-key. Puzzled that it was missing, she hunted through her handbag and brought out a duplicate key that was attached to a ring containing an assortment of others. She opened the door and almost stepped back in shock at the sight of the beaming Trauber who had cleaned himself up and was waiting in the semi-darkened hall to greet her, alerted as he had been by the sound of the key in the lock. The girl dismissed the night porter at once. 'Yes, it is quite in order. I'd forgotten they were coming tonight,' she said as calmly as her excitement at seeing her Horst again would allow. The old man shuffled off, grumbling to himself about how he wished people would let him know what was going on, but relieved that he'd not made a mess of things, for he knew he should always check visitors' passes and authority. It was what he was paid to do.

Trauber held her to him tightly, and kicked the door so that it closed behind them. 'Irene, *schatz, schatz,*' he whispered hoarsely in her ear. Irene sighed as she hugged him and nestled closely to his chest. '*Meine* Horst,' she cried, stifling back sobs of joy and relief at seeing him once more. Trauber found her eager lips and kissed her with a burning passion. Irene pushed herself free for a moment to gaze up into those earnest grey eyes that she had thought would never again look into hers. Then she kissed him with a restless fervour that wildly expressed her need and longing for him. This time it was Trauber who broke free.

'*Liebling* — there are others with me,' he said, nodding in the direction of the lounge. 'Let us go into the kitchen— I have much to tell you.'

'The kitchen?' Irene's eyes held a provocative question. 'Wouldn't the bedroom be more suitable?'

Trauber kissed her neck several times. 'Much more, but my friends are in there, catching up on sleep,' he said in a low voice. Irene pouted disappointedly. 'How inconsiderate!'

In the kitchen Trauber watched Irene preparing the coffee. Her severely cut dark blue suit only seemed to emphasise her sinuous feline figure as she moved about. Trauber ached for her. Irene poured the boiling coffee into paper-thin china cups and handed one to Trauber. He took it, placed it on a nearby shelf and pulled Irene to him.

'Drink the coffee.' Irene fought him away with a giggle. Trauber shrugged with a smile and did as he was ordered. Trauber tasted the coffee approvingly. 'Mmm, it's good.'

'Yes, it's real coffee,' Irene said, sipping hers. Trauber nodded.

'Now then,' Irene said, settling herself on a high kitchen chair. 'I want you to tell me what you've been up to.' She elegantly crossed her long, smoothly stockinged legs and gazed up at Trauber, noticing for the first time his drawn, lean features.

Trauber told her as much as he felt she would want to know, but he carefully avoided explaining the real reason why he'd been reduced to the rank of sergeant. She would certainly not have taken kindly to his act of unfaithfulness, general's wife or not! In fact, that confession would only have heightened her jealousy. Instead, he related a story of how he had discovered corruption and intrigue in high places, reported his findings to his superiors and had, without the benefit of a military tribunal to hear his evidence, been stripped of his commission and posted to Sachsenhausen Concentration camp as a sergeant clerk. He then told her briefly of the massive counterfeiting operation he had witnessed there, and that when he eventually deserted, rather than be sent to the Russian front and almost certain death, he planned to gain his revenge in a very materialistic way: to return to the camp, steal a fortune in British currency, and sit out the remainder of the war, a rich man, in Sweden. He also told her that with the help of his friends in the other room he had planned everything down to the minutest detail, and he concluded his account by informing her that he desperately needed her aid, and what form that aid should take. Irene swallowed his story, hook, line and sinker, but looked concerned about the part she was expected to play in its further development.

'*Liebling*,' Irene stared at Trauber thoughtfully, 'is there no other way to do what you propose?'

Trauber held her hand and gazed deep into her eyes. 'We must have the right papers. We have to appear to be absolutely bona fide.'

Irene seemed decidely worried. 'But I have no right to be in the vicinity of Doktor Kaltenbrunner's office — no reason,' she said hoping that Trauber would be able to provide a solution to her dilemma. But, instead, Trauber tried a different approach. 'You know I spoke of the corruption of men possessed of unquenchable thirst for power and money, men who have been lining their pockets for a future far away from Germany. A Germany where most people will be under the heel of Russian oppression for the rest of their lives?' Irene nodded woodenly.

'Who do you think has master-minded his own escape, as well, I might add, as of a few of his privileged cronies? Who do you think will certainly not be here when the Russians come?'

Irene stared at Trauber quizzically.

'Kaltenbrunner,' Trauber breathed dramatically.

Irene was clearly taken aback. 'Yes, and while most of us at the arse end of the SS pecking order will be flung up against a wall and shot, or at best sent to rot in one of their accursed Siberian camps, Kaltenbrunner and his gang will be lazing under the sun of some South American haven, where there are no extradition treaties. I know myself, from money transfer notes, how much has already found its way into numbered Swiss bank accounts. I leave it to your own common sense to guess who holds the keys to those accounts.'

182

The statement was purely surmise on Trauber's part. True, he did have suspicions that something of that order was taking place, but his heartfelt accusation that night was purely for Irene's ears. Irene sat quite still for a while. Trauber's revelations were making her have doubts about her ideology concerning the party, loyalty and honour. Trauber could see that Irene was teetering on the brink, but needed just a little more persuasion. After all, why should he expect her to capitulate so easily? Deception of any kind was completely alien to her nature.

'The Russians are closing in on Berlin as we speak, and when they come who will be here to help you then? Time is of the essence,' Trauber emphasised with passion. Irene silently acknowledged the truth of his words. Now that all was lost, her allegiance must surely be only to the man she loved. Whatever he asked of her she must do. Trauber bade her stand up and, holding her slender shoulders, stared intensely into her eyes. 'When you return with the paper and a few other office items which I will specify in detail later, you will go to your mother's in Westphalia immediately. You can arrange that?'

'Yes, I believe so, but . . .' Irene began to argue. Trauber squeezed her tightly. 'You must get out of Berlin the moment we've gone — understand?' The urgency in his voice and his obvious concern for her safety stopped any further protestations. She reached up on her toes and kissed his mouth tenderly. Trauber nuzzled her neck, felt her goose-pimples rise. He smiled to himself. It always did that to her. Trauber moved away from her slightly. 'We had a dream, a wonderful dream,' he said softly, 'of a Germany that, like Rome of old, would rule and influence the world for a thousand years. That dream has finished in ruins in little more than a decade. Now we must consider our own future.' He kissed her nose, her eyes, her ears, and then, savouring her lips, he pressed his own hard against them and held her to him for what seeemed an age. She broke loose, weakly. 'You must be very tired, *Liebling*,' she said breathlessly.

'I am tired,' Trauber whispered huskily, 'but not that tired!' He undid the top buttons of her blouse, and slowly slid his hand inside. Clumsily at first, with one hand he unhooked the bra fasteners and heard Irene gasp as he held first one of her smooth firm breasts, then the other. As her nipples sprouted, so his trousers crotch became more uncomfortably restricted.

Suddenly Irene pushed him away.

'How dare you — a common *Shütze*,' she said with mock seriousness.

'A *Shütze*?' Trauber questioned, not quite on Irene's wavelength.

'You are dressed as an ordinary *Shütze* of the Wehrmacht,' Irene replied in haughty good humour. 'I am used to being taken by an SS officer!'

Trauber grinned roguishly and began to strip off. 'Then I shall be an SS officer again,' he said as he stepped out of his underpants. 'A naked officer true — but an officer!'

Irene giggled but without any embarrassment as she gazed at Trauber's rigid manliness and quickly started to shed her own clothes. 'We have made love in some odd places in the past, but never before on a kitchen table,' she said as she hoisted her firm buttocks on to the bare pine top. Trauber came over her at once and nibbled her ear. 'Well, why not? I cannot imagine a tastier morsel ever being served on this table!'

Outside, all over the city, the wail of sirens began their warning message, but Trauber and Irene were too wrapped up in their own consuming desire to pay any heed. The animal sounds of the hungry lovers, as they writhed and twisted, were soon augmented by the massed droning of overhead bombers, but they only felt and heard each other.

In the bedroom it was a different matter. Shaw, awoken from a light doze on the bed, suddenly shot up and listened to the throbbing engines of the planes above. He looked around him and saw that Harris, seemingly oblivious to everything, was sitting in front of a small antique table on which he had meticulously laid out different items in readiness for his night's work. In the centre of the table was a smallish typewriter. At one side of it were magnifying glasses, pens, ink, several nibs of varying thickness; on the other side, ink pads, some razor blades and a rubber lettering set which Harris was now painstakingly placing on the little wooden shelves of a box into alphabetical order. Shaw then turned his head to the open door of the bathroom and saw Leder in front of the mirror, carefully going about his toilet as he happily hummed the strains of a tango. Without breaking the refrain of what Shaw now recognised as 'Jealousy', Leder delicately plucked at his fine nostril hairs with a pair of tiny tweezers, wincing as he tugged at each one.

'Dunno where you're going tonight, Les,' Shaw whispered to Harris, 'but I think Elsie's going to a dance.'

Harris looked up from the table, followed Shaw's gaze at Leder's total preoccupation with his appearance, lifted his eyes heavenwards in a 'God help us' expression and went back to his work.

As Shaw struggled and cursed, trying to get his size ten feet back into German boots two sizes smaller, Trauber entered the room, buttoning his shirt and looking mightily pleased with himself. Shaw knew at once, by his expression, that Irene had agreed to help.

'Irene is leaving now,' Trauber said almost smugly, 'and I strongly suggest we also get ready. There is no telling how long this air raid will last.'

Leder, who had completed his lengthy toilet only a few minutes earlier, showed his eager willingness by coming to Trauber's side at once. The idea of donning an officer's SS uniform again had been uppermost in his mind for the best part of the evening.

Understandably, only Harris showed any reluctance to move, and was still stooped over the box of rubber letters, placing some of them in a franking stamp with the tweezers he had now retrieved from Leder. Shaw, doing up his greatcoat, leaned over his shoulder. 'Come on, Les. You don't want to be a Jerry private all your life, do you?'

'Well, being a German corporal's been known to pay off,' Harris growled acidly, as he stood up to get ready.

A stick of bombs falling nearby shook the contents of the room noisily. 'Don't bet on it, son,' Shaw quipped, as he stared up at the rattling chandelier. 'If we don't shift our arse, the only pay-off we're likely to get is a Kraut bugler blowing the Last Post!'

18

Irene walked swiftly past the heavily sandbagged entrance of the Reich Security Headquarters, stepped crisply up the marble steps, and received an eye's inward sign of recognition from the otherwise motionless steel-helmeted guards who stood rigid to attention as they flanked the pillars of the ornate doors. She pushed the doors, and strode confidently along the plain blue-carpeted corridor that led to her office. She glanced quickly over her shoulder, checked that the floor was quite deserted, then, walking much faster, turned right into another corridor and hurried along it until she stood facing a large mahogany door. She stared for a moment at the highly polished brass sign, which read 'REICHSSICHERHEITS-HAUPTAMT'. Her heart started to beat faster as she saw the name in smaller lettering beneath it, 'SS, Obergruppenführer E. Kaltenbrunner.' She knew there was always the possibility that someone might be working late, so she knocked firmly on the door and waited. There was no answer. She screwed up her courage, grabbed a large brass doorknob, turned it and quickly entered. She closed the door gently behind her and stood, with her back against the wall, allowing her eyes to get used to the dark that enveloped her. She took a deep breath to control the nerves that had caused perspiration to prick at her skin, and felt around the wall for the light switch. A blaze of light revealed that she was in the reception area of Kaltenbrunner's suite of offices. A curved receptionist's desk with a canvas cover over its typewriter stood just a few feet in front of her. She went round behind it and nervously opened one of the drawers. Her heart raced as a copy of a list of names for the day's appointments caught her eye. It was signed 'E. Kaltenbrunner'. She snatched it up and placed it in her coat pocket. She hastily searched through all the other drawers, but there was no sign of any official notepaper. Just a few plain brown envelopes, some spare typewriter ribbons and some boxes of paper clips and pins.

Irene realised that she must now enter Kaltenbrunner's outer office where his secretary, Hilda, worked. She knew the woman only vaguely, had nodded to her in the corridor, and had conversed briefly with her at the odd office party. She was a stuck-up little bitch, full of her own self-importance. Irene opened the door with a trembling hand. The lights in this office were already on, obviously linked to the ones in the reception area. Stealthily she crept across the parquet floor to the biggest, most orderly desk of a group of three. 'Oh, please God, let this be the one,' she offered up a silent prayer as she tugged at the top drawer. It was locked. Breathing heavily now, she tried the second drawer. This one was not locked, and there, neatly stacked, were several sheets of Reichssicherheitshauptamt black-lettered notepaper. In another corner of the drawer were a quantity of expensive-looking cream-coloured envelopes, which were embossed on the flap with the SS Runes, ringed in a small silver circle. Her heart beating like a drum, she folded about six sheets of notepaper, took a similar number of envelopes, and unclasping her handbag laid them carefully inside. She closed the drawer and opened the slimmer centre one. It revealed some inkpads, a rubber date stamp and an official Sicherheitsdienst rubber seal. Irene was filled with excitement. She'd got everything her Horst had wanted. Taking care not to soil the paper, she wrapped the rubber stamps, some still moist with ink, in a handkerchief, and put them in her pocket. With a solid click the outer office door opened. Irene whirled round to face the questioning stare of Sturmbannführer Froben who stood framed in the doorway. She felt the colour drain from her face and her mouth went dry.

'Irene, what are you doing here?' the Sturmbannführer asked her politely, his cold eyes looking twice their normal size, magnified as they were by the powerful lenses of the steel spectacles he wore. Irene moved away from the desk, and quickly tried to regain her composure.

187

'Oh, Herr Sturmbannführer, you quite startled me,' she said with an overbright smile and put her hand to her hair, patting it into place, as though this typically feminine gesture would lend credence to the compromising situation she found herself in.

'Obviously,' the Sturmbannführer smiled back pleasantly.

'Earlier today, I was helping Hilda with some work,' Irene heard her voice pitched far higher than normal, and she lowered it as she continued, desperately trying to act calmly, 'It's my notebook — I've mislaid it. I thought I could have left it in here. It is, of course, very confidential.' Irene gave a self-conscious giggle.

The Sturmbannführer made no reply. The smile still played on his lips, but his cod-like eyes continued to bore humourlessly through her.

'I was so worried,' Irene went on airily, 'that I came back to look for it.'

The Sturmbannführer glanced at his wristwatch. The muffled sound of explosions in the distance were a pointed reminder that there was still an air raid taking place. 'So you did.'

'It doesn't seem to be here after all. I must check my office again.'

'What a good idea,' The Sturmbannführer stepped aside as Irene made it plain she wished to pass.

'Aren't I foolish?' Irene laughed, just a shade too loudly as she reached the door.

'Quite possibly,' the Sturmbannführer replied softly with that same courteous smile, as she left.

19

The bomb's awesome whistle, increasing in volume by each shrieking second, produced an instantaneous response from Shaw and his companions. They hurled themselves full-length into the meagre protection of a kerbside gutter and awaited the explosion. It did not come. Instead, a wall of fire shot up from a big department store across the road and the remainder of the stick of incendiary bombs fell a hundred yards or so behind the building, the havoc they wrought therefore being out of Shaw's view. Trauber motioned for him and the others to follow him over the deserted street, and to a parade of small exclusive-looking shops. In the bright illumination of the flames that devoured the blazing store, Shaw saw that Trauber was leading them into the narrow doorway of a military outfitters which, according to the gilt numerals on its black glass door, had been established since 1775. The glass door, which had survived all of the recent bombing, was not to survive any longer as Shaw turned his head away and crashed his rifle butt through it. He reached in, carefully avoiding the jagged edges of splintered glass, lifted the latch and, with Trauber's flashlight to guide them, they stepped into the shop. Although Trauber had not been to the shop for some time, he was vaguely familiar with the layout of the interior, but it took a little while for him to find his bearings as the place looked different in the light of a torch. Eventually he located what he was seeking — a rail containing a dozen or more SS officers' black uniforms.

'Right,' Trauber hissed, holding the uniforms in the flashlight's beam, 'these are what we need. Let's make sure they are a decent fit.' Shaw selected several without much success. If the jacket was comfortable, the trousers were too short, or vice versa. Finally, by taking the trousers from one and the jacket from the other, he was fairly satisfied that it looked passable. They all seemed to have a similar problem, but with the addition of some good fitting jackboots and leather cross-straps that were on display in another section of the shop, they looked as well turned out as they were ever likely to be under such bizarre circumstances. Then, Trauber informed them, they would have to wear the correct insignia. He moved to a glass counter and pulled out one of the long drawers. It contained a bewildering variety of colourful flashes and emblems. Trauber let the beam play on the contents of the drawer while he slowly scrutinised the selection, and, sorting through them, he eventually made his choice and picked up the regulation number for each man. They included collar patches, death's-head cap badges and campaign strips.

'I've made us Third Panzer SS Tötenkopf,' Trauber whispered as he stuffed them into his pockets.

'Is that good?' queried Shaw. He was slightly puzzled as to why Trauber had attached so much importance to this particular aspect.

'Well,' Trauber answered with a wry smile, 'most of this division is fighting at the Russian front. Only our own regimental brother officers would be likely to spot us as bogus and they, as I said, are otherwise engaged!'

Shaw chuckled softly and turned to Harris. He was sitting in a high-backed chair, twirling his peaked cap around his forefinger and looking thoroughly disgusted. A sharp contrast to Leder who was standing in front of a mirror admiring his own dim reflection. There was no doubt, Shaw silently conceded, the SS officers' 'walking out' dress was not only superbly tailored, it was also designed in every way to give its wearer a feeling of inner power.

Back at Irene's apartment, Shaw, Harris and Leder were all sitting around the lounge looking for all the world like a group of needlewomen as they studiously followed Trauber's instructions for sewing on the emblems in the appropriate places. As they worked, Trauber paced up and down. Shaw could see by his drawn features that he was worried, and knew the cause of his concern was Irene, who had not yet returned.

Trauber came over to Shaw as he bit the white cotton away from the stitched-on collar patch. 'Yes, that's good,' Trauber said, but his mind was elsewhere.

'You reckon she's all right?' Shaw asked, echoing all their thoughts.

'God, I hope so!' Trauber replied gravely. 'Anyway, whilst we wait for her, let's go over these ranks again. I am in charge, an SS Obersturmbannführer. In your army, not quite a colonel. You, Martin?'

'Untersturmführer,' Leder answered proudly. 'It was my own rank before . . .' Leder tailed off, his enthusiasm suddenly waning as he remembered the circumstances that had led to his court martial. He looked up and saw Harris glaring at him with hate-filled eyes.

'Yes, that's a pity,' Trauber said solicitously. 'Strictly speaking, you should be no more than an Unterscharführer if you are to drive the car.' He turned to Shaw. 'That is a corporal. However, on this occasion we will have a second lieutenant chauffeur. They usually only drive generals. We shall consider ourselves honoured. Now you two are . . .?'

'Haupsturmführers,' Shaw answered.

'Good, captains,' Trauber nodded.

Shaw noted that Harris had remained stonily silent throughout the entire conversation. In fact, he'd said very little since they'd dressed in the black uniforms back at the military outfitters. Every reference to the SS seemed to wound him and add to his inner turmoil. Shaw decided to switch to another, less painful, topic.

'Where are we going to get a car, anyway?' Shaw asked lounging back in the plush comfort of the big armchair.

'That, Wally, is no problem. I thought I'd mentioned it earlier. Irene has the use of her employers' staff car. The Oberführer she works under entrusts her with its care. Part of her duties are to see that it is regularly taken in for servicing and maintenance.'

Shaw appeared satisfied; then Harris spoke up at long last. 'What kind of car is it?' It seemed an odd question, but at least he'd broken his silence.

Trauber seemed puzzled by the query as well.

'I mean, if it's one of those slow-crawl inspection jobs and anything goes wrong, we're sitting ducks,' Harris said gloomily.

'Oh, I see, yes . . . No, it's very much the opposite. They are usually Mercedes ot Steyrs. These *Kommandeurwagens* can really shift, believe me,' Trauber said, glanced absent-mindedly at his watch and, with a flicker of a smile walked out of the room.

Harris leaned over to Shaw when Trauber had gone and whispered quietly in his ear, 'Say, ol' buddy boy seems pretty jumpy, huh?' Shaw shrugged his shoulders without answering, but, like the others, he was only too aware of how much depended on Irene's safe return. Her unaccounted-for delay was very worrying. Anything might have happened to her. She might have been caught stealing the paper, or indeed, even killed in the air raid. Absolutely anything — no everything — could have gone wrong. But Shaw knew it would be foolish to discuss his own anxieties with Harris; not in his present edgy state anyway. The next hour or so was spent distinctly uneasily. Their pensive mood was only interrupted by the odd polite remark and, ironically, by the siren sending out the All Clear signal.

The sudden urgent tapping at the apartment front door sent all four men instinctively rushing for their guns. They stood still, scarcely daring to breathe. Another knock, a little louder this time, and a girl's voice in not much more than a whisper. 'Horst, it's me!'

'It's Irene!' Trauber turned to the men, his brow a furrowed frieze.

'Wait — she got a key?' Shaw whispered, holding Trauber's arm. Trauber nodded. 'Then be careful! She might have company.' Shaw shot a warning glance at the door and unclipped the safety catch on his automatic rifle. Trauber approached the door warily. 'Irene, are you all right?' 'Yes, yes, — let me in!'

Trauber unbolted the door, and to his immense relief saw that she was alone. She brushed past him, her lovely face flushed and a look of panic in her eyes. Trauber hastily peered down the corridor to see that she was not being followed and then closed the door, and threw the bolt.

'What happened to your key?' he asked and tried to embrace her, but she was too flustered, and pushed him away. 'I didn't want to open my handbag,' Irene was very strung up. 'I've got what you wanted, I think.' Irene unclasped her hand-bag and gave the paper and envelopes to Trauber. 'Here — oh,

192

these too.' Irene searched in her pockets, brought out the rubber stamps wrapped in the handkerchief, the ink pad and the appointment list signed by Kaltenbrunner. Trauber ran his eyes over the items. 'That's wonderful — but I was worried sick about you. Why so long?'

'Give these to your friend, and I'll tell you.'

Trauber looked at her anxiously for a moment, then went into the lounge and handed the paper and rubber stamps to Shaw and Harris, who pounced on them eagerly, remembering Trauber's instructions not to speak, as the beautiful Irene stood in the doorway and acknowledged them with a warm smile. She was certainly a stunner, Shaw observed, as he returned her smile with his own, but it was only a brief greeting as Trauber took her elbow quickly, and once more wheeled her to the kitchen, leaving Harris, Shaw and Leder to go to the bedroom and commence the delicate job of forging the SS permits and money-transfer authorisation that was going to get them in and, hopefully, out of Sachsenhausen the richer by several million pounds.

Shaw leaned back on the bed, propped up by a bulky pair of cushions, and with a glass of Schnapps in his hand, watched Harris at work. Harris's head was tilted at an angle as he pored over a sheet of paper that lay on the small writing table and carefully scrutinised it under the powerful glare of a bedside lamp from which he had removed the shade. The document to which he was paying so much attention was the wording of the authorisation letter that had been composed and written in bold handwriting by Leder, who stood nearby, and who, every so often, would gaze over Harris's shoulder to observe his progress. Harris, after each brief period of concentrated study, would straighten up, and facing the typewriter in front of him, peck at the keys with two fingers. This slow excercise had taken almost an hour, but with the help of the Sicherheitsdienst stamp obtained by Irene, he had already produced four, in Leder's words 'very acceptable' permits that would explain their presence in the area if they were questioned and asked why they were not with the rest of their comrades in Russia. In precise Teutonic terms, the permits vouched for their being assigned to carry out a highly secret, 'Geheime Reichssache', mission under the direct orders of Ernst Kaltenbrunner.

Now, the all important money-transfer instruction was being ponderously prepared. Harris paused, scratched the back of his head and turned with a puzzled look to Leder. 'What's that?' Harris queried, as he pointed to some words on the paper he did not understand. Leder sprang to Harris's shoulder, stared at the words, and then he broke into that thin-lipped smile that was somewhere between a sneer and a snarl. '*Unternehem,*' he said superciliously, and spelt it out slowly letter by letter as Harris typed: 'U-n-t-e-r-n-e-h-e-m B-e-r-n-h-a-r-d-t.' Leder lifted his head grandly when Harris completed the word. 'Operation Bernhardt — the whole reason for our being here!' Leder turned away and this time sat down in a nearby chair. Harris threw him a disdainful look and then continued typing. 'The world hates a smart ass,' he muttered under his breath.

'Operation Bernhardt — the whole reason for our being here' — Leder's words echoed in Shaw's mind, but it wasn't really true, Shaw reflected. They were here because Fate's warped sense of justice had thrown them together, and given them a chance to turn one last card from a hand where all the others had been irrevocably played. Here they were, four desperate men, with only their lives left to gamble. A quartet of totally individual people, from vastly different backgrounds, with unbridgeably differing attitudes about almost everything, linked by a bond as frail as a spider's web; and where the common denominator was shame, because desertion and shame were intrinsically bound together, and Shaw knew that, for all their bravado, each one of them was painfully aware of it. Wealth, he felt was his own one salvation, money being a soothing balm for wounds inflicted by a scornful society whose rules he had broken, rules which he had had no part in making. With money to embark on a new way of life he could regain his self-respect, the wounds would one day heal and the memories of his shame fade away. Self-examination did not come easily to Shaw. No man could follow his roots deep down without finding twists in them, and the revelation could wither him if he dwelt upon it too long. Yet there were moments of meditation like this, when to look down from the leafiest branch and to trace again the seasons it took to get there, could also be a rewarding experience. Memories, sorrowful and joyful, came flooding back, the body blow of his father being killed; being torn away from an education he'd been constantly told to value; his mother's dependence on him which turned into a suffocating clinging;

his friends, whose youthful faces he saw flashing past him; the girls, and his constant search for love which he confused with conquest; his business, an embryo fleet of three cabs until, in a moment of patriotic madness and a restriction on petrol, he decided to sell up and volunteer for the paras; and Sylvia, his great happiness. His mind went back again to that poignant first meeting when she was in a dazed and tearful state of shock brought on by the sudden death of her young brother who had contracted meningitis, and then to his own crushing moment of tragedy, when, in a muddy foxhole at Salerno, he learned that his lovely Sylvia and his baby son were no more. And that bloody haze at Arnhem, and now this, and although it was happening at this moment, it was the most unreal part of his life. It had an almost dreamlike quality . . . It all seemed like a dream . . . a dream . . . With the noisy clattering of the typewriter keys in the background, he fell asleep.

Trauber paced up and down in the lounge, clenching and unclenching his fist, his face grey with concern.

'Sit down, *liebling*, you're like an expectant father,' Irene chided him good naturedly. 'I'm sure I will be able to smooth it all out in the morning.' But Irene's voice did not carry conviction. Trauber shot her a troubled glance. 'A Sturmbannführer, you say?'

'Yes, Froben, a real crawler, everyone loathes him,' Irene replied, as a picture of his cold eyes staring out of that impassive, smiling countenance spun across her mind.

'I don't like it; I don't like it one little bit!' Trauber punched his clenched fist into his open palm.

'Then, as I told you, I went round to Hilda's apartment, but she was out.'

'Yes, but even if you'd seen her, how can you be sure she'd back up your story? You said yourself she dislikes you.'

'Worse — she hates me!'

'Well, there you are then!'

'But she's having an affair with Oberführer Hollerbach. I've seen them together in little intimate restaurants, billing and cooing like a couple of doves.'

'So?'

'So, she knows I know!'

Trauber frowned, wondering what Irene was coming to. 'She also knows I am acquainted with the devoted Hanalore Hollerbach, his wife.'

'Ah, I see,' Trauber nodded conspiratorially, 'I'm beginning to be with you now.'

'Now, at the moment, Hollerbach is the Reichführer's blue-eyed boy,' Irene continued. 'If I blow the whistle on their sordid little affair, there'll be one hell of a scandal, and you know how Himmler deals with that sort of thing in the SS.'

Trauber nodded. He'd fallen foul of the man's hypocrisy himself. Himmler acted as though he were a uniformed Pope, and indeed was a devout Catholic, but everyone at HQ knew that he'd also deserted his wife, and was a frequent visitor to the notorious SS brothel 'Salon Kitty's'.

Trauber's frown faded somewhat, but he was still worried. 'Look, that's all very well, but I don't think you should take any chances.'

'But I could still telephone Hilda before I go to the office tomorrow,' Irene said reasonably.

'No,' Trauber ordered her sharply. 'Just phone the office in the morning, say you're not feeling well and won't be in for the day. You must leave when we do. You dare not risk a visit from the Gestapo for all our sakes.'

Irene was silent.

'Irene,' Trauber snapped.

'Don't shout at me, Horst. I don't see you for more than a year, and already you're quarrelling with me,' Irene pouted.

Trauber softened and with a tender smile came over to where she was sitting. 'I'm sorry, *Schatz*, it's just that I'm worried about you,' he said with a sigh, and kissed her softly on her head.

'Please don't be. I'll do as you ask,' Irene murmured, and snuggled into his arms.

*

'It's almost perfect!' Leder exclaimed, as he held the finished letter under the light and examined it gleefully.

'What do you mean — almost?' Harris scowled. 'It is perfect!'

'Well, it's just the way you have this 'E'. The shape is faultless, yes, but perhaps it looks as though it is just a little too deliberate. A busy man like Doktor Kaltenbrunner would have signed it with a more hurried stroke.'

'Crap!' Harris grunted.

'I think the ones you executed on the permits are more convincing,' insisted Leder.

Harris silently took the letter from him and studied it. Although Leder had hurt his professional pride, he had to admit the son of a bitch was right. The initial did look a bit stilted. He took his pen, and with an artist's delicate touch, flicked the curve of the 'E' down to make it seem as though it had been scribbled in a rush. He didn't show it to Leder again, but compared it with the sample Irene had brought and seemed to be more satisfied.

The typewriter's intermittent clacking and the low murmuring of voices had, with the Schnapps, lulled Shaw into a pleasantly restful state. But now the silence had awakened him. It was such a dead silence that for a moment Shaw felt he was alone in the room. He opened his eyes wide to stretch away the sleep and saw Harris quietly working, carefully using an eradicator to restore the spotless state of the document he had now finished forging. Leder turned from his position in the chair and nodded to Shaw with just a glimmer of a smile. The bedroom door handle rattled as Trauber opened it and entered. He seemed to be somewhat harassed. 'How long to finish now?' he enquired of Harris anxiously.

Harris, without turning but still rubbing the paper and blowing away the fragments, paused for a moment while he thought. 'About twenty minutes,' he replied.

'Sooner, please, if possible,' Trauber said urgently.

Shaw looked up at him questioningly, and Trauber caught his expression. 'We can't stay here any more. I have this feeling inside here, you know.'

Trauber turned and started to pick up the glasses and the nearly empty Schnapps bottle. 'We must make it look as though we have not been here.'

Shaw swung his legs off the bed and helped him to straighten up the room, clearing away all traces of their presence, but leaving Harris undisturbed as he added little finishing touches to his work.

Fifteen minutes later, three SS officers were standing smart and ready, impatiently waiting to take their leave of Irene's apartment as Trauber took her lovingly in his arms to say his farewell. Standing at a discreet distance with Leder and Harris, while Trauber spoke softly to her, Shaw felt the adrenalin beginning to surge through his veins, that heady mixture of nerves and excitement he knew so well had never been more acute than it was at this moment.

'As soon as we've gone, understand?' Trauber gazed at Irene adoringly.

'I promise.'

'The car?'

'At the back of the block, by the garages. In front of the one with this apartment number on it, number 44. Oh, I almost forgot— the keys.' Irene felt in her pocket and handed them to Trauber as tears began to fill her eyes. 'It's got a full tank,' she said sniffing.

Trauber nodded and held her to him tightly. 'Goodbye, my love. I will find you again soon, I promise.'

Trauber kissed her hard and long. Shaw signalled with his head to Leder and Harris to leave them alone, and the three men walked softly by as Trauber and Irene clung together in a tight embrace. Shaw quietly opened the door and followed by Harris and Leder crept into the corridor. A moment or two later Trauber had come to their side while Irene stood in the shadow of the darkened hall to watch them go, too overcome with emotion to say anything.

198

20

Irene pursed her lips as she gazed at herself critically in front of the bedroom mirror, then applied a touch more lipstick. Satisfied, she wound the lipstick back in its holder, made some final adjustments to her civilian two-piece costume, and casually glanced into the corner of the mirror at the reflection of the chair that stood by the door. On its brocade-covered seat lay a small weekend valise and resting on that was her handbag and umbrella. Over the back of the chair her folded check top coat was neatly draped. She stood up and went towards it as the shrill unexpected ring of the door bell startled her, making her jump as it shattered the silence of the small hours. She froze in her steps, not daring to move, held her breath and waited. The strident sound of the bell penetrated the stillness again; this time the caller was more insistent. Irene grabbed her long dressing-gown from the wardrobe, kicked off her shoes and cursed under her breath as she vainly hunted for her slippers, remembering suddenly that she had already packed them. The bell was still ringing as Irene closed the bedroom door and walked, in her stockinged feet, to the front door. She hastily wiped off the lipstick with her fingers, made sure the safety chain was secure, and opened the door as far as it would go. Through its restricted gap she saw a tall, youngish man wearing the black leather-belted coat of the Gestapo.

'*Geheimstaatspolizei,*' the gaunt-faced official snapped. Irene's heart started to pound as she unlocked the chain from its retaining slot.

'Yes?' Irene said, with the feigned sleepiness.

'You are needed at SS Headquarters.'

'Oh, why didn't you telephone me?'

'The lines are down.'

'Can't this wait until the morning?'

'It is the morning!'

'Oh, very well,' Irene tut-tutted irritably, 'wait here while I get dressed.'

As Irene turned to go into the bedroom, the Gestapo officer immediately stepped into the hallway, but made no attempt to follow her, just stood politely by the open front door. Shaking all over, Irene snatched her coat off the back of the chair, took her weekend valise and umbrella from the seat and hastily slid them underneath the bed. She put her coat on quickly, then, almost as an afterthought, she unclasped her handbag and with quivering hands took out a small red address book. She turned to the back page and ran her eyes quickly down a column of telephone numbers until she saw the one she wanted. She crept to the bedside telephone and lifted the receiver. There was a steady dialling signal. The Gestapo official had lied. The telephone was in working order. She hurriedly dialled the number in the book, tapping her foot nervously as she waited for the other end to answer. But after what seemed an interminably long time without a reply, she replaced the receiver. She walked out of the bedroom and smiled apologetically at the implacable-looking young man, then casting a loving glance down the hallway at an apartment she felt in her heart she might never see again, Irene followed him into the corridor and closed the door. She fell in step beside him, trying to keep up with his brisk strides as he marched purposefully ahead, and then her heart plummeted as, just at the end of the corridor, she saw a second Gestapo official and, to her terrified surprise, standing beside him, a tear-stained and trembling Hilda!

'Hilda!' Irene uttered woodenly. Hilda made no reply, but stared at her in watery-eyed accusation. Silently the little party walked down the stairs towards a waiting car.

21

Trauber had not exaggerated, Shaw reflected, the big black Steyr command car could really shift. They were travelling at a speed of some sixty-five miles per hour, and yet it seemed they were barely cruising. As Leder drove smoothly along the broad flat road, heading north of Berlin in the half light of early morning, Shaw, sitting in the front passenger seat, glanced over his shoulder at Trauber and Harris in the back. 'How long now?' he said, addressing Trauber who, in contrast to his earlier display in the apartment of strained anxiety, now looked surprisingly calm and collected.

'We are nearly at Oranienburg and it is just a little way from there.' Trauber's flat reply seemed to be the cue for an uneasy silence. Shaw remembered Trauber's grim warning that they were going to witness some rather unpleasant sights at the camp. He did not try to justify it — just told them flatly and unemotionally what to expect. He'd also said that success or failure in this raid would quite simply decide whether they lived or died. That moment was now rapidly approaching. All at once Leder slowed down and turned into a narrow, winding road, and there, looming up ahead of them, mist-shrouded in the dawn's grey awakening, were the sombre watch towers of the dreaded Sachsenhausen concentration camp. Shaw swallowed dryly as he read the stark black lettering on the square signpost 'Sachsenhausen Kz.' The car glided to a halt and Shaw gazed up at the great forbidding iron gates and at the inscription *'Arbeit Mach Frei'* that arched above them, and although he didn't understand its meaning, his stomach felt as if it had turned to jelly. Two guards, wearing dark olive-green greatcoats and carrying sub-machine guns came up to the car and gave a smart salute primarily for the benefit of Trauber, whose high rank they'd observed through the car's windows. Trauber made no attempt to return the salute, but wound down his window and thrust the forged permits and letter of authorisation into the hand of the senior-looking of the two SS guards. The guard studied the permits closely, lifting his head occasionally to glance at each of the car's four occupants in turn. With the utmost difficulty, Shaw, Harris, Leder and Trauber all managed, with varying degrees of success, to exude an air of haughty confidence. The guard then came to the letter of authorisation. Shaw watched his lips moving silently as he read it. When he finished, he stepped forward, bent stiffly at the window and handed the four permits back. Trauber's hand was still outstretched as he awaited the return of the letter, but it was not forthcoming. Trauber hesitated for a moment, then changed the gesture to a formal salute. He leaned across to Leder and brusquely ordered him to drive on. The guard folded the letter, stood back and, with a snap of his heels, saluted as Leder put the car into gear, and slowly moved forward. The second guard, in the meantime, had rushed to the heavy gates and with an obvious effort pushed them apart to allow the car to pass through.

Leder, following Trauber's directions, drove at little more than walking pace along a broad gravel road that was walled on both sides by electrified barbed-wire, and headed towards the inner gates. No one spoke, such was the atmosphere in the car, all of them deeply absorbed with their own last-minute doubts and fears. The awful realisation of wittingly going into the heart of a concentration camp, putting one pair of closed gates behind them and now approaching a second pair. An SS, Sturmmann guard flagged them down as the car drew up at the inner gates. He jabbed out his arm in a salute when he saw that the four occupants were all officers, came to attention but made no move to open the gates. He was obviously waiting for some kind of instruction or even, perhaps, a code word. There was an agonising moment of tension and Shaw's hand dropped to his coat pocket and to the comforting bulge of a grenade. As far as weapons were concerned they were well supplied. They had, over their travels, accumulated enough to fill a small armoury. There was Shaw's trusty collapsible Sten gun, and two Erma sub-machine guns concealed under a heavy car rug in the space between the front and rear seats. In addition, each man carried in his pockets two grenades as well as holstering the standard SS PO8 Lugers. The guard stood still, patient as a milkman's horse. It was plain that something had to be said or done. Trauber had either forgotten a procedure or it had been introduced after he had been posted from the camp. Trauber wound down the window, 'Well?' he barked at the guard. The guard seemed puzzled for a moment, then felt obliged to say something.

'We are required to insist on being informed of the nature of all visitors' business.'

Shaw's finger slipped into the loop of his hand grenade.

'I am very well aware of that,' Trauber snapped, 'I have already shown our permits and letter of authorisation to the sentries at the front gate. We are here on business concerning Unternehem Bernhardt.'

The guard visibly relaxed when he heard the password he'd been waiting for.

'Yes, Obersturmbannführer.'The guard snapped to erect attention again. 'When you go through the gates turn right by the factory compound and . . .' Trauber interrupted him sharply. 'I know the way to Blocks 18 and 19. Just allow us to pass, if you please.'

'Of course, at once, Obersturmbannführer,' the guard clicked his heels, then turned and raced to the gates. He fiddled and rattled the bolt which the ice cold of the early morning had made stiffly resistant. Shaw felt droplets of sweat roll from his armpits down his side as he slowly eased his finger out of the grenade pin. In a few seconds — though to those in the car it felt as though time had decided to stand still — the guard managed to work the gates free, and the car slid past his statue-like saluting pose into the SS Command compound.

Shaw and Harris gazed in stunned stupefaction at the sight that confronted them. A group of men who seemed to be totally devoid of flesh and who were all dressed alike in coarse, shapeless, long, striped coats, were being marched along to a large hut that looked like a factory or workshop. Four armed guards came up at the rear and prodded the shaven-headed internees with their guns, shouting abuse as they did so. The guards raised their arms in unison in a proud Nazi salute as the car passed and screamed to the internees to stand to attention as a sign of respect. Shaw caught just a glimpse of some of the haunted faces as they stared with listless eyes at their 'masters' in the car. They all seemed to have the same empty expression, the same blotchy grey skin and hollow cheeks. They no longer looked like living men, just spindly walking dead. Shaw turned round to catch Harris's eye, but Harris just gazed in horror at the unnerving spectacle of these pathetic human creatures and burned with a barely contained inner wrath as he saw men he knew to be mostly fellow Jews reduced to this pitiful degradation. They were watching men being vilified as something less than sub-human, and whose sole crime, it seemed, was that they were not fortunate enough to be born of pure Aryan stock.

A few of the grimly gaunt figures would occasionally glance in their direction, but their great round bovine eyes registered nothing. A guard bellowed a command, and all at once, like a troupe of macabre dancing skeletons, the prisoners broke into a creaking trot and doubled towards the workshops. Shaw eventually caught Harris's attention and gave him a reassuring nod, knowing how utterly meaningless the acknowledgement was. Harris nodded back understanding and appreciating Shaw's concern for his feelings, and Shaw once again turned to face the front as Leder swung the car hard left and drove into another curved row of hutments.

'This is it,' Trauber said excitedly pointing to two longish buildings approximately in the centre of a group of some sixteen similar blocks. Leder slowed the car down and stopped.

Shaw noted that although from a distance Blocks 18 and 19 seemed the same as the other huts in the curved row known as Group One, they were, on closer inspection, quite different. Blocks 18 and 19, unlike the adjoining hutments, were linked together by a communicating extension that had the effect of combining the two into a single unit. Access to either hut was thus gained by a large central door. Surrounding this camp within a camp, was a seven-foot-high wooden wall surmounted by heavy barbed-wire. The overall appearance of the complex was not dissimilar to a giant chicken coop. It was, Shaw thought, the most unlikely place imaginable as the production plant for millions of pounds' worth of British banknotes, and a million light years away from the City of London's image of how a respectable Royal printing house should look.

Trauber got out of the car first and, with Shaw, Harris and Leder following him, marched with a strutting gait into the noisy, bustling workshop. As the four SS officers entered, a hushed silence descended on the inmates who had, until this unexpected intrusion, been animatedly conversing while they worked. They stopped what they were doing and stood respectfully to attention. Shaw could see in the brightly lit area that the contrast between these men and the other, scarecrow-like, unfortunates in the camp was quite startling. These internees were decently dressed in their own civilian clothes and looked surprisingly well fed.

Trauber quickly took in the surroundings, and with an impatient sweep of his hand ordered the men to recommence their work. Then he arrogantly strode down the centre gangway between the benches and work tables. Shaw was a few paces behind him and noted with a silent whistle of admiration the stacks and stacks of neatly piled banknotes that were at various stages of development. In a corner laboratory bubbling retorts were being used in the manufacture of special printer's ink; there were engravers wearing thick jeweller's eye-glasses engaged on perfecting plates; ink-stained typesetters slotting numerals into lead containers as they prepared for a new run of serial numbers. Some of the internees were chemically treating the paper, while others were preoccupied with dirtying the notes to speed up the all-important ageing process. Shaw marvelled at the brilliant organisation and efficiency of the counterfeiting factory. The whole operation, it seemed, was being conducted under the watchful eye of a small grey-haired Slavic-looking man who wore thick horn-rimmed spectacles which, coupled with his pronounced stoop, gave him the appearance of a slightly eccentric scientist. He walked towards the approaching Trauber and stopped abruptly in front of him at the regulation distance of three paces. With a silent bow of the head that hunched his shoulders still further, he introduced himself.

'Good morning, gentlemen, I am Klinger, the book-keeper, and I am responsible for output,' he said, in a broken German accent that immediately betrayed his Polish origins.

Trauber flashed the special permits under his nose and Klinger leaned forward to take them, still not moving his feet.

'These documents from the Office of Obergruppenführer Kaltenbrunner will verify that we are on a highly secret mis-

205

sion, and are to remove your present stock of British bank-notes without delay,' Trauber said curtly.

Klinger, with a polite nod, took the permits and read them carefully, but as he slowly scanned the contents his face clearly showed that he did not agree with Trauber's interpretation of these directives. Shaw realised that the letter of authorisation that, for some reason, the guard at the gate had retained, was the kind of document that should have been produced, not these deliberately ambiguous permits. Shaw hoped to Christ that Trauber, even with his limited knowledge of procedure, would now be able to bluff his way through.

'We have urgent Reich business which is very pressing. You will open the safe, select a team of men who will pack the notes in the prescribed manner in wooden cases, each one to contain the full quota of £500,000, and convey them speedily to our car. You may commence. That is all!' Trauber dismissed Klinger offhandedly as though that were the end of the matter, but Klinger stood his ground as a look of astonishment spread across his face.

'All of it?' he said incredulously, handing back the permits.

'Do they not teach you manners here? You refer to me at all times as Obersturmbannführer, is that clear?'

'Yes, Obersturmbannführer.'

There was an uncomfortable shuffling and murmuring among the rest of the workers. It had been some time since one of their master craftsmen had been rebuked in such a manner. That sort of talk was for the others surely, not for them. Had they not been awarded special medals by the Obergruppenführer Kaltenbrunner himself for good service on behalf of the Third Reich and thus become the only Jews ever to be so honoured? Trauber rounded on them angrily. 'And you, old women, get back to your work at once. What is this — a tea party?' The men started to occupy themselves immediately, and soon the factory was once again a hive of industry.

Trauber turned once more to Klinger who was still looking extremely agitated. 'How much is in the safe?' he snapped

'More than nine million pounds . . . er . . . Herr . . . Obersturmbannführer,' Klinger stammered.

'Quality-one notes?' Trauber exclaimed, unable to contain an element of surprise in his voice.

'Five million in quality-one notes, sir . . . er . . . Obersturmbannführer,' Klinger replied a trifle proudly.

Shaw raised his eyebrows. He had been watching Harris during the exchange between Trauber and Klinger and had seen him bristle whenever Trauber shouted and made Klinger cower. There was even a point when he thought that Harris might have done something stupid. But now as he turned to Shaw his expression indicated that he was equally impressed by the amount that was apparently available. Even with their limited German, Shaw and Harris were able to understand the figures being referred to by Trauber. Trauber remained calm, but was plainly as excited as the others by the staggering quantity of notes.

'You will require ten cases. See to it at once,' he commanded Klinger.

Shaw saw that Klinger, frightened as he was of this tall, officious SS Obersturmbannführer, intended to play it by the book; and it was becoming patently obvious that he considered the permits were not sufficiently detailed to warrant him to act as Trauber ordered.

'But . . . Obersturmbannführer, I very much regret, indeed my orders forbid, that I transfer money without explicit instructions from my commandant. I can only act on his express authority.'

Trauber was furious. 'Your orders! Your orders! You scum!' Trauber brandished the permits. 'What does this say, eh? This is SS Obergruppenführer Kaltenbrunner's instructions. Do you understand?'

Klinger went pale and started to shake. 'I am very sorry, sir . . . er, Obersturmbannführer. It is forbidden to open the safe unless the Camp Standartenführer himself is present.'

'You know the combination?' Trauber said, glowering down at the trembling Klinger.

'Yes, sir, but without the Standartenführer I cannot under . . .'

'There is a chimney out there!' Trauber shouted and pointed out towards the window.

'I will go to the phone and call him for you, sir,' Klinger said, dry-lipped and in a quavering voice. 'It is early for him, he will be still asleep I expect, but I am sure he will be able to clear things up to your satisfaction, Herr Obersturm. . .' Klinger stopped speaking and his eyes widened in horror as Trauber unholstered his Luger. He prodded Klinger in the ribs with the gun and motioned him to move to the door. 'Come with us at once.' Trauber beckoned Leder to go with them outside and indicated that Shaw and Harris were to remain in the hut. Trauber shoved the terrified Klinger through the door. A bellow of agony from outside brought the workers to a sudden standstill. Shaw stood looking at Harris, whose face was drawn and tense, and shrugged his shoulders with resignation to show that he felt that under the circumstances Trauber had little choice. Then another even more penetrating scream of pain, and Harris made for the door. Immediately, Shaw dived after him, grabbed him by the ankle and brought him down in a badly executed rugger tackle. But it did the trick. Harris got to his feet, but made no attempt to leave the hut. Nevertheless, Shaw was taking no chances and put a firm restraining hand on his arm. The workers looked at each other in utter amazement, they had never seen SS officers act in such an unseemly way before. A low buzz of conversation began as Harris angrily tried to free himself from Shaw's grip, but Shaw held on tightly.

'I'll kill the bastards!' Harris's voice was choked with emotion.

'Les, Les! For Christ's sake! There is nothing you can do,' Shaw gritted between clenched teeth as yet another tortured cry was heard from outside. 'Except screw it all up like you're doing now. Look, I know how you feel — I'm your friend.'

Harris turned to Shaw, distraught, broken, bursting with pent-up rage. 'Wally— my best friend you'll always be, Jewish you will never be! How can you know how I feel?'

Shaw had no answer to that. Even if he had, it would have been drowned by the loud long moan that came from outside and tailed off into an ominous silence. Harris made another attempt to break free from Shaw, but was stopped by the hut door opening as Trauber and Leder dragged in the semi-conscious, battered and bleeding Klinger. Harris turned away, so that only Shaw was able to see him desperately trying to suppress tears of impotent fury. Shaw released his grip on his arm and placed his hands consolingly on Harris's shoulders. 'Let's just get the money, and get out of this place, that's all!' Shaw whispered.

'You! You! You! And you!' Trauber barked pointing at some of the workers near him. 'You will come with Klinger and us to the safe. You will also bring ten banknote-transportation cases. Move! At the double!'

The terrified men jumped to obey while Trauber and Leder pushed Klinger, barely able to stand, to the huge safe that stood at the far end of the room. Shaw noted the high flush of colour that Leder had in his cheeks and the look of satisfaction in his eyes. The sadistic bastard had really enjoyed the brutal thrashing he'd handed out to the old man, Shaw thought bitterly. As Harris was regaining his composure, Shaw motioned with a tilt of his head towards the safe. 'Come on, Les,' he said with an encouraging grin, 'It's payday!'

*

The Sachsenhausen Commandant SS Standartenführer Kaindl softly hummed a tune to himself as his razor scraped over his chin, gathering up tiny black hairs in the highly cologned lather. He looked up from studying his face in the mirror. He was certainly a good-looking man for forty-eight years of age, he felt; who could possibly believe he was a day over thirty? He continued to shave and picked up his song where he left off. He was in a splendid mood. He'd had a night of love-making with a hot little Polish Kapo, plenty to drink and yet no hangover, that should show how fit he was! And to look this good at six o'clock in the morning, eh?

Yes, he was a remarkable man, all right. Little wonder women could not resist him. The woman prisoners just fought to be serviced by him. There was a gentle tapping on the bathroom door. His batman with his morning coffee no doubt.

'Leave it in the bedroom, Shusnig,' he said amiably.

'Begging your pardon, my Standartenführer.' A voice the commandant did not immediately recognise spoke respectfully from the other side of the door. 'This is not Oberschütz Shusnig, it is Unterscharführer Meyer.' The commandant frowned, put down his razor on the sink shelf, and opened the bathroom door.

'Well?' he said, studying the red-eared, cold-looking Unterscharführer who wore full guard dress and pack.

'I have been temporarily replaced at the main gates, my Standartenführer, in order to show you this letter presented by four officers who arrived in a staff car about fifteen minutes ago.' The Standartenführer looked puzzled as he took the letter.

'And the officer in charge did not request to see me?'

'No, sir, that is why I became a little suspicious. I beg forgiveness if I am in error, sir, but they did not act according to standard procedure.'

The commandant was not listening, he was already reading the letter. It was not the usual money-transfer authorisation note, yet it certainly seemed genuine enough, the paper, the signature. But why had he not been told about this before? It was very annoying. Perhaps there had been a communication he had not yet received? He would certainly check it at once, and if some idiot in Berlin had forgotten to notify him of this he'd be in trouble, that was for sure. The commandant looked at the letter again. There was no mention of what quantity was to be transferred. Responsibility for the movement of the money was his, and of course Bernhardt Kruger's, no one else's. Ah! Wait a moment, the commandant thought, could Kruger be one of the officers? The question was worth asking.

'Would you recognise Gruppenführer Kruger?'

'Yes, sir. I have seen the Gruppenführer many times.'

'Is he one of the officers?'

'Definitely not, sir. I would not have troubled you if he were there.'

The commandant rubbed his freshly shaven chin as he walked pensively towards the bedside telephone. He paused for a split second, then lifted the handpiece.

'Get me Berlin!' he snapped when the operator's voice eventually responded to the signal. 'The Reichssicherheitshauptamt.' He cleared his throat. 'I want to talk to SS Obergruppenführer Kaltenbrunner personally.' While he waited to be connected the commandant looked slowly up and down at the Unterscharführer who stood motionless to attention.

'That is all!' the commandant said, dismissing the NCO.

'Yes, sir!' the Unterscharführer shouted, saluted, span on his heel and marched out of the room.

*

Doktor Kaltenbrunner pushed aside his morning mail when he spotted the envelope marked 'Urgent and Confidential' that leaned against the silver inkstand on his desk. It was an internal communication, there being no stamp on the envelope, and surely that was Froben's writing. What was the

210

fool panicking over now? He opened the letter and began to read its contents when the ring of the phone broke the morning quiet. He was getting irritable now, he'd left strict instructions that there were to be no phone calls before eight a.m. He needed the time to catch up with his correspondence. What was the matter with Hilda these days? He studied the letter again, concentrating this time, while he fingered the sabre scar on his left cheek: the scar he'd 'won' as a young university student. The phone rang again, more persistently this time. Kaltenbrunner, tutting impatiently, placed the letter on the table and picked up the telephone receiver.

'Yes? Kaltenbrunner speaking.' Kaltenbrunner listened attentively while the voice at the other end crackled out a series of questions that were liberally laced with apologies for disturbing the Obergruppenführer at such an early hour for something that was probably just an oversight on his part. After all, he knew what a busy man the Obergruppenführer was . . . Kaltenbrunner cut him short when he'd got the gist of the message and spoke softly and firmly.

'Now listen, Kaindl, you may take it from me that the document you are referring to is a forgery. I have signed no authorisation for the transfer of Bernhardt notes for the last two weeks.' The voice at the other end became very agitated. Kaltenbrunner was tiring of this conversation.

'Yes, yes. It seems that some official paper was stolen from my office in the early hours of this morning. It is probably connected in some way.' He listened again. 'Well where are these officers now?' He smiled slightly before continuing. 'Indeed. Still in the camp, eh? Then I would have thought that that was the best place for them!' Kaltenbrunner put the receiver back in its cradle.

*

The group of internees Trauber had selected had just managed to squeeze the last case of banknotes into the Steyr's luggage boot. Trauber then gave them a brief stern warning that they must not speak to anyone of this highly secret SS mission and that to do so would result in a mandatory sentence of death. He then ordered them back to the workshop. Shaw, barely managing to conceal his excitement as he contemplated the fortune that the boxes contained, rearranged them so that

211

the boot cover could just be closed. With Leder at the wheel and Harris and Trauber now already in the back Shaw raced round the car and got into the front passenger seat as Leder slowly started to pull away.

'I think I frightened the life out of them,' Trauber said. Shaw reached over the back seat, unfolded the car rug containing the guns and lifted an Erma from among them.

'How come?' Shaw said, now facing front, cocking the Erma and laying it gently across his knee.

'I just thought we might gain a little time,' Trauber replied without expanding on the threats he had made to the internees.

'Good,' Shaw grunted, and then turned to Harris and winked broadly. 'All right, Les?' But Harris didn't answer, he just stared woodenly ahead.

He'll come out of it soon, Shaw thought, especially when the amount of money he's got coming dawns on him. Leder started to speed up when he saw the first set of gates ahead of him.

'Slow down, for God's sake!' Trauber snapped at Leder. 'You must stick to the same speed as when we came in.'

'Sorry,' Leder mumbled trying to control his nerves.

'Look, we have to act calmly. Anything we do to arouse their suspicions will mean the end for us. Believe me, I know these fellows. They shoot first and ask questions after,' Trauber said grimly.

The first set of gates were wide open, and as they came nearer Shaw could see that a large truck with its consignment of new prisoners had just arrived. Shaw saw their bewildered faces as they stumbled out of the back and were roughly handled by half a dozen SS guards who pushed them into a waiting line. They were all dressed in travel-crumpled civilian clothes and each clutched a shabby suitcase as though his very life depended upon it. They were standing right in the approaching car's path.

'Sound your horn,' Trauber ordered Leder, 'Loud!'

Leder responded at once, and blasted the horn angrily. The prisoners jumped aside and the guards stepped back and saluted. Shaw turned round to face a smiling Trauber. They were through the first set of gates without a hitch.

A wall telephone impatiently summoned the SS Haupscharführer who stood at the guard house just behind the main

212

gates. He stepped inside and lifted the receiver.

'Guard house, main gate,' he said casually, but his face and posture changed when he heard the voice of the commandant himself at the other end. 'No, sir — yes, sir.' The guard, still holding the telephone receiver tightly to his ear, peered out through the window and saw a big black car approaching. 'This could be the car coming now, my Standartenführer. Yes, sir, at once, sir!' The guard slammed the phone back so hard that it fell from the wall and hung loose. He rushed out and shouted across to his comrade at the other side of the gate.

'This car must be stopped!' And making good his words, he stepped forward and raised his right hand. Shaw already had his window down, and seeing the guard stepping into their path he thrust the muzzle of the Erma out and opened up with a stuttering burst of fire. The Haupscharführer gave a surprised look as he tried to raise his gun, but fell dead before he could complete the movement. As the other guard steadied his sub-machine gun, Leder rammed his foot down on the gas pedal and went straight for him. It was too late for the guard to get clear or take his finger from the trigger he was squeezing, and a spray of bullets went skywards as the guard went downwards, screaming in agony as he was crushed beneath the wheels of the car. Shaw felt the jolting bump as the car rode over the guard and headed towards the big iron outer gates that were only a short distance away but firmly and menacingly barred their exit. Shaw reached into his pocket and pulled the pin from the grenade. Almost as though by telepathy, Trauber followed Shaw's action, and while the grenades hissed for a second in their hands, pandemonium broke loose. Their car had arrived at the precise moment a change of guard was due, and a fresh contingent of four guards was marching from the picket duty billet near the gates to take over the patrol from their comrades. The raucous escape siren which had started just a moment earlier, and the sight of the speeding car firing and being fired at, alerted them at once. The guards took whatever available cover they could find and began firing at the car as it came alongside the guardhouse. The guards quickly tried to scramble away as a blinding flash and two thunderous explosions came from the grenades that were lobbed from either side of the car. When the smoke cleared the four guards were laid out in crumpled, lifeless heaps, but the gates still remained steadfastly closed. Leder brought the car to an abrupt halt just a few feet in front of them. Shaw peered in the mirror and could see behind them a truck full of SS troops and at least one other car was speeding towards them as the siren continued its wailing message of oncoming doom.

'Ram 'em!' Shaw bellowed at Leder, who seemed at a loss to know what to do.

'No — the engine will be smashed to pieces,' Trauber screamed. He reached out of the window and threw a German stick grenade straight at the gates. With a great roar one of the gates lifted completely up into the air, while the other still remained solidly in position, leaving just enough space for Leder to scrape the car by. In a split second he had steered it through the gap and they were racing away, leaving the Oranienburg Road, heading north as they had planned, for the Baltic seaports of Stralsund and Sassnitz.

Harris had suddenly come to life, grabbed Shaw's Sten and he, Trauber and Shaw were leaning out of the windows, keeping up a continuous barrage of fire at the truckload of soldiers who were in hot pursuit. But the Steyr *Kommandeurwagen* was fast, and the heavy truck coming up at the rear was no match for it. Metre by harrowing metre, amid the constant exchange of whistling bullets, some of which thudded harmlessly into the car, they pulled further and further away, and after almost a kilometre the pursuers were rapidly fading into the distance. Shaw, Harris and Leder quickly dispensed with the finger-burning spent magazines, and with a simultaneous slamming snapped home new ones. Shaw looked in the driver's mirror, then stuck his head out of the window. The road behind was deserted. With a joyous yell Shaw sat back in his seat and kicked his legs in the air like a toddler.

'Rich, mate! Do you hear? We did it!' he whooped. Leder threw back his head and laughed as he pushed the pedal flat on the deck, exhilarated by the hair-raising speed of the command car as it screeched along the autobahn at almost a hundred miles per hour.

'Yes, we did it!' Leder cried out jubilantly. Harris's face was as black as thunder. The sight of Leder rocking back and forth with uncontrolled mirth seemed to prise the cap off his bottled-up emotions. He saw again a picture of Leder and Trauber dragging in the beaten-up and bleeding Klinger. 'Yes, you bastards, and what did you do to that poor old guy, eh?'

Leder, still keeping his eyes glued to the road, half turned his head towards Harris and with a biting edge to his voice shouted over his shoulder, 'Him? That stinking old Jewboy? I wish we'd had more time— I'd have given all those filthy Yids the same medicine.'

Suddenly, without warning, Harris lunged hysterically forward and grabbed Leder by the throat. The Steyr swerved dangerously as the choking Leder desperately clung to the wheel and lifted his foot from the accelerator to reduce the tremendous pace of the car. Shaw immediately sprang to his aid and struggled to release the hold Harris had on Leder's neck as he saw his face turning bright purple. Harris, like one demented, was slowly squeezing the life out of him as the car zig-zagged crazily. Trauber leapt from his rear seat and, stretching his long length forward, grabbed the steering wheel just in time to prevent the car from plunging over the steep embankment that ran alongside the autobahn. Shaw, unable to free Leder from Harris's vice-like grip, frantically smashed the butt of his Erma across Harris's white knuckles, incessantly hammering at them until the pain, penetrating to Harris's brain, made him unclench his fingers. Leder, spluttering and coughing violently, slammed his foot on the brake and brought the car to a screeching halt, spinning it round so that it almost faced the opposite direction. Shaw, with a massive effort, restrained the wildly struggling Harris, but had not anticipated Leder's anger. All the vicious hatred Leder had contained erupted like a volcano of venom as he flew screaming at Harris and started to pummel him with clenched fists. Shaw let go of Harris to allow him to defend himself against Leder's berserk attack. Harris and Leder locked together in a whirlwind of flaying arms and legs as in a frenzy of furious fighting they burst through the car door, out onto the road and tumbled down the grass bank, kicking, punching and tearing insanely at each other.

'Help me stop them,' Trauber pleaded with Shaw and raced with giant strides towards the catherine wheel of flying fists. Shaw, tightly gripping his Erma, came plummeting down behind him. Trauber grabbed Leder by the shoulders and tried to pull him off. Shaw almost simultaneously managed to get a tenuous hold on Harris's shirt but was struck in the face by a wild punch that sent him reeling backwards still clutching part of the shirt. With a resounding rip it tore away to reveal the glittering gold Star of David medallion that hung round his neck. For a split second everything stopped. Leder's jaw fell as he stared at the Jewish emblem with wide-eyed astonishment. The pause was just long enough for Harris to scramble to his feet and with a murderous kick of his right foot he struck Leder squarely in the crotch. Leder keeled over, yelling and writhing in pain. As he hit the ground he quickly unclasped his holster, pulled out his Luger and fired at Harris. Trauber's cry of 'Don't!' was too late, as two steel-jacketed bullets tore into Harris's guts. Harris, dropping to his knees, clutched his stomach and turned to Shaw who stood helpless and stunned just behind him.

'Wally,' Harris moaned, then he held out his hands and his eyes begged Shaw with a silent plea to give him the Erma. Shaw tossed it to him. Leder, horror-struck, knew what was coming, and turned with a superhuman effort onto his stomach and darted forward. Harris fired a long lethal burst at the retreating Leder who spun round like a top, twisted on to his back and lay quietly groaning. Shaw leaned over Harris, saw his blood-soaked tunic and knew in one grief-stricken moment that his friend was beyond help.

Trauber was the first to see the truck load of SS and the two fast moving cars that escorted it, approaching rapidly over the rise. He hesitated for a moment and then ran up towards the Steyr, leapt behind the wheel and started the engine. The noise of the motor turning over made Shaw look up. He saw the convoy of troops on the horizon, and then turned to see Trauber wrenching at the steering wheel, trying to get the car round. Shaw cast an agonised and despairing glance at his friend, and tenderly tried to lift him to his feet. Harris shook his head and, looking into Shaw's sorrowful eyes for a moment, smiled weakly, winked, and then, turning his face aside so that Shaw could not see it knotted with pain, waved him away.

Harris looked over his shoulder and watched Shaw bounding up the slope and jumping into the car just as Trauber straightened it out. A second later the car was roaring off into the distance. Harris smiled to himself. Then he turned his mind towards Leder and a moment of sweet revenge, the irony of which even in his state of throbbing agony, had become a final obsession. With twisting stabs in his belly he willed himself forward and with each grunting breath he came closer to the paralysed Leder who stared up helplessly. With the convoy now less than half a kilometre away, Harris dragged himself the last few feet to sit at Leder's side. He was barely alive, quite unable to move; only his eyes showed life, burning into Harris's, their hatred undimmed even near death.

Harris, tortured now by the sharpness of pain, gazed down at his victim and summoning up all his strength managed a faint chuckle. 'May God forgive,' Harris murmured sincerely, and with another mighty effort that made him gasp, he slipped the Star of David chain over his head and with beads of sweat breaking out on his brow, he lifted Leder's head, and placed the Star of David around his neck.

'Gotta make sure ... ' Harris panted heavily, ' ... they don't give you ... no SS funeral ... you stinking Nazi shit.' Harris coughed up a mouthful of blood as he lifted a shaking hand to ensure that the gold symbol of Judah was nestling squarely against the fine black linen of the SS uniform.

Leder's features, immobile as they were, still managed to register an expression of horror as he realised what Harris had done. Powerless to do anything about it, his eyes filled with tears of bitter humiliation.

The truck and cars descended the bank and came to a grinding halt. The Obersturmführer in charge of the pursuit clambered out of his car and, accompanied by a platoon of SS men with machine guns at the ready, strode briskly to where Leder lay prone on the ground. He stood above him, feet astride and gazed down in shocked wonder at the Star of David on his chest. These men who had dared to impersonate SS officers were not only thieves but to add insult to injury were Jews as well. He spat contemptuously into Leder's face, unholstered his Luger and fired a single shot into his skull, almost resenting the waste of a bullet. This would have been Harris's real moment of triumph but he never saw it because a few seconds earlier he had toppled sideways — dead.

22

'Weren't thinking of going solo, were you?' Shaw still panting heavily, eyed Trauber suspiciously. Trauber, hunched over the wheel, foot hard down on the gas pedal appeared hurt by the suggestion and frowned disapprovingly.

'Wally!' he said eventually in a loud clipped voice, trying to make himself heard over the drumming of the wheels as they traversed the joins in the concrete slab surface of the autobahn. 'We could do nothing for them, they were hellbent on destroying each other,' Trauber shook his head sadly. 'You know that.'

Shaw made no reply. He was thinking now of Harris, his face racked with pain as he bade him goodbye, then he saw his face again wreathed in smiles, full of fun, always making with the wisecrack. There would never be another like Les. Shaw felt a deep sense of loss, which in itself surprised him. He had witnessed so much slaughter, seen so much death. He believed he was immune from forming any kind of strong emotional attachment again, but the shock of seeing Harris dying unnecessarily had numbed him and had even blotted out the enjoyment he should be feeling now about the immense fortune they were carrying in the luggage boot of the car.

'Did you know he was a Jew?' Trauber asked suddenly.

'No,' Shaw answered, and was shaken by his own quick denial. It wasn't that he was concerned by what Trauber might or might not think. He couldn't care less what the hell he thought now anyway, so why had he answered as he had? The story of Peter denying Christ three times before the cock

218

crowed suddenly came back to him. He understood now how Peter must have felt.

'Damn it, they're still on our tail,' Trauber said, staring into the driver's mirror. Shaw instinctively tightened his grip on the Erma that lay across his knees, and leaned over so that he too could see in the mirror. There was no sign of the truck but the two SS cars that had accompanied it were very definitely in pursuit, and were steadily closing the gap. It would not be much longer before they had the Steyr within firing range.

'How're we doing on petrol?' Shaw shouted to Trauber anxiously, not taking his eyes off the mirror. Trauber glanced at the fuel gauge.

'With a bit of luck — no, I'll rephrase that — with a lot of luck we could just make Stralsund,' Trauber smiled grimly, 'but that means sticking to this road. If we have to take a detour to try and shake them off, we could be in real trouble.'

Shaw poked his head out of the window and looked back down the road. There was no doubt that the two SS cars were travelling at a greater speed than they were and were getting nearer by the second.

'Can't you go any faster?' Shaw yelled. Trauber shook his head. 'I don't think I can.'

'Can the car?'

'Well, Martin seemed to be able to.'

'Shift over — I'll make the bugger go.' Shaw quickly clambered over Trauber whilst Trauber still held on to the wheel, enabling Shaw to take his place behind it. As Shaw moved across him, Trauber managed awkwardly to slide into Shaw's vacated seat. The Steyr wobbled violently at the erratic twisting and turning of the wheel as the switch was made.

The years of nipping in and out of London traffic, the invaluable experience of getting a fare to an appointment on time with only minutes to spare, had made Shaw a very capable driver indeed. Once behind the wheel he felt the latent power of the Steyr's engine that Trauber had not managed to extract. In a few minutes the speedometer needle was quivering at 110 m.p.h. and only the leading SS car was still in sight. Shaw turned off the autobahn onto a long, winding country road, bounded by spruce, scots pine and oak. He drove with a maniacal disregard for life and limb, not easing off for a second as he willed the car to go faster and faster. Trauber held on to his seat tightly and glanced at Shaw's face, taut with concentration as they tore round bends, mounted verges, flattened bushes and shrubs, roared through farmlands, scattered startled geese, knifed through streams sending up voluminous clouds of spray, cracking down fences and almost every other obstacle that stood in their path.

Shaw peered out of the window behind him. There had been no sign of their pursuers for some time now. He eased his foot off the accelerator, dropping their speed to around seventy, and turned to Trauber with a smug grin that implied, 'If you had driven like that they would never have got near us in the first place.' Trauber seemed to uncoil with relief.

'I think you've missed your vocation. You should have raced at Brooklands.' Shaw chuckled and then saw a slip road that led back to the autobahn. He steered the car in its direction, hoping to resume their route. As they came nearer the unspoiled country scenery changed dramatically. Instead of tall proud trees to grace their journey, there were convoys of stationary Wehrmacht vehicles along the roadside. Some burnt out, some simply abandoned, already beginning to rust. But there was also plenty of activity. Streams of battleworn stragglers, despondent, dejected, and with defeat clearly showing on their grimy faces were retreating westwards to take up yet further inland defensive positions. Mingling with them were dazed groups of German refugees, some carrying their pathetic possessions in hand-held bundles, other 'luckier' ones wheeling carts and prams. In the distance Shaw could hear the ominous sounds of the approaching Russian guns. He blasted his horn loudly and flashed his headlights full on as several of the legions of homeless wandering refugees filed slowly across the road and blocked the car's progress. Shaw was forced to slow down to little more than a crawl. He impatiently thumped his hand hard down on the horn again but no one took a blind bit of notice.

Shaw glanced in his mirror and could hardly believe his eyes at the reflected images that had suddenly appeared. Not just the one, but both the SS cars were coming over the hump of the hill. Shaw nudged Trauber in the ribs, jolting him out of a dreamlike lethargy as he sat watching the faces of his fellow countrymen drift past his window. Once the unbeatable, glorious victors they were now reduced to these stumbling, vanquished souls. Trauber followed Shaw's gaze as he turned round and saw the cars.

'They don't give up easily, do they?' Trauber grunted anxiously bending forwards to pick up the machine gun that lay at his feet.

'Nor would I, if someone had nicked five million quid from me,' Shaw quipped sourly, sounding the horn once more. This time a little space was made and he inched the car slowly through the milling throng. Then he saw it! Among the lines of deserted vehicles was a Wehrmacht fuel tanker with its wheels firmly entrenched in a muddy ditch. Shaw turned to Trauber and pointed a finger at the tanker. 'If there's any juice in that, we're in business, mate.'

Driving some yards beyond the tanker, he pulled up and, allowing the engine to tick over, fiercely wrenched the hand-brake on, flung the door wide open and, without stopping to close it, raced across to the tanker. Trauber had no idea what Shaw had in mind, but followed him quickly out of the car. Shaw stared at the gauges at the side of the tanker with its maker's name 'Opel Blitz' on a small brass disc above them, and turned with a puzzled expression to Trauber, who every so often would glance nervously over his shoulder at the progress of the oncoming SS cars. Trauber averted his attention to the gauges and, hastily examining their markings, turned to Shaw excitedly:

'It's brimful of petrol!'

'Bloody marvellous! That's all I need to know,' Shaw said. In an instant he had hauled himself up into the driver's cabin and sat down behind the wheel. He ran his eyes along the dashboard but, as he had feared, the ignition keys were missing. He looked around quickly and noticed just in front of the co-driver's seat a large, rusting starter handle. He picked it up and tossed it out to Trauber who was just below. Although there had been no time to explain, Trauber began to realise what Shaw's plan was. He caught the handle and rushed round to the front of the vehicle, found the socket and shoved the handle home. He then found the catch at the side to release the bonnet, raised it with one hand as he hastily studied the inside, resting the bonnet on his shoulders. With trembling fingers he ripped out two wires that led to the lights, attached one of them to the live terminal of the battery and the other one to the ignition coil. He slammed the bonnet down, then gripping the starter handle tightly he feverishly cranked it. The engine coughed and spluttered briefly for a second, then was silent. He tried again, this time peering apprehensively down the road, and saw that the SS cars were no more than two or three hundred metres away, but finding the same difficulty that they had encountered in making headway. He could even hear the frustrated, constant hammering of their car horns as they vainly tried to get through. With a deep breath and a silent prayer Trauber wound the starter handle again. As the mighty engine roared into life he smiled fleetingly and stepped briskly out of the way. Shaw gave Trauber a thumbs-up sign, pushed the long gearstick into first and, wrestling with the huge steering wheel, he cautiously urged the tanker forward, dispersing a handful of refugees who were walking in front of it. He then drove diagonally across the road and brought it to a juddering halt. He heaved the handbrake up and jumped from the cab. Tilting his head to Trauber to follow him, he dashed to the side of the tanker and grabbed one of the pair of adjacent fuel cocks. Quickly he wrenched the iron wheel anti-clockwise and in a few seconds the trickle of petrol that dripped out soon became a gushing stream. Trauber was trying to turn the second cock, but it was proving stubbornly resistant. Shaw pulled him away. 'Don't worry about that. Let's go!' he said breathlessly, and darted back to the Steyr with Trauber on his heels. He reached into the car and grabbed the Erma, while Trauber took a grenade from his pocket and went round to join him. Shaw was already crouched behind the car's long, high bonnet waiting for the SS cars to approach. As he and Trauber gingerly lifted their heads above the protective shield of the bonnet, they saw the shimmering haze on the road as the fuel tanker cock belched out its cargo of gasoline. A moment later the two SS cars, driving virtually bumper to bumper, came into view and warily halted just in front of the obstructing fuel tanker. Shaw greeted their arrival with a continuous stream of bullets from his blazing gun. There was a hasty scurry as the occupants of the two cars, nine in all, got out and, using the tanker as a cover, returned Shaw's fire with sporadic bursts from their machine guns. While Shaw pinned them down behind the tanker, Trauber ripped the pin from the grenade and with a skill that would have been envied by a crack bowls player, rolled the grenade along the road where it stopped just inches short of the tanker. Less than a second later there was a blinding flash followed by an ear-splitting explosion. The blast threw Shaw and Trauber onto their backs and sent the tanker, the SS men and one of the cars, hurtling in pieces in all directions. Shaw and Trauber held their hands over their heads as flying pieces of shrapnel hummed over them. The area around them suddenly became a white-hot inferno as flames leapt to an incredible height. Thick black smoke and fumes curled upwards and darkened the air. Even Shaw had not expected the frightening chaos that ensued. He rose shakily to his feet; Trauber had already done so, and was dusting himself down more as a shock reflex reaction than a desire to appear immaculate. Miraculously the Steyr's engine was still running, but the car itself was moon-pitted with myriads of dents that had been caused by sharp fragments of metal descending on it like a torrent of tiny meteors. Shaw observed that, apart from the odd, barely recognisable SS corpse sprawled out in the road, there were a few other bodies too, refugees who had been hit in the cross-fire or had just been unlucky enough to be near the tanker as it blew up. It somehow took the edge off the success of the ambush. He had no beef with civilians, especially women and kids, whatever their race. He got back in the car and resumed his position behind the wheel as Trauber clambered into the front beside him.

As Shaw drove off, the road slowly came to life again; he saw that the seemingly ceaseless flow of refugees and troops were now weaving their way round the obstructing holocaust and were numbly continuing their journey. They were both silent for a long while. It had been one hell of a day — a day that seemed to commence a year ago that morning and had still not ended.

With most of the immediate danger now behind them, Shaw permitted himself the luxury of relaxing for the first time and a feeling of well-being surged up inside him and he felt a smile creeping to his lips. He saw himself and Trauber like those crazy comic characters he used to read about as a boy. The pair of ne'er-do-wells, usually down-and-outs, who got kicked from pillar to post by everyone, but mostly by one toffee-nosed twerp in particular who appeared regularly and who represented authority. Then, just as things were at their black-est, the lovable hobos would suddenly strike it rich, discover some buried treasure, or find that one of them was the long lost heir to 'Lord Moneybags' and would inherit millions. The final square of the strip would always show them fabulously dressed with immense diamond stick pins jutting out of their ties as they were served a slap-up banquet at the 'Hotel de la Posh', waited on hand and foot by smiling waitresses, whilst, in vivid contrast, the man who was constantly rebuking them got his come-uppance, and was invariably reduced to rags. There was a moral there somewhere but its profoundness eluded him and he was too buggered to philosophise anyway. With a smile on his face Shaw turned to Trauber. 'How do you feel?'

'Very tired. How do you feel?'

'Very rich,' Shaw started with a huge grin which graduated into a guttural chuckle. It was enough to set Trauber off. Great peals of laughter jerked his long neck backwards and forwards like a racehorse nodding over a stable door. Watching him Shaw was at once reduced to a state of near helplessness as he collapsed into a shaking fit of laughter. With the utmost difficulty he tried to keep the wheel steady. The months of tension, the planning, the plotting, the constant danger, never knowing a moment when they could feel safe, the necessity of living in claustrophobic surroundings, wondering all the time what the others might be thinking and whether, despite their bond of unity, they could ever really trust each other — all this just rolled away, like a great storm-cloud evaporating in the near hysterical release of uncontrollable laughter; laughter that had little to do with humour, but a great deal to do with relief.

23

In a high, wooded area, not far from where the black Steyr was maintaining a less than steady course, winding its way up the hill in the shadow of the majestically tall rows of fir trees that flanked the road and spread back in dense profusion to the summit, was another vehicle. The clanking of its tracks was strangely muted as it crunched its way over the thick bed of pine needles and lumbered slowly and laboriously down the slope. The commander of the Russian T34 tank was in good humour as he stood none too erectly in the turret. He had two good reasons to feel happy. The first was that he was well away from the centre of the battle action and was proceeding westwards at the southern end of the USSR's 49th Army sector. The second was the more obvious one which he exhibited with the almost empty bottle of Slivovitz that he held in his gloved hand.

Shaw brushed the back of his hand across his eyes to wipe aside the tears of laughter that filled them. The road ahead was clear. There was nothing to obstruct their steady progress as the car climbed smoothly up the hill. The clear upward road seemed to symbolise for Shaw the new life he could now look forward to. He was rich enough to indulge himself to the very heights of pleasure, young enough to enjoy it, old enough to appreciate it, wise enough to have the knowledge that when he had got it out of his system he would feel like settling down again. It was an exciting heady feeling. The hilarity in the car had been exhausted, but not the jocular mood.

'Know what I reckon?' Shaw said, grinning broadly.

Trauber smiled silently and waited for him to continue. 'I reckon South America's the place,' Shaw paused and then continued in a series of clipped, monosyllabic words. His eyes twinkled with anticipated pleasure, seeing at once a vivid mental picture of himself lazing on a faraway golden beach. 'All that sun . . . meat . . . tarts!' He paused a little longer this time. 'Shag like bloody rabbits, they do down there . . . 's all that sun . . . and the meat I expect.' He chuckled roguishly and began drumming a rumba beat on the steering wheel whilst humming the tune of 'Besome Mucho'.

The solitary Russian T34 tank rumbled cumbersomely down through the lower wooded slopes and straightened out with noisy squeaking tracks as it made contact with the flat east–west road. The commander looked towards the west. He blinked his eyes, not quite believing what he seemed to be seeing. He raised his binoculars and focused them on the vehicle which was moving up towards his angular position. It was not the contents of the bottle of Slivovitz playing tricks, it was there all right. A German staff car, and in the front — he could almost pick out the details of their faces — were two black-uniformed SS officers.

Trauber's thoughts were also well planted in the future. He turned to Shaw gleefully.

'Like yourself, I too shall have a little fun and then I shall marry Irene.'

'Good on yer, mate!' Shaw nodded approvingly, and then, as an afterthought, but without any real sincerity, 'You should both come down and visit me when I get settled in Rio.'

'Yes, of course, that would be splendid,' Trauber responded good-humouredly, but with equal lack of sincerity, 'and naturally you will come and see us when we decide where we will live.'

'You try and keep me away,' Shaw said with no intention of making good the invitation. 'After all, we're mates now — allies!' The incongruity of the word suddenly hit him. 'That's bloody rich, that is. Do you realise that, Horst? You and me,' Shaw laughed loudly, he was tickled silly by the thought, 'bloody allies!' He punched Trauber playfully on the shoulder and set himself and Trauber off on another spasm of ringing laughter.

The tank commander picked up his lip microphone and briskly gave the range and direction of the approaching car.

226

Slowly the long 85-mm gun swung to the right and locked with a heavy click as it fixed position on the car that had just come into the gunner's sights. Shaw's eyes widened in horror as he turned the bend and saw the tank and the gun pointing straight at them. He attempted in a split second to steer the car into a ditch, but the attempt was only a thought, as yet still in his brain. The brain's message was never transmitted to his hands. The huge shell was bang on target. The Steyr lifted a full ten feet into the air and five million pounds in British banknotes hurtled skywards with the flaming twisting metal and fabric of the vehicle. What was left of the car crashed down on a grass verge while a massive snowstorm of white paper fluttered gently down above it.

The Russian tank crunched its way forward and stopped just metres away from the funeral pyre of the car. The commander climbed down from his turret and walked towards the blazing wreckage, his sub-machine gun hooked easily over his arm, his bottle still clenched firmly in his other hand. One of the men, having been blown out of the car, was inconceivably still alive, screaming at him as he lay doubled up on the road, his clothes in flames.

'British! British!' the voice croaked. It sounded like a curse. The commander shrugged his shoulders indifferently. He couldn't understand German anyway. He lifted his gun and fired a long burst. The SS bastard stopped cursing now all right!

A tubby gunner squeezed his large girth out of the tank, and hesitatingly walked towards his commander who stood over the dead German officer, with his sub-machine gun still smoking.

'Excuse me. May I take a few moments to have a shit, comrade commander?' the gunner said with a feeble smile. The tank commander turned to him with a frown, not sure that he'd heard it right.

'I think I had a little too many herrings last night,' the gunner offered by way of excuse as his stomach grumbled noisily, and his face contorted with the pain of the wind that seared it. He tried desperately to squeeze the cheeks of his arse together to contain the blast he felt coming. Another head popped out of the tank's turret.

'For God's sake, let him go!' yelled the non-commissioned crewman to the commander. 'He's been farting all day. It stinks like Hades in here.' The gunner grinned stupidly at the tank commander. The tank commander grunted to him without smiling back.

'Go on then. Don't be long.' He tilted his head towards the hedgerow, then turned back to walk to the tank lifting the bottle and draining it as he did so.

The gunner bent down, his stomach thundering with a sound like a storm over the Steppes, and gratefully gathered up six or seven sheets of fine white tissue paper that bore the legend 'five pounds'. Hastily unbuttoning his trousers he rushed towards the bushes.

Epilogue

Bank of England,
Threadneedle Street,
London
The Boardroom,
Thursday, 9 a.m. — 1945

Those present:
The Governor, Lord Catto; The Principal of the Issue Office, W.K. Paget, representing the Bank of England; the Chancellor of the Exchequer, Sir John Anderson; the Permanent Secretary of the Treasury, Sir Richard Hopkins, representing the Government.

Four distinguished-looking men sat, grave-faced, at the top end of the long green-baize-covered table in the magnificently gilded and chandeliered room. Just to the right of the Governor, who chaired this hastily called for extraordinary meeting, sat a slim, middle-aged woman who, with her head bent over a notebook, was furiously scribbling the minutes in shorthand. The meeting had been convened to examine, discuss and arrive at a preliminary policy on the best way to deal with some bizarre facts that had been presented to them, under a veil of great secrecy, the previous day. The quorum had started civilly enough with a friendly exchange of small talk over the early morning tea, but was now becoming considerably more animated as the full implications became apparent.

'What makes it so embarrassing, quite apart from anything

else, was that it was the Americans who had to bring it to our attention,' Hopkins started sourly, flicking his cigarette into the black ashtray in front of him.

'I'm sorry if I might appear to be stupid, but I don't see the relevance,' Paget said. 'Why should that be so embarrassing?'

Hopkins rounded on him fiercely. 'Well, good God, man! How much confidence do you think Wall Street is going to have in our sterling when this lovely piece of news breaks, eh?'

Paget appeared a trifle taken aback by the outburst, while Anderson frowned and absent-mindedly tapped his pencil against his teeth and looked thoughtfully at Hopkins as he continued. 'There's obviously millions, billions for all we know, in circulation right now!' he said, staring pointedly at the Chairman.

'I think that could be a wild exaggeration,' Catto replied evenly, trying to remove some of the acrimony that had begun to creep into the meeting. He unfolded a buff folder in front of him. 'We've got some figures here on what amounts are likely to be involved.'

But Hopkins would not be pacified. 'Look, I've read those figures. They're purely guestimates from the most unreliable sources.'

'Now, I take a very strong exception to that,' Paget retaliated hotly. 'We had a team of our own experts on the spot almost immediately after Major McNally had conducted his own enquiry. They spent a considerable time with the internees involved in the production of the notes, as well as examining the plant itself. They interviewed the personnel employed, studied the type of press used, the quantity of paper, etc., etc., and they were able to ascertain, with a great degree of accuracy, just how much could have been produced there. Believe me, gentlemen, our experts are highly experienced in this sort of thing — these figures are very far from being guestimates, I can assure you.'

Catto cleared his throat. 'Yes, well now, I think William has allayed most of our fears.' He took some horn-rimmed spectacles from his breast pocket, placed them precariously on his nose, and turned to address the Chancellor. 'In all, it appears we are likely to be talking in the region of some two hundred million pounds, ten million of which has been accounted for.' He withdrew a sheet of paper from his folder. 'The breakdown is as follows: £50 notes . . .'

'Yes, yes, we've read all that,' Anderson interrupted irritably, 'but I can't help sharing Richard's concern here that we may only just have scratched the surface.' He looked at Paget. 'May I ask, were these experts you sent from your Issue Department?'

'Naturally — who else would be qualified to do the job?'

Hopkins opened his buff folder and thumbed through a sheaf of papers until he found the one he was looking for, then he carefully removed it and held it in front of him. 'Would these be the same experts from the Issue Office who wrote to the Swiss Bank Corporation in Zürich, and I quote from their authoritative letter dated 26th February, 1941: "These banknotes are unquestionably genuine." Do you know what banknotes these *experts* were referring to, Chancellor?' Anderson made no reply. 'Well, I'll tell you; Bernhardt notes! British banknotes produced in their tens of millions in a couple of wooden huts in Sachsenhausen Concentration Camp. Notes that our so-called experts have stated categorically are Bank of England issue. I ask you, gentlemen, how can we take any of their findings seriously after that, mmm?'

Paget shifted uncomfortably in his chair.

'Look, I'm not trying to score points here, William,' Hopkins went on, 'but these so-called experts of yours are responsible for an enormous blunder, one which the Germans must really have laughed up their sleeve at! What worries me now is the tremendous repercussions it could have on our desperately shaky economy. We could have a situation on our hands like Germany did after the First World War, where money was meaningless, where people paid ten million marks for a loaf of bread! I have also heard that we still haven't recovered the plates.'

'Well, we've every confidence we will locate their whereabouts soon,' Paget replied.

'How soon? Next week? Next month? Next year?' Hopkins said. 'Gentlemen, I tell you, we've got to act now, otherwise billions of pounds more of these undetectable notes will be flooding the world's money markets. We've got to decide what to do right now.' He emphasised his words by thumping the table. 'And take drastic steps if need be.'

The meeting continued until late that evening, at which time a course of action was finally agreed upon, and which resulted in the Bank of England taking the unprecedented step of calling in all banknote currency above the one-pound-note denomination.

On the 1st May 1945, the £50, £20, and £10 notes were withdrawn from circulation, and on the 1st May 1946, the famous white 'fiver'.